HISTORIAN'S NOTE

At the time of this writing (mid 2020), France was involved in counter terrorist operations in the Republic Mali. This changed in February of 2022 when all French troops were withdrawn as a result of a coup d'état in May of 2021. Also, between the completion of the final draft and publication, Her Majesty Queen Elizabeth II passed away, so I made all appropriate changes to reflect the start of King Charles III reign.

NAUTICAL STRIKE

THE GARGOYLE TRILOGY
BOOK 1

ROBERT A. ADAMCIK

To the late Commander Joseph Acevedo, Supply Corps, United
States Navy
And
The late Senior Chief Engineman (Surface Warfare) Judge Haugen,
United States Navy (Retired)
Rest in Peace, Shipmates
We Have the Watch

PROLOGUE

M/V *Kobiashi Maru*
3,000-ton container ship
East China Sea
Position: 30°42′07″ North by 125°34′54″ East
Course: 200° True
Speed: 12 knots
Time: 0200 local

Captain Hoshi Sato stood on the starboard side bridge-wing of his small container ship. His eyes and thoughts centered on the coast of China, several hundred kilometers over the horizon. He'd spent his career running illicit cargo; this voyage was no different. Well, maybe one difference – the special cargo. The Chinese and American navies don't send you to the ocean floor for running cigarettes and booze. They would not like what he carried in his ship and getting caught by either meant a death sentence. In addition to her normal cargo of consumer goods bound for the Middle East, the Kobiashi Maru carried a special cargo bound for the Iranian port, and naval base, of Jask. He didn't know the exact nature of the cargo but considering the obscene amount of money his North Korean customers offered, it had to be very important to the mullahs in Tehran. The Americans, of course, didn't like anything that increases Iran's power and influence in the region. The Chinese? Well, they hated any activities not sanctioned by their government, specifically the Ministry for State Security, and this cargo was definitely not sanctioned.

Captain Sato opened the door into the pilothouse and walked over to his American-built Sperry navigation system display passing by both the helmsman and his Second Officer who currently stood as Officer of the Watch. So far, his ship was right on track heading for the Straits of Taiwan. From there, they'd sail through the Straits of Malacca and on into the Indian Ocean, like the hundreds of commercial vessels that ply these waters. *What is it the computer hackers say, "Security through obscurity?"* Moreover, since Jask sat on Iran's Gulf of Oman coast, they'd avoid the prying eyes of the Omanis, Emiratis, and Americans by not having to transit the Straits of Hormuz.

Sato looked out over his ship's cargo deck, stacked three high with containers and began to think about his plans once this voyage is over.

After this trip, I'll have enough money to retire somewhere sunny and warm. Bali perhaps?

He felt the change in the deck's vibrations first and looked up to check the Sperry's speed display. Just as he thought, they were slowing down. He turned to yell at the helmsman when he saw the man's head explode in a pink spray of blood and brain matter. He turned in time to see his Second Officer suffer the same fate as the helmsman. As the Second Officer's body dropped to the deck, Sato saw the figure dressed all in black holding a suppressed pistol pointing at his head.

Fifteen minutes before Captain Sato's soul-searching moment, a group of swimmers laid in wait along the *Kobiashi Maru*'s intended track. Lieutenant Commander James Robert Morgan, United States Navy Reserve and his handpicked team of U.S. Navy SEALs and Special Warfare Combatant-craft

Crewmen (better known as the Dirty Boat Guys) moved silently towards the container ship's hull. Morgan had to get this right. This was his first mission since the CIA's Special Activities Center chain of command allowed him back in the field since his injury. He had been transferred to the Agency's Analysis Branch during his convalesce, and while he enjoyed the work there, he preferred being out in the field.

Normally, the Agency used operators from the Maritime Branch for missions of this nature. The Maritime Branch consisted of former SEALs, SWCCs, and U.S. Marine Corps Force Recon personnel, just like Morgan's team. However, unlike Morgan's team, the members of the Maritime Branch were at a greater risk of compromise. Morgan learned that lesson the hard way, and it had cost him an eye.

The team reached the *Kobiashi Maru*, executed a "bottom up" assault, and began to scale the black, barnacle crusted hull by using magnetic handholds carried by each member. They moved silently aft towards the ship's superstructure and once there divided into smaller groups and moved toward their initial objectives. Morgan and his team had to be very careful. According to the intelligence, the first requirement to serve on this freighter was a criminal record, making all of the crew members very dangerous.

Morgan and his partner, Special Boat Operator Second Class Jose 'El Fantasma' Hernandez moved silently along the deck. A noise to his left suddenly caught his attention. As Morgan turned, a crewmember attacked Hernandez with a knife, executing quick stabbing and slashing motions. Hernandez countered as best he could. As the knife ripped the sleeve of Hernandez's right arm, he let out a grunt as the blade cut skin, Morgan fired. The Glock spat once and the silenced nine-millimeter slug dropped the crewmember with a round to the head before he could raise the alarm.

"You okay?" Morgan asked quietly.

"I'll live," Fantasma said, pain etched his face. The wound on his arm bled a lot but wasn't too deep. Morgan tied a tourniquet and gave him a slap on the opposite shoulder. Despite his precautions, Morgan's extended blind spot nearly cost one of his men his life.

"Roger, let's go."

Morgan and Fantasma crept up the ladders attached to the exterior of the ship's superstructure. Morgan's team were now in position awaiting his word. Once Sato passed though the pilot-house doors, Morgan pressed the transmission button on his throat microphone twice, the go signal.

Down in the ship's engine room, three members of the team, led by Special Boat Operator First Class Martin 'The Judge' Haugen entered ship's engineering control station. They eliminated the two watchstanders, took control of the engine's throttles from the bridge, brought the ship to a stop, and then headed into the engine room. They found a mechanic working on one of the ship's main propulsion diesel engines. A single nine-millimeter round struck the man in the back of the head and the body fell into the bilge. The three then searched the remainder of the engine room and found no additional threats. Judge then checked over the local control panels for both the main propulsion and electrical generator diesel engines and saw that they were working properly. The Judge and his men now had complete control of the ship's engineering plant.

Lieutenant Doug Kroll, the no-nonsense SEAL platoon commander, and two of his men checked the crew's staterooms. They quietly and quietly opened doors as they moved down the passageway and fired silenced nine-millimeter rounds into any sleeping crew members they encountered. He and his men ensured no one awoke to raise the alarm.

The final four members of the team, led by Chief Special Boat Operator Michael 'Dallas' Shaw, swept the dark, cool, and damp cargo hold looking for their primary objectives. They moved around the forty-foot-long, eight-foot-high rectangular cargo containers in search of a specific one and its contents. Looking for the proverbial needle in the haystack amongst the three-high stacked containers laid out in rows stretching from the aft super-structure to the bow. They also looked for any members of the opposition lying in wait while also dodging rusted sections of the deck. The last thing Dallas needed was to become trapped after stepping into a hole.

Morgan and his partner crept towards the starboard-side pilothouse door while two more members of the team did the same along the port side. They both entered the pilothouse, simultaneously shooting the helmsman and watch officer. Captain Sato took a swing at Morgan. Morgan easily ducked the blow and responded with a right cross to the jaw that knocked Sato to the deck. Before Sato pulled himself up off the deck, Morgan pressed an anesthetic syringe into the captain's neck ensuring Sato's cooperation for the trip to come. With that, Morgan and his team now had complete control of the *Kobiashi Maru*, well almost.

Morgan looked at the navigation display's speed indicator and verified that the ship had come to a full stop.

Nice work, Judge.

He then stepped through the open door and out onto the portside bridge wing. He keyed his throat mic.

"Dallas, Gargoyle. How are you doing?"

"Stand by, sir." Chief Shaw said as Morgan heard the sounds of gunfire in his earpiece.

Down in the hold, Dallas and his men engaged four of the ship's crew in a gun fight around a group of containers separated from the rest of the cargo. One of his SEALs pulled a flash-bang grenade from his belt then caught Dallas's attention. He nodded and after a three count, the SEAL tossed the grenade. It rolled to the gap between the containers Dallas hid behind and where the bad guys were, then detonated. The screams of the opposition served as their cue, and Dallas's team attacked. Four suppressed nine-millimeter rounds impacted four skulls, perma-nently eliminating the threat.

After a moment, Morgan heard Chief Shaw and his distinctive Texas twang come back on the radio. "Cargo hold secure. Search in progress."

"Roger, Chief." Morgan took another quick look around and seeing they were all alone in the inky blackness of night, changed his radio's channel, and keyed his throat mike.

"Gargoyle to Buckeye, we're ready."

About a mile from the ship, a hulking, black shape emerged from the star lit depths. U.S.S. *Ohio*, SSGN 726, came to the surface. Morgan spotted one of the guided-missile submarine's lockout chambers opening, the one he and his team swam out of less than an hour ago, followed shortly by several sailors moving about her broad turtleback.

Lieutenant Kroll joined Morgan on the bridge-wing.

"Sir, we've secured the deck logs, manifests, and our guest."

"Very well, Doug. Get everything to the port side and deploy the pilot's ladder."

"Aye, aye sir."

On the cargo deck, several large boxes came up through an open hatch from one of the lower cargo holds while the unconscious form of Captain Sato moved down the port side ladders courtesy of two of Doug's SEALs.

"Gargoyle, Dallas. Sir, objectives secured."

"Thanks, Chief. Get them to the port side of the ship." Morgan called back to *Ohio*.

"Buckeye, Gargoyle. Send the CRRCs, and we need the corpsman to meet us on the turtleback."

Two five-meter combat rubber raiding crafts made their way from the sub towards the port side of the cargo ship. Morgan switched his radio back to his team's frequency.

"Judge, open the engine room main drainage system discharge and suction valves and get you and your team back up here."

"Yes, sir," Morgan's engineer replied. Morgan had worked with Petty Officer Haugen before while serving as Officer in

Charge of a Mark V Special Operations Craft detachment. The Judge was a U.S. Navy Engineman specializing in main propulsion diesel engines before transferring to the SWCC community and knew his way around a ship's engine room. Morgan trusted him to get the job done.

Morgan joined his team on the cargo deck and looked over the gunwale at the incoming CRRCs. He felt a slight tilt to the deck as the ship began to settle by the stern.

Looks like Judge is finished.

He heard footsteps to his left and saw Judge and the other two members of the engineering team walking towards him.

"All drainage valves opened as are all the watertight doors in the cargo holds, sir."

"Outstanding, Judge." Morgan turned towards his senior SEAL, "Doug, are all our people accounted for?"

"Yes, sir."

"Good, then let's get out of here."

Morgan's team began climbing down the ship's pilot's ladder towards the CRRCs with two members using a stokes litter to lower the unconscious form of Captain Soto into the boat. Once he was sure everyone from his team left the *Kobiashi Maru*, Morgan climbed down the ladder and boarded the last CRRC.

The two CRRCs came along side *Ohio* with some of her crew assisting Morgan's team with hauling their new acquisitions onboard as well as the boat's independent duty hospital corpsman tending to Petty Officer Hernandez's injury. After climbing on the turtleback, Morgan watched as the two CRRCs came up on deck for deflation and storage. While the sailors worked to clear the turtleback, Morgan looked back towards the *Kobiashi Maru*. The ship's superstructure still showed barely above the surface of the water.

The last of the deck crew started down the ladder back inside the boat. Morgan took one last look at the *Kobiashi Maru* before she sank. *Mission accomplished.* The North Koreans might now think twice about smuggling nuclear triggers to Iran. The doubts he'd had about the informants who provided the information were proved wrong. The mousy rat had seemed to be only out for a payoff as so many informers were, but not this time. He'd like to know what else the informant knew, because the North Koreans would try again, and it was wishful thinking to suppose otherwise. They always tried again.

The *Kobiashi Maru* finally dipped below the ocean's surface, the last of the air bubbling to the surface disturbing the otherwise glassy surface of the water.

So much for the no win scenario…, he thought to himself with a smirk.

He descended the ladder, closing the lockout chamber hatch behind him. Time for debrief in the boat's Battle Management Center and a quick and well earned 'Hollywood' shower. Then rack time. Surface Warfare Officers, even former ones, never had enough sleep. As he nodded off in the troop berthing area, *Ohio*'s diving alarm sounded with the traditional "Dive! Dive!" passing over the boat's announcing system, and the eighteen-thousand-ton submarine slipped silently beneath the waves.

CHAPTER
ONE

Headquarters,
2nd Foreign Parachute Regiment,
French Foreign Legion
Gao, Mali

Jerry Biggs, call sign Logan, stood atop the regimental headquarters building and looked west towards the sun setting over the Niger River. Over his shoulder, to the east, lay Gao's airport. Its lights were the only sign of modern civilization in northern Mali.

Another desert shithole, lovely.

Between Logan's years in the U.S. Marine Corps and his work as a consultant for Constellis, he'd been in Afghanistan, Iraq, Syria, Kenya, Chad, Libya, and now Mali. Still, he shouldn't complain too much; the money was excellent. Way more than he earned as a United States Marine Corps officer. Still single in his mid-thirties, Jerry used that money to enjoy himself wherever, and with whomever, he wanted. His 'don't give a shit' demeanor, tough, cruel features, black curly hair, and stocky build were irresistible to many women around the world.

He particularly liked the ladies he met when stationed at

Camp Courtney, Okinawa while on the staff of 3rd Marine Expeditionary Brigade. A bevy of Japanese, Korean, and Filipino women came into, and out of, his life at a substantial rate while out in the Western Pacific.

Just like that little Filipina hottie Bob Morgan married. Wonder how ol' Bob is doing these days. Hadn't heard from him since his divorce and return to the boat teams...

Jerry shook his head and took one last look around before headed back into the building and its blessed air conditioning. He headed to the lounge and saw the parachute regiment commanding officer, Lieutenant Colonel Jean-Charles Bethune, smoking a cigarette. Jerry liked working with the Foreign Legion. They were tough, smart, and very professional operators who didn't take to the politically correct agendas of the other armed forces back in Europe or in the States. The regiment Jerry advised had, until recently, gave the Islamic insurgents, like the Jama'a Nusrat ul-Islam wa al-Muslimin, a run for their money. They'd wiped out several cells in their area of operations. The effort supported the overall French-led anti-insurgent campaign known as Operation: Barkhane. The operation began on August 1st, 2014 in cooperation with five countries, all former French colonies that spanned the Sahel: Burkina Faso, Chad, Mali, Mauritania, and Niger.

Lately, the JNIM has counter-attacked French forces all over the country with results deadlier than expected. The French intelligence folks out their headquarters in Niamey, Niger worked day and night trying to figure out how this was happening and more importantly how to stop the onslaught.

"*Bonsoir, Mon Colonel*," Jerry said.

"Good evening Monsieur Logan. How are things outside?"

"Same as it was yesterday. Hot, dry, dusty, and thankfully quiet."

"Good, I like quiet."

"Any word from H.Q. on JNIM activity?"

"No, those JNIM *bâtards* seem to have melted away. Our drones out of Niger haven't found their base of operations yet."

"Could satellite imagery help?"

"Maybe. Do you have some handy?"

"Not quite, but I know who to call…"

Explosions suddenly rocked the building, knocking Jerry and Colonel Bethune off their feet. A siren wailed. The Colonel grabbed a radio off his belt.

"Voici le Colonel Bethune. Que se passe-t-il?" (This is Colonel Bethune. What's going on?)

"This is Caporal-chef Vannier. We're taking artillery and mortar fire and armored vehicles are approaching the fence line."

The two men exited the lounge and stared dumbfounded at the utter carnage they saw. Flaming buildings lit the compound. Bombs and artillery shells had flattened others. Smoke hung thick in the air, stinging Jerry's eyes. Outside the fence, they saw five German-built Boxer armored fighting vehicles rumbled towards the gates. Each eight-wheeled vehicle mounted an Israeli-made Samson Mk II turret complete with 30-millimeter cannons, 7.62-millimeter machine guns, and Spike anti-tank missiles. The Boxers smashed through the gates and the surrounding fence. The turret guns spat flame, the detonations thumping loudly, laying down suppressing fire as the rear doors opened. Eight JNIM insurgents exited from each vehicle firing their AK-47s as they moved. Three of the regiment's *Véhicule de l'avant blindé* armored personnel carriers attempted to reach the battle, but the Boxer's Spike missiles made short work of them. Behind the Boxers, additional insurgents poured through the now flattened fence. They used the Boxers as initial cover, then spread out over the base. A single Puma helicopter gunship approached the Boxers, but a sixth Boxer responded. That Boxer was equipped with a Swiss-built Oerlikon Skyshield 35-millimeter anti-air cannon. It thundered once and blew the Puma out of the sky.

Colonel Bethune and Jerry launched into the fight. They

engaged the insurgents with their FAMAS Valorisé and M-4 assault rifles, but the heavy fire from the Boxers drove them back into the regimental headquarters. More reports crackled over the Colonel's radio, sounds of machine gun fire drowning out the Legionnaire's voices. The insurgents were overrunning French positions with cries for help coming in fast and unheeded. The Colonel looked out the door.

"*Merde*! Where the hell, did they get those things?"

Logan looked out and saw a swarm of insurgents heading their way.

"Don't know, but I'm taking as many of those sons-of-bitches with me before I go. You with me?"

"*Oui*, let's go my friend."

The pair opened the door and charged out into a hail of gunfire, firing as they ran. Colonel Bethune received a barrage of 7.62-millimeter rounds and was dead before his bullet ridden body hit the desert floor. Jerry responded with a three-round volley from his M-4, killing the insurgent that took his friend's life. He knelt down on one knee and continued to fire until his weapon ran out of ammunition. He threw the now useless M-4 on the ground and drew his K-Bar fighting knife, a souvenir from his days in the Marine Corps. He plunged the blade into the abdomen of the first insurgent within reach, a quick zig-zag move disemboweled him. Before the body hit the ground, he was already striking upwards, into the soft palate of the next insurgent, as he raised his AK-47. Moving swiftly towards the third insurgent, his body jerked as several rounds struck him in the torso. He kept going and when he finally fell from the rounds aimed at his legs, he caught a glimpse of eight bodies surrounding him.

Ha! Eight to one, nice kill ratio…

CHAPTER
TWO

CIA Headquarters
Langley, Virginia
Two Days Later

CIA Deputy Director of Intelligence, Ronald Bailey, strode through the seventh floor hallway towards his office. Seating his tall, athletic frame behind his desk, which held the day's newspaper and a file folder next to a picture of his family.

"Jags still finding ways to lose," the Jacksonville native said to himself as he scanned the sports headlines. He'd played corner back for Austin Peay, and he followed the ups-and-downs, mostly downs, of the Jaguars since the team's founding.

He opened the file and perused the dossier on an operative that, he hoped, was best-suited for the escalating Mali situation, James Robert Morgan.

The file told story of an officer with extensive background in maritime intelligence, naval operations, and both Navy and Agency special operations. An injury suffered while on mission with the Maritime Branch led to his transfer to the Analysis Branch.

"Hmph, allegedly transferred to the Analysis Branch…" Director Bailey said aloud.

Bailey skimmed the rest of the file. It told him that Morgan, on paper, was the man to handle the current crisis, quirky (Morgan's psychological profile said he was very introverted almost to the point of misanthropy), but very effective. He'd have to see if reality matched the history. The file contained Morgan's official CIA photograph, taken after his injury that led to his transfer. It showed a young man with a close-cropped head of brown hair with a hazel colored right eye, a patch over his left eye, and a Van Dyke beard. The right side of his mouth curled into what could only be described as a smirk. It reminded him of the 1970s era comic-book hero, the Green Arrow. The eyepatch also gave him a somewhat piratical look.

The Deputy Director picked up the phone and dialed his secretary.

"Coleen, where is Commander Morgan?"

"Virginia Beach, sir. He's on his two-week active duty period at the Navy and Marine Corps Intelligence Training Center."

"Please get me NMITC's commanding officer on the line."

"Yes, sir."

We need Commander Morgan back up here as soon as possible.

Morgan sat at his table at his favorite restaurant in Norfolk, Streats. He could have gone to one of the many places on the Virginia Beach oceanfront much closer to where he was staying out at Dam Neck. However, they all had the same problem, too many people. He preferred the smaller, relatively quieter places in Norfolk's Ghent neighborhood, with Streats being his favorite. After all, they had the James Bond martini on the drink menu. Add in a raisin-free bread pudding du jour, and the results were spectacular.

Streat's owner, Mr. Neil Boden, handed Morgan the check.

"How was everything this evening?" he asked.

"Great as always, Neil." Morgan replied as he handed Neil his government issued travel credit card.

As Neil turned away to finish the transaction, Morgan's phone rang. Looking at the caller ID, he knew he had to answer and not let it go to voice mail, as was his preference.

"Morgan," he answered.

"Bob! It's Clint Peters." the voice on the other end replied. Clint was Morgan's boss in his new home at the Agency's Analysis Branch. "How's the vacation?"

"Wonderful. Anytime I can spend outside the cubicle farm at Langley is great. However, I would not call my annual two-week active duty period a vacation, exactly. Putting in some serious work at NMITC."

"What are they having you do?"

"I'm revamping their curriculum for the basic intelligence course. It is way out of date, especially concerning what the Agency can bring to the table."

"Outstanding. We could use all the good word we can get. However, I need to cut your trip short. Deputy Director Bailey wants to see you back up here as soon as possible."

"I still have a week to go…"

"I know, but the Director has contacted the C.O. there, and you're cleared to finish up with full credit given for your annual training."

"I'll be back tonight."

"I'll let the General's office know to expect you first thing tomorrow morning."

"Any idea what's going on?"

"Not a clue."

Morgan ended the call as Neil handed the check and card back to him.

"You look rather annoyed, sir. Everything alright?" Neil said with a look of concern as Morgan passed him back the signed check with his customary high 'glad I don't have to deal with the people you do' tip.

"Unexpected work-related news. Have to get going a little sooner than I planned."

Morgan climbed into his 2013 Corvette Grand Sport parked across Twenty First Street from the restaurant and headed back to the beach. The car's Cyber Gray Metallic paint and red heritage stripes on the front fenders shining brightly in the early evening light.

CHAPTER
THREE

Morgan arrived at CIA headquarters early to beat the horrible morning traffic in and around the D.C. area. He wore dark grey dress slacks, a light grey button-down dress shirt with a scarlet and grey regimental-style stripped tie. He also sported an Omega Seamaster 300-meter diver's watch on his left wrist. A sharp, tailored navy-blue blazer with two distinct lapel pins rounded out his attire. The first was a gold pin showing a ship's bow over two crossed swords, the emblem of a United States Navy Surface Warfare Officer. The second was silver, showing a patrol boat over a crossed cutlass and flintlock pistol, the emblem of the U.S. Navy's Special Warfare Craft Crewman community. Two miniature versions of the pins he wore on his Navy uniform representing two of the three warfare specialties Morgan had mastered. He was currently working on his third.

Morgan walked, or as his ex-wife Julie used to say, swaggered, along the seventh-floor hallway and into General Bailey's outer office. His eyes widened as he first saw the attractive, brown-eyed brunette sitting behind the secretary's desk.

"Good morning. I have an appointment to see the Director Bailey."

"Name please?" the raven-haired young woman asked as she stared at her computer screen.

"Morgan, James Morgan. My friends call me Bob," Morgan offered his hand.

The secretary looked up, smiled, and shook Morgan's out stretched hand and replied, "Colleen Biggins and my friends call me Colleen. Director Bailey is finishing a teleconference, but he'll see you shortly."

"A pleasure Colleen and thank you."

Morgan began to wander around the office, stealing a glance now and then at Ms. Biggins, who bore a very strong resemblance to the singer Shania Twain.

Director Bailey's outer office held many souvenirs from his time in the service. One item in particular caught Morgan's one good eye. It was a framed, green t-shirt with a distinctive logo at the upper right, a numeral two pierced by a Marine K-Bar combat knife. A small plaque mounted to the bottom of the frame read:

To Colonel Ronald Baily, USMC,
Commanding Officer, 2nd Regimental Combat Team,
Task Force TARAWA,
Operation Iraqi Freedom, 2003

Morgan recognized the unit's name. He had taken some of those Marines up the Euphrates River during the drive towards Baghdad.

He then wandered over to a series of photographs showing the Director during various times in his Marine Corps career. The pictures showed him from his time as a young second lieutenant and platoon commander to his retirement ceremony at the rank of lieutenant general.

While looking at a display of several dozen challenge coins over on a sideboard, the door to General Bailey's inner office opened and the Deputy Director stuck his head out.

"Commander Morgan, come on in," the General said.

Morgan enter the Deputy Director's office and found himself facing the tall, athletic, African American former Marine. As the pair walked further into the office, Morgan shook the General's offered hand.

"Please, James, take a seat."

"Thank you, sir, but I go by Bob."

"Bob?"

"Yes, sir, middle name. My late father was James, and I went by Bob in order to know which one of us my late mother was yelling at."

"Ah, very good. Now for the business at hand, I heard great things about your recovery of those North Korean nuclear triggers. Well done."

"The North Koreans should have used a ship with a better name. Didn't they watch *Star Trek*?"

"You'd think," replied General Bailey. "The head of the Special Activities Center had some issues with how the mission proceeded. He seemed concerned that your physical condition led to a team member's injury, and he doesn't want you back in SAC."

"That doesn't surprise me. Malcom Stone and I never got along very well."

"How so?"

"Well before he joined the agency, he was my first Commanding Officer on the *Winston S. Churchill,* and he slept with my now ex-wife."

"What!?"

"Yes, sir. Julie was a cousin by marriage of my leading petty officer, and I met her at a divisional party early in my tour. We hit it off well, and we married a few months later. She met Captain Stone during a ship's Christmas party, and feeling command-at-sea made him more handsome and more charming, he proceeded to seduce her. The whole thing ruined my marriage, his marriage, and almost ended Stone's Navy career. Only his patrons in the Navy kept him from being court-martialed, and since he had already been selected for promotion to Captain, he put on his new rank, but had to retire way earlier than he planned. Since then, he's had a bit of grudge against me."

"Holy crap! That's terrible! I've always felt Stone is a bit of an arrogant ass, but damn." The General continued, "Well, never mind him, but I need your maritime analysis acumen." The General handed Morgan a file folder covered with several colorful classification markings.

"We received a request from our French colleagues in the DGSE," the General continued. "The counter-insurgency operations against Jama'a Nusrat ul-Islam wa al-Muslimin and other Islamic extremists in Mali are not going as well as expected. Two days ago, the Jama'a Nusrat ul-Islam wa al-Muslimin attacked headquarters of the French Foreign Legion in Mali inflicting heavy casualties. Drone and satellite imagery showed the insurgents using weapons much heavier, and more expensive, than an insurgent group should have. Self-propelled artillery, armored infantry fighting vehicles, and the like. The DGSE are at a loss as to where these are coming from, and they have requested our assistance."

"Where do I come in, sir? Last I looked, Mali is land locked, not exactly a big maritime player."

"The nature of these weapons and the fact they are manufactured by countries all over the world, China, Russia, the European Union, and even the US, suggests they have to be arriving by sea. These are not the type of things one can smuggle in the back of a Toyota Hilux pick-up truck, and we have all the potential air supply routes covered. I need you to start digging around the financials and ship tracking data to find out where these things are coming from and, more importantly, who's bankrolling the whole thing."

"Yes, sir. Anything else?"

"Not right now. We will discuss further action once you figure this out."

Morgan rose up from his seat and turned towards the office door.

"Oh Bob, one more thing."

"Sir?"

"Your call sign, Gargoyle?"

"From then-Commodore Allard, my C.O. while I served on the Amphibious Squadron Eight staff. He was a previous A-6 and F/A-18 pilot, so he assigned everyone on his staff a call sign. Mine came from the brand of sunglasses I wore at the time, and it stuck."

"Marty Allard?"

"Yes, sir."

"Sounds like something Mallard would come up with. I like it. Carry on."

"Yes, sir."

Morgan entered the outer office and saw Colleen hard at work.

"I hope to be seeing more of you in the weeks to come."

"Same here, but I do have one request."

"Oh?"

"Could you please smile?"

"Excuse me?"

"Well, you're smirking in all the pictures of you in your file, and, if you don't mind me saying, a man as handsome as you are should do more than smirk."

"Actually, I never smile. It scares people, especially small children."

"Scares people?"

Morgan looked Colleen right in the eyes and drew his lips

into a smile revealing his abnormally large canine teeth making him look, in a word, malevolent. This, plus the cold, narrow look in his one remaining eye made Colleen gasp.

"Oh, my! You're right. That is frightening."

"That's why I smirk. Much friendlier don't you think? Good day, Colleen." Morgan tilted his head and smirked.

"Good day, Bob." Colleen replied with gleam in her lovely brown eyes.

CHAPTER
FOUR

Morgan left the seventh floor and headed to his desk down in the Analysis Branch. Once there, he set his World War 2 Victory-style coffee mug under his desktop Nespresso machine and made his first cup of the morning. Symbols of his Navy career adorned his mug. On one side, a surface warfare pin, and 'Gargoyle'. On the other, the emblem of PHIBRON Eight and his old N2 office code. He drank it black, no sugar. After the first sip, he turned to his computer monitor. He checked his email and seeing there was nothing needing immediate attention, opened his Automatic Identification System, or AIS, program. AIS, via on board radio transponders, tracked ships anywhere on the Earth, if the transponder worked properly.

There has to be a pattern, Morgan thought as he looked at the hundreds of ship icons crossing his screen.

He adjusted the display to focus on the West African coast. If those weapons came via ship, this would be the most logical place to come ashore as it is closest to the Malian boarder. After a few minutes of looking, however, Morgan came to the realization that he needed some assistance. He took a fresh sip of his coffee, reached for his desk phone, and pushed one of the speed dial buttons. After a couple of rings, a male voice answered.

"Cyber Intelligence, this is Lloyd."

"Good morning, Lloyd. Bob Morgan here."

"What can I do for you?"

"Quick question, how much AIS information do we record?"

"We usually keep six months or so on hand, and we archive a year's worth."

"So, we have enough for a trend analysis."

"Sure. What do you have in mind?"

"Swing by my desk and I'll give you the rundown. I received some tasking from the DDI, and I could use some help."

"Sure. On my way."

A few minutes later, a tall gentleman with salt and pepper colored curly hair and round wire-framed glasses appeared at Morgan's desk. Morgan and Lloyd Decker had worked together before on the North Korea operation, and now he was Morgan's go-to-guy on all things computer related.

"Damn, Bob! Never understood why's your desk all the way back in the corner?"

"I like it back here. It's private. Keeps people at arm's length."

"Fair enough, what can I do for you?"

"Some heavy weapons made their way to Jama'a Nusrat ul-Islam wa al-Muslimin forces in Mali. My working theory is they came via ship from various points of origin then made their way inland, possibly by barge up the River Gambie, then overland through Senegal and into Mali. What I need is an analysis of the past twelve months or so of AIS data showing any deviation from the normal merchant traffic patterns in and around the area."

"Yeah, I can do that. Have an area in mind?"

Morgan passed Lloyd a series of latitudes and longitudes to narrow the search area into something more realistic.

"When do you think you can have this ready?" asked Morgan.

"Will twenty four hours from now work?"

"That'll work. Owe you one, Lloyd."

"Actually, you owe me about 512," Lloyd said. "But who's counting?" He smiled and turned back towards his office.

With the work on how now underway, it was time to begin figuring out who might be able to pull off such a task. Morgan popped his ear buds into his ears and while listening to one of the works of John Williams began researching shipping firms with fleets large enough to move bulky cargo, yet small enough that smuggling weapons might be financially attractive. Companies like A.P. Moller-Maersk Group, Hapag-Lloyd, and Evergreen did not need the additional income gunrunning brought, while firms like Pt Salam Pacific Indonesia Lines did not have the numbers to hide smuggling behind its legitimate shipping efforts.

Later in the morning, Morgan heard a knock on the side of his cubicle. He paused his music, looked up, and saw Clint Peters standing there.

"Can I bum a cup of coffee from you?" Peters held out an empty CIA-branded coffee mug.

"Sure." Morgan grabbed the mug.

As the Nespresso machine filled the cup, Morgan turned to his friend and boss.

"You here to talk, or indulge in my superior brew?"

"Both, the coffee in the cafeteria is like the swill my ex-wife used to make, and we haven't had a chance to talk since you returned from the *Ohio*. How are you doing?"

"The mission went fine at my level, but one of my team came within inches of losing proper use of his left arm due to the knife attack by a crew member I missed. The guy's blade came close to the tendons."

"Not your fault, Bob."

"Tell that to Stone."

"Stone is Stone. You need to put that behind you and concentrate on the now. And I have some news that will help with that."

25

"Oh?"

"The documents you recovered from the *Kobiashi Maru* may shed some additional light on what's going on in Mali. The ship was the property of RDS Shipping, a company based out of Copenhagen with offices in the US, London, and Singapore. The ship's logs showed that while the property of RDS, she made several voyages to the West African coast. Conversations with Captain Sato, who is quite talkative since you snagged him, mentioned picking up several large cargos he subsequently dropped off in West Africa. This was all before the ship was bought by that North Korean shell company you uncovered for their use."

"Indeed. RDS is one of firms I have my eye on. Lloyd Decker is working an analysis of AIS data to check for any anomalies. Anyone running the company's financials?"

"Should have an analysis in the next day or two."

"Lloyd's analysis is expected tomorrow as well."

"Thanks for the coffee, Bob," Peters said as he walked away from Morgan's desk.

Morgan kept working until the end of the day with a list of potential firms locked up in his safe as he prepared to leave for the day. He left his navy blazer hanging on a hook in his office and slipped on his green U.S. Navy CWU-36P flight jacket, which was covered in patches reflecting his time on active duty before heading out to the parking lot.

Morgan drove his Corvette Grand Sport down Virginia Route 123 away from Langley and towards his home in Burke, Virginia. Looking at the traffic display on his after-market Panasonic info-tainment system, he saw patches of yellow and orange indicating the flow of traffic, or lack thereof.

Who the hell are all these people, and why are they all in my way?!

Finally, he saw his street coming up and slid to his assigned parking spot in front of his condominium. He slipped his everyday carry Beretta Nano out of the car's center console and into his Alien Gear inside-the waistband holster before heading to his front door.

After checking his mailbox for snail mail, Morgan unlocked the door and stepped inside. One thing he learned from his ex was how to decorate. His living room was minimally decorated in a 1920s art deco style while the kitchen, which was open to the living room, had wood cabinets with nickel pulls, green granite countertops, and stainless-steel appliances. He proceeded to his home office to check email and social media sites on his personal computer. As he sat behind his desk, he admired the nautical themed office he assembled. Behind him a brass ship's clock, which chimes the bells of the watch, and a matching barometer hung on the wall. Along another wall hung Morgan's Shellback, Bluenose, and Order of the Ditch certificates for sailing over or through the Equator, Arctic Circle, and Suez Canal, respectively. Other mementoes of his time in the service either hung on the walls or sat on his bookshelves and desk.

That's one thing about my job at the Agency, there are no souvenirs of my travels.

Morgan headed to the kitchen to put some dinner together. He pulled some leftover tempeh and broccoli and a bottle of water out of the refrigerator, sat on his couch, and turned on his 65 inch, 4K Sony television. He watched the evening news as he ate his dinner. Morgan's diet turned more towards plant-based proteins since his parents passed away from a combination of heart disease and complications from type 2 diabetes. He still loved the occasional steak, especially the wagu New York strip from BLT Steak in the District, or a bacon cheeseburger, but not as often as he used to.

Morgan's phone rang. He looked at the caller ID and saw who it was.

Christ, Julie. What the hell does she want?

He let the call go to voice mail. No one interrupts a SWO while he's eating, unless the ship's on fire or under attack.

Morgan cleaned up his dinner dishes and headed up to his

bedroom. As he changed out of his work clothes, he looked at himself in a full-length mirror. Not bad for a guy in his mid-thirties. Three things stood out in the reflection of Morgan's somewhat lanky five foot ten inch frame; first were the scars on the left side of his face where his eye used to be, with the second and third being his two tattoos: the octopus emblem of the Special Executive for Counter Intelligence, Terrorism, Revenge and Extortion (better known as S.P.E.C.T.R.E.) on his upper left arm, and the stylized eagle emblem of the Strategic Homeland Intervention Enforcement and Logistics Division (better known as S.H.I.E.L.D.) on his upper right arm. Both tattoos reflected his love of both the classic James Bond films and the modern Marvel films. He put on a t-shirt and sweatpants and played Julie's message.

"Hi Bob, its Julie. I'm lonely, could you please come over? I miss you, baby! Call me. Bye!"

"Ha! Fat chance! I'm not that desperate," Morgan said aloud.

After reading a few more chapters in Ian Toll's amazing book *Six Frigates* while relaxing to one of his favorite musical pieces, Jerry Goldsmith's score to *Star Trek: The Motion Picture*, Morgan went back to his bedroom. He stripped off his t-shirt and sweatpants, climbed into bed, and drew up the covers. Shutting off the light on his nightstand, Morgan switched on his white noise generator. After years in the Navy, he needed some background noise to sleep. On board a ship, if it was silent, something was wrong. Once the lights were out and the white noise started, Morgan immediately surrendered to sleep.

CHAPTER
FIVE

After slogging through the typical Northern Virginia morning traffic, Morgan arrived at the parking lot at CIA headquarters, parked his 'Vette, and headed inside. As he did on most mornings, especially if he did not have an early appointment, Morgan stopped briefly on the CIA seal embossed on the floor. He then turned his head towards the Memorial Wall and its anonymous gold stars. He threw a silent salute towards the wall and to all those memorialized there and headed through the security checkpoint.

Arriving at his desk, Morgan logged into his computer, opened his email, and immediately noticed the message from Lloyd with the subject line "CALL ME!" Grabbing his phone, he dialed Lloyd's extension.

"This is Lloyd." Morgan heard after a single ring.

"You bellowed?"

"The AIS analysis program finished its run last night. Can you swing by my desk?"

"Sure. I'll see if Clint Peters is available and we'll both head up."

"See you in a bit."

Morgan stopped by Clint's desk with a spare coffee mug

filled from his Nespresso machine. He grabbed the man's attention by waving the cup under his boss's nose.

"Good morning, boss! Here, a little life's blood for our walk to Lloyd Decker's office. His AIS data analysis is ready."

"Perfect," Peters replied. "The financials are ready as well. We can compare notes and see what we have."

The pair walked to the CIA's Office of Analytic Production and Dissemination, home to the Agency's cyber analysts, where Lloyd's desk resided. Seeing the pair approach, Lloyd waved them over.

"Gentlemen. I have some news," said Lloyd.

Peters replied, "So do we. Is your conference room available?"

"This way," Lloyd said as he grabbed his laptop and notes.

The trio set up in the conference room, and Lloyd projected an AIS display on a big, wall-mounted screen.

"I took a look at a year's worth of AIS data," Lloyd began. "I wrote a program looking for any anomalies, especially disappearing tracks, tracks out of expected positions, etc. in the area of West Africa we're interested in. There was one group of ships that stood out." Lloyd switched the screen to a list of several ships.

"These ships," Lloyd went on, "all tracked normally along the African coast from both the north and south. They disappeared once they reached the coast off The Gambia, specifically, at a position 30 nautical miles due west of Serrekunda. The tracks then reappeared further along their intended track. However, if you compute the time distance problem, they all were not where they supposed to be based on the course and speed they showed prior to their disappearance. The discrepancy equates to several hours of dead time. To the casual observer, it appeared normal or at worst a temporary loss of AIS data, but there are too many of them to be a coincidence."

Morgan looked at the ships up on the screen. Each ship was a medium sized container ship equipped with on board cranes. He noticed the owner of all these ships was RDS Shipping.

"So, none of these ships sailed into Serrekunda or maybe Dakar, Senegal?" asked Morgan.

"No, they went nowhere near those ports nor any other in the area."

"Interesting." Morgan said. "Clint, what did the financial folks find?"

"They ran RDS Shipping's numbers for the past few years. The company was in fairly dire straits until recently. Their revenue stream is now quite steady, at least on paper."

"Meaning they could have revenue streams off the books supplementing their legitimate income to make it look normal."

"Correct. And the numbers began to improve shortly before the French began having setbacks in Mali."

"It sounds like we have the 'who'," Lloyd said. "But I don't understand the 'how.' None of the ships went anywhere near a port."

"They don't have to," Morgan said. "Each ship has on board crane capability, and if you use shallow draft lighterage, you can move a lot of cargo. The Gambia River is navigable for at least 350 miles inland. Set up a crane somewhere up-river or put a crane on the barge; unload the cargo, finish the move inland, and you're good to go. Never use the same place twice and you can keep everyone guessing."

"Makes sense," Lloyd said. "Who's in charge at RDS Shipping?"

"This gentleman," Peters pulled a picture out of a file folder. "Edward Rasmussen, age 60, Danish citizen, second generation owner of RDS Shipping after the passing of his father fifteen years ago."

The picture showed a tall man with short, grey hair cut in a military style and wearing an expensive, well-tailored, suit, standing behind a podium. The one word which best described him would be 'distinguished.'

"He's quite well known in social circles as a contributor to several animal-related causes. Pet adoption, animal shelters, spay/neuter clinics, that sort of thing," Peters continued. "He's grooming his only child, a daughter, as his successor." Peters pulled a second picture from the file. It showed a strikingly beautiful woman with long, black hair, olive complexion, and Scandinavian facial features sitting on a stage apparently at the same function as her father.

"Lady Aurora Essenhigh, widow of the late Sir Ian Essenhigh, and sole heir to his substantial estate. Her dark hair and complexion come from her Italian mother, Martina, deceased."

"Guess she's the light of her father's life?" Morgan said. His two friends turned towards him and gave him an evil look for the obvious pun.

"What?" Morgan asked as he shrugged his shoulders.

"Lady Essenhigh shares her father's love of animals, and she's a major patron of the UK's RSPCA and the Humane Society International in Denmark."

Tearing his gaze from Lady Essenhigh's picture, Morgan gave his head a quick shake and looked at his companions. "Okay, we have a shipping company which is the right size to hide a smuggling operation amongst legitimate business, a company with a near miraculous financial recovery from near certain bankruptcy, and a company whose ships appear and disappear from AIS. As the saying goes 'Once is happenstance, twice is coincidence, the third time it's enemy action.' I recommend we see General Bailey."

The trio picked up their materials and headed to the seventh floor.

Morgan, Peters, and Decker entered General Bailey's outer office and checked in with always-lovely Ms. Biggins.

"Good morning, Colleen. Is the General available?"

"He has nothing on his calendar this morning…," she looked at her computer monitor. "Okay, he's clear until noon," she continued as she picked up her phone. "General, Mr. Peters, Mr.

Morgan, and Mr. Decker are here to see you." She paused a moment, "Right, sir. Okay gentlemen, please go in."

Morgan looked straight into her eyes, "Available for lunch?"

"Not today I'm afraid, raincheck?"

"Please." Morgan turned towards the inner office.

As the three entered Bailey's office, the General looked up from his computer. "Gentlemen, what do you have for me?"

Peters being the senior member of the three took the lead on briefing the DDI on the team's findings. After Morgan closed out the briefing, the General smiled and congratulated them on a job well done.

"So, what's our next course of action?" General Bailey asked.

"Simple, we get someone on the inside." Morgan said. "Someone who can get a hold of RDS's schedules and manifests to find the next shipment meant for Mali."

"Sounds good," said Bailey. "When do you leave?"

"Excuse me, sir? Did you say me?"

"Bob, you're perfect for this mission. You know the intelligence inside and out, you're an expert on maritime operations, and you're a trained operations officer."

"Yes, sir, but Stone won't sanction this, not with my injury and my performance on the *Kobiashi Maru*."

"Stone can kiss my Marine Corps ass! I'm about to go over his head so hard he'll have my combat boots' prints on his scalp for the next year." The DDI reached for his phone.

"Colleen, please ring Admiral Fitzpatrick's office," Bailey said. Admiral Dennis Fitzpatrick currently served as the CIA's Deputy Director of Operations, or DDO, and was General Bailey's opposite number on the Agency's operations side.

After a brief pause, Bailey continued, "Denny! Ron Bailey here. I have a lead on that request from the DGSE and I need your concurrence with my intended course of action... You know Bob Morgan, call sign Gargoyle? Yeah, that's him. I want him out in the field. I feel this is none of Malcom Stone's business, and I prefer it if he didn't know about this. Great! I'll send him there right away. Thanks, Denny."

Bailey said to Morgan, "I'm sending you to see Admiral Fitzpatrick's assistant, Ms. Frances McCulloch. Brief her on what you briefed me earlier, and she'll work with you on a plan of action, an appropriate cover and any equipment you may need."

Morgan looked at the General with a very wide eye and said, "Aye, sir. Thank you."

"Don't thank me yet, this is just beginning."

"Yes, sir," Morgan and the rest began to head out.

"Bob, could you stay a moment? Please."

"Catch you guys later," Morgan said as Peters and Decker left the General's office.

When alone, General Bailey continued, "Bob, before you see Ms. McCulloch, I may have some bad news. Do you happen to know a Gerald Wayne Biggs?"

"Jerry? Yes, sir. We're high school and Ohio State classmates. He earned a Marine Corps commission the same time I earned my Navy one. He was also best man at my wedding, but we lost touch after my divorce and return to the boat teams. Why?"

"I thought so, I noticed the high school's name in both his file and yours. Jerry worked for me when I commanded the 3rd Marine Expeditionary Brigade out in Okinawa. He left the Corps shortly thereafter and joined Constellis."

"The private military company?"

"The same. He worked as a consultant around the globe and since I started here, would pass me information from time to time. Lately, he worked with the French Foreign Legion in Mali and acted as an unofficial conduit between the Agency and the French. Unfortunately, he was in Gao during that last attack and was killed. I'm sorry, Bob."

Morgan looked at General Bailey with an expression of shock and sadness.

Jerry? Dead? I can't believe it. Growing up, he seemed invincible.

He hardened his expression.

"Thank you, General. His passing makes getting to the bottom of this that much more imperative. Anything else, sir?"

"Not right now, good luck."

Morgan got up and left the General's office. He passed Colleen's desk, skipping their usual flirtations, and headed to Ms. McCulloch's office with a look of grim determination on his face.

CHAPTER
SIX

Morgan headed down the hall to the office of the Deputy Director of Operations, the Agency's senior field operative. Before he arrived at the DDO's office, he saw a woman standing by the door. Frances McCulloch. She had glasses, grey hair, and stood no taller than five feet two. She looked like someone's grandmother, and she was a legend in the Agency. She cut her teeth in covert operations during the waning days of the Cold War in both Moscow and Berlin Stations. She used her harmless, maternal appearance to run several agents right under the noses of both the Soviet-era KGB and East German Stazi. With the increase in tensions with a newly resurgent Russia, her experiences and resourcefulness led her to the number two spot in the Operations Directorate. All in all, a formidable woman.

"Hello, Gargoyle, or do you prefer Bob?"

"Bob please, ma'am. I save Gargoyle for the field."

"Very well. Let's step into my office."

The pair entered a well-appointed office filled with pictures of her family, including, appropriately enough, grandchildren. She sat at her desk and directed Morgan to a seat in front of it.

"What do you have for me?"

Morgan gave Ms. McCulloch a rundown of his findings.

Afterward, she looked at him with a thoughtful expression. She stood up and walked over to a sideboard.

"Coffee?" she asked.

"Yes, please, black, no sugar."

"Ha! Just like the Admiral. What is it with Navy guys and black coffee?"

"Keeps us going during the midwatch," Morgan replied. "Nothing keeps you awake better than coffee so strong it'll turn the inside of your mug jet black within a month."

"The mug you never wash?"

"Yes, ma'am. Washing removes hard earned flavor."

Frances let out another laugh as she passed a mug to Morgan. "So that explains the mug on Dennis's desk. It looks like a science project in there." She continued, "Do you have any ideas on how you can get inside RDS?"

"Yes, ma'am, two of them actually. First, I pose as a potential customer looking for a large scale, yet discrete, means of moving some cargo. Or two, I go in via either Rasmussen's or his daughter's charitable works."

"Have you thought about both?"

"It *would* provide two opportunities for access."

"Correct, doubles your chances of success. Provide me your plan by close of business, and I'll send you down to my man in Global Services to plan logistics and discuss equipment."

"Will do, ma'am." Morgan said as both he and Frances stood up.

"One more question. General Bailey was most insistent we keep Malcom Stone out of this? Why?"

"Well, Stone and I haven't seen eye-to-eye since he ruined my marriage and I ruined his Navy career."

Ms. McCulloch rolled her eyes. "That would do it. See you this afternoon."

"Yes, ma'am."

Morgan went back to his desk with a plan forming in the back of his mind. After some further research on Mr. Rasmussen and his all too attractive daughter, he finalized his ideas enough to pick up his phone.

"Hey, Clint! I have a plan of action, but I'd like to run it by you for a sanity check…"

Morgan retuned to Ms. McCulloch's office at 16:00 with Clint Peters in tow. After quick introductions, the pair gave Frances an outline of the plan. She looked at the two men sitting in her office and smiled. She took a quick sip from her water glass.

"What's your timeline?" she asked.

"Both father and daughter are hosting an invitation-only fund raiser for the Humane Society International in Copenhagen in two weeks," Morgan said. "A 100,000-dollar donation is required for an invite. A suitably large donation above and beyond the 100 grand should secure me an introduction to the pair."

"Steep, but doable. I'll authorize the expenditure along with an expense account necessary for your cover. Anything else?"

"No, ma'am."

"Good. I'll give my man in Global Services a heads up you will be seeing him first thing in the morning. I think you will like Joe. He's been with the Agency almost as long as I have, and you both have similar taste in coffee." Frances winked as Morgan left her office.

CHAPTER
SEVEN

CIA Headquarters
The Next Day

Morgan headed down to the basement of CIA headquarters to meet Ms. McCulloch's point of contact in the Global Services division, the Agency's supply department. He opened the door and entered some sort of combination workshop/storage area. Walking up to one of the folks running around, he caught her attention with a gentle tap on the shoulder.

"Good morning. I'm looking for Joe," Morgan said.

The harried young woman turned and cupped her hands around her mouth, "Hey, Chop!" she shouted. "You have a visitor!"

A Hispanic gentleman about 65 years of age with grey hair streaked with black and a pencil moustache came out from behind a stack of pallets. Looking at Morgan he said, "You must be Gargoyle. I'm Joe Acevedo."

The two men shook hands.

Morgan asked, "Chop? Are you former Navy?"

"Retired Navy Supply Corps Commander. I started out in the

Surface Warfare community before transferring to the Supply Corps in the mid-80s."

"Destroyers?"

"U.S.S. *Conolly* and U.S.S. *John Hancock*."

"Outstanding! I served on *Winston S. Churchill*."

"Thought so. Coffee? Let me guess, black, no sugar?" Joe asked with a smile. "Come on, let's head to my desk and we'll see how I can help out a fellow tin can sailor."

For the next few hours, Morgan and Joe worked out the details for his mission including weapons, transportation, communications, and other odds and ends. As they finished up, Joe took a critical look at Morgan's eye patch.

"I understand your injury caused some problems during your last mission?"

"Yeah, one of my team was injured because I missed someone in my blind spot."

"Hmmmm," Joe said looking lost in thought. "One of my folks may have something for you. Let me take a picture of your right eye."

Morgan leaned over Joe's desk as Joe took a close-up picture of Morgan's good eye. Joe continued, "Okay, that's all for now, but here, you'll need this if you're going to look your cover's part." He handed Morgan what some consider the holy grail of credit cards, an American Express Black Card. A card so exclusive, it had no spending limit. This particular one had his cover name and employer embossed on it.

"It's linked to your Agency expense account, so save any receipts," Joe said with a smile. "I recommend obtaining the appropriate wardrobe."

"I have just the thing in mind." Morgan said. "Thanks, Chop!"

Morgan exited the building and started the Grand Sport. The 'Vette's 436 horsepower LS3 V8 engine screamed out of the parking spot and towards the headquarters' outer gate while ignoring the indignant look from the gate guard.

Morgan walked through the tailor shop's door and immediately came to the attention of the proprietor, Mr. Mark Levinson.

"Mr. Morgan. Haven't seen you in a while. Still enjoying the blazer?"

"Very much. It lends a bit of class to my somewhat boring job," Morgan replied. "Can you do a couple of bespoke suits and a tux in less than two weeks?"

Mr. Levinson's eyes widened to the size of dinner plates, "No, sir. The patterns alone take two weeks. Will a made-to-measure garments work?"

"Sure. Let's see what you have."

Morgan and Levinson spent about 30 minutes going over available styles and took Morgan's measurements. Morgan left the store with an appointment for his first fitting in 5 days' time, and a few new ties to go with the shirts he also ordered.

I love expense accounts.

Morgan climbed in the 'Vette for the trip home.

CHAPTER
EIGHT

Leesburg, Virginia Executive Airport
Ten Days Later

Morgan sat and enjoyed a quiet, people-free wait for his flight to Copenhagen in the Leesburg, Virginia airport's departure lounge. As he read a novel in his e-reader, a rather attractive auburn-haired woman in a pilot's uniform attracted his attention.

"Mr. Morgan? I'm Susan, your First Officer. We're ready for you."

"Thank you, and please call me Bob."

Morgan got up, grabbed his personal and garment bags, and followed Susan to the tarmac.

She doesn't look like any of the aviators I've ever served with, shit hot! Or as my aviator friends would say, sierra hotel!

Morgan caught his first glimpse of his ride to Copenhagen as he exited the terminal, a brand new, CIA owned Cessna Citation Longitude. The 72-foot long, 20-foot wide aircraft with the 69-foot wingspan gleamed in the early morning light. The Agency's Air Branch's latest aircraft cruised at .84 Mach in industry leading quiet comfort. The best part, Morgan was the only passenger.

Oh yeah, way better than flying commercial!

As the pair approached the boarding ladder, a gentleman in a dark suit and even darker sunglasses approached Morgan.

"Compliments of Ms. McCulloch," he said as he handed him a padded envelope.

"Thank you."

Morgan boarded the aircraft. Once up the ladder, he turned to his right, and looked into the well-appointed cabin decorated in varying shades of light and dark greys. Morgan moved to take the first forward-facing seat on the aircraft's starboard side. As he did so, Susan grabbed his two bags. She hung his garment bag in the aircraft's forward closet and placed his personal bag on the seat in front of him. Susan turned, gave Morgan a quick smile, and headed into the cockpit.

Morgan sat in his seat, grabbed his personal bag, and pulled out his e-reader and iPod. He placed the bag in the compartment under his seat, the padded envelope, iPod and e-reader in a pouch mounted to his right on the aircraft bulkhead, fastened his seatbelt, and prepared for takeoff. The Citation began to taxi towards the runway and the aircraft's announcing system came to life.

"This is the Captain. We are cleared for immediate take-off. Once airborne, our flying time to Copenhagen will be approximately 9 hours. Thank you for flying with us today." The Captain spoke with a slight mid-western accent.

The Citation rolled to the far end of the airport's runway 35. The aircraft lined up with the runway's centerline at which point the Captain gunned the throttles. The Citation accelerated quickly to its takeoff speed and leapt into the sky. The crew turned the aircraft onto the appropriate heading for Copenhagen and climbed to its cruising altitude of 35,000 feet. Once there, Susan exited the flight deck.

"Would you care for some breakfast, Bob?"

"Please, if you'll join me." Morgan said.

With a smile and a tilt of her head, Susan went to the galley to prepare the two meals while Morgan pulled the padded envelope from the bulkhead mounted storage bin. He tore it open and saw a letter in a smaller envelope and a new Samsung Galaxy S-22 cell phone wrapped in a black Otterbox Defender phone case.

Ha! Chop must have heard that I was hard on my cell phones. I hate gravity.

He read the letter first:

Bob,

 Enclosed you will find your cell phone. It's loaded with 'certain optional extras' above and beyond a normal Galaxy S-22. Once airborne, and out of sight of the aircraft's crew, enter 48991007 for the PIN and play the video file shown on the phone's home screen. It contains further instructions. Good luck, Gargoyle!

 Frances

Morgan folded the letter back into its envelope, tucked it into one pocket of his jacket, and placed the phone in the opposite pocket. By that time, Susan had returned with small trolley holding two steaming plates and a thermal carafe of coffee. Susan deployed two tray tables from a hidden compartment in the starboard bulkhead, placed one plate on each, and then sat in the seat facing Morgan's.

"Coffee?"

"Please."

Susan poured cups for each of them as they then tore into their surprisingly good bacon, egg, and cheese omelets with home fried potatoes and toast.

"Is this your first time flying private?" Susan asked.

Morgan looked up from his meal with a slightly embarrassed expression, "Is it that obvious?"

"I've been flying these aircraft for the past eight years. Folks who have never flown on one of these before always have a certain look of awe about them."

"I can imagine. My awe is not only for this magnificent aircraft and its wonderful crew," Morgan said with a nod towards Susan. "It's that I'm not used to the opulence. Last time I flew it was in the back of a cargo plane. Also, for the fact I didn't have to put up with any people either here or at the airport. Flying's great, but crowded airports suck!"

Susan nodded in agreement and the pair finished their meal quietly. Afterward, Morgan helped Susan clean up, and then she took a plate with her to the cockpit, leaving the carafe of coffee behind. When certain Susan was not returning right away, Morgan pulled the Agency issued phone from his jacket pocket as he sipped his coffee, powered it up, plugged in the accompanying ear buds, entered the personal identification number, and pressed play on the video file found on the home screen. After the Agency's logo, the smiling image of Joe Acevedo graced the screen.

Good morning Gargoyle! Before we begin, please pause the video, head back to the aircraft's luggage area, grab the attaché case, and return to your seat. Don't worry, I'll wait.

Morgan smirked to himself, unbuckled his seat belt, and headed aft to the walk-in luggage area. He found a gorgeous navy-blue Globe-Trotter Centenary attaché case atop a matching navy-blue trolley bag. Grabbing the attaché case, Morgan returned to his seat, set the case on the tray table, and opened it. Inside he saw a file folder, a lap top computer, and four small cases. Opening one of the small cases, he saw a pair of silver framed Matsuda aviator-style sunglasses with blue-grey lenses. Looking at the exquisite eye ware, Morgan wondered what the hell he was going to do with these. He closed the case, put his ear buds back in, and re-started the video.

You're back? Excellent! Let's continue. Inside the file folder, you'll find further detail on your cover as well as your hotel reservations. If you grab the small tab at the bottom of the case, you can lift off the bottom and expose the x-ray proof area with space for the three weapons we discussed last week. Your Agency laptop and charging cables for all your devices are also in the attaché case. As far as ground transportation is concerned, let's say I hooked up a shipmate and 'you're welcome.'

Now, grab the plain black case and the case with the Frost eyewear logo and head to aircraft lavatory. Again, I'll wait.

Morgan grabbed the two cases and his phone and headed into the lavatory. He put the items on the sink and pressed play.

Open the plain case, inside you'll see my solution to your injury. An eye prosthetic that will fit in your socket. When you put it in and wear the glasses, the image from the prosthetic is projected on the upper left side of your right lens. This should eliminate the blind spot. Go ahead and put it in, it's designed to be worn 24/7 so you can even sleep with it.

Morgan never used a glass eye before, he never saw the point of one, and the eye patch made him look cooler. Looking in the mirror, he removed his eye patch, pulled the new prosthetic from its case, and placed it carefully in his left eye socket. He kept his left eye lid closed as he placed the stylish Frost eyeglasses on his head. He opened his left eye and the image from the prosthetic automatically appeared in front of him. He waved his left hand in front of his left eye, and he saw it in front of him. He moved his hand around towards the left side of his head, and the prosthetic followed it instinctively until his hand disappeared behind what was his normal, binocular blind spot. "Holy crap!" Morgan said aloud. He turned his head left and right, admiring his new look while stroking his Van Dyke. He never thought he'd look like this again. The prosthetic even matched his somewhat unusual eye color. He resumed the video.

Awesome, right? The prosthetic works with the Frost eyeglasses, the Matsuda sunglasses, and the Gatorz Magnum tactical glasses included in the attaché case. You'll like the Gatorz, the lenses are photochromic, so you can use them either day or night. Additionally, if you blink three times rapidly, you'll activate the prosthetic's recording and streaming capability. Images can either stream via your phone back here to Langley or recorded on your phone or laptop for future viewing. Blink three times rapidly again, and the recorder shuts off. The trolley bag contains the clothing and toiletry items you dropped off with us, and per your schedule, you should have your formal and business wear already. It also has tools you may need for certain nocturnal activities in a hidden compartment accessed the same way as the weapons.

That's all for now. Clint and Ms. McCulloch are awaiting your arrival and first check-in. Good luck and be careful, shipmate!

The video ended, and Morgan returned to his seat. He pulled the file folder and reviewed his legend. He would be Mr. Robert L. Curry, the COO of Raptor Microsystems, looking for a shipping company to move consumer electronics from Malaysia out to the rest of the world. His identification papers, passport, Virginia driver's license, etc. with his Robert Curry identity were in the file folder. The papers even had his pictures with two eyes and the Frost eyeglasses, an amazing Photoshop-generated image.

Not bad, Chop.

The file also contained several business cards with real phone numbers and e-mail addresses that when contacted would be either answered by someone with the company or forwarded to Morgan's Agency account with any replies sent with the appropriate address. The Agency also spared no expense with his accommodations, with an executive suite reserved for him at the Nimb Hotel in Copenhagen's city center. The boutique hotel was part of Copenhagen's famous Tivoli Gardens, site of the fundraiser.

Nice!

Definitely beat the ships, patrol boats, or hard ground Morgan usually slept in, or on, while on a mission.

Checking again for the flight crew, Morgan pulled his

personal bag from underneath his seat. He opened it and the special compartment in his attaché case. From his bag, he pulled out two hard plastic cases. The first case held two of his weapons; one was his personal Beretta Nano nine-millimeter with a seven-round magazine with one round in the chamber, and the second was his Gerber Guardian II fixed blade knife he had inherited from his late father. He placed both those items in the attaché and opened the second plastic case. Inside was his second handgun, an over thirty-year-old Smith & Wesson model 6904 nine-millimeter. The 6904 had also belonged to his father, and it was the first weapon he ever shot. With a 12 round staggered magazine, and one in the chamber, the 6904 was ideal for heavy use but with its bobbed hammer was still quite concealable if necessary. He waited his entire career for an opportunity to use it on mission, and this was finally it. He added the 6904 plus additional magazines for both handguns into the attaché case. He pulled his Kirkpatrick shoulder harness with leather holsters specifically fitted for each handgun and the Alien Gear inside-the-waistband holster for his Nano out of his personal bag and took them and his attaché back to the luggage area. He placed the shoulder holsters in the trolley bag and placed the attaché back in its place. Morgan returned to his seat, closed his eyes, and, like all good sailors, immediately fell asleep.

CHAPTER
NINE

Copenhagen Kastup Airport
Copenhagen, Denmark

First Officer Susan shook Morgan's shoulder as he slept soundly in his chair.

"Bob," she said softly. "We're preparing for landing."

Morgan opened his eyes, and the attractive pilot's surprised expression greeted him. He forgot for a moment he still wore his new eye prosthetic.

"Good morning," Morgan replied as he slipped on his glasses. "Looks like I now only have eyes for you," he added with a smirk.

Susan smiled and shook her head at the pun. "We'll be touching down in twenty minutes. Local time is 10 PM."

"Nice, thank you." Morgan adjusted the time on his Seamaster.

The Cessna landed and taxied to a private hangar. Once the aircraft came to a halt, Susan and the Captain opened the door and lowered the steps while Morgan headed aft to grab his luggage. Once at the door, Morgan pulled his garment bag from the front closet and turned to the flight crew.

"Thanks for the smooth flight, folks. I'm looking forward to the return trip."

"You have my number?" Susan asked with a gleam in her eye.

"I'll be sure to call you when I'm ready to leave, or perhaps for other reasons," Morgan added with a smirk.

Morgan descended the ladder and walked around the front of the aircraft. Past the starboard wing, Morgan caught sight of a striking dark-skinned woman, hopefully his Agency contact.

"Good evening, Mr. Curry." She used his cover name. "I'm Ms. Nyo with the firm's Danish office. Welcome to Copenhagen."

"Good evening to you, Ms. Nyo," Morgan said. "Please lead on."

The pair walked towards the rear of the hangar. They exited via the back door and Morgan saw something that made his jaw drop.

Gleaming under one of the hangar's external lights stood a brand-new McLaren Artura. The sleek, 671 horsepower, plug-in hybrid, mid-engined super car, was painted in an amazing Burton blue. It looked fast even standing still. He walked around it with a look of astonishment.

Hooked a shipmate up indeed. Thanks Chop!

The interior had dark gray leather seats with a dark gray leather-covered dashboard.

Dove grey interior with Flux green accents, Joe has exquisite taste.

Looking up, he saw Ms. Nyo smiling with something in her out stretched hand.

"We knew you would love it, sir. Here's the key fob."

He took the fob in his hand with a sense of awe. He pressed the McLaren logo in the fob's center, the Artura's lights flashed, and it unlocked with a chirp. He pressed the lower portion of the fob that opened the car's front trunk. He placed the trolley bag in the truck and closed it. He placed the attaché case behind the seats and draped the garment bag across the passenger seat. He turned towards Ms. Nyo.

"You've made my year," Morgan said.

"Good luck with your business trip." Ms. Nyo turned to leave.

Morgan opened the Artura's dihedral door and climbed inside carefully. He noticed an envelope with his name on it sitting on the center console. He opened the envelope and read the email printout inside.

Gargoyle,

Here's the vehicle I spoke of, hope you're liking it. I think it fits with your cover identity. The windows are coated in a bullet-resistant film which can withstand small arms fire up to 7.62 millimeter NATO with a double coating on the windshield and rear glass, just in case. There are protected storage areas in the doors for your weapons. Otherwise, it's a standard McLaren, as much as a McLaren can be described as 'standard.' Please be careful with it and return it in one piece, we'd like to use it again for future operations. Have fun!

Chop

"Love you too, Chop." Morgan said aloud. The envelope contained a stack of local currency, so he tucked the envelope into his jacket's inside pocket. He turned on the car's accessories and entered his hotel's location into the McLaren's on board navigation system via its Android Auto interface. He lowered both windows before pressing the brake pedal and starting the engine.

"Ooooooooo, that's nice!" Morgan said as the sounds of the car's exhaust filled the cabin.

Smooth! Much smoother than my Corvette, not as visceral.

He paired his electronics to the car's Bluetooth system,

selected his 'Driving Tunes' playlist, and pressed the random play button. A familiar base line began to thump through the car's Bowers and Wilkins speakers.

"Hmmm, 'In the Air Tonight,' appropriate," Morgan said.

He put the Artura in gear and took off from the hangar.

Morgan drove carefully as he left the airport property, using the Artura's front nose lift system to go over the all too numerous speed bumps. Finally, he reached the public roads where he let the car loose as he headed towards Copenhagen's city center. The navigation system recommended two possible routes, so Morgan chose the longer one. He told himself it was for a surveillance detection purposes. But in reality, he just wanted extra time to drive such a remarkable machine and explore its unusual quirks and features.

He turned left onto the E20 motorway and accelerated quickly to the posted speed limit of 130 kilometers per hour. No sense being pulled over by the local police. As he traveled west along the E20, Morgan checked his mirrors and didn't notice anyone following him, yet. He decided he would not drive a surveillance detection route like he learned at the Farm since his cover was as a tech company executive, but he would keep an eye out just in case.

The motorway made a gentle sweeping right hand turn as Morgan exited the E20 and merged onto an access road followed quickly by a left exit onto the Sjaellandsbroen where the terrain became urban. When he turned right onto the Scandiagade, he noticed an Audi A4 falling in behind him. It wasn't too close, but also not too far away for someone trying to tail him.

Since he wasn't supposed to be looking for a tail, Morgan didn't immediately try to lose him. Instead, he intentionally missed the left turn onto the Bernstorffsgade and proceeded into the parking lot of the Copenhagen Marriott hotel. With Queen's 'Don't Stop Me Now' coming out the stereo, he drove towards the hotel's entrance slowly while keeping an eye on the Audi. Once he watched the Audi continue down the Kalvebod Brygge,

Morgan floored it past the hotel entrance and the confused parking valets. He turned right onto the Kalvebod Brygge, made a U-turn, and turned right onto the Bernstorffsgade and onward towards his hotel.

A flight of two French Air Force Mirage 2000D fighter-bombers flew through the night sky over Mali. Operating from their base in the Malian capital of Bamako, their mission was as simple as it was imperative, find the location of the JNIM forces that attacked Gao and destroy them. French losses in the campaign were mounting, and the political leadership in Paris wanted payback, yesterday.

Each of the two delta-winged aircraft carried two, GBU-12 laser-guided bombs, two R550 Magic air-to-air missile, and a Forward Looking Infra-Red camera pod with laser targeting capability. The Mirages flew at 35,000 feet. High enough to avoid the Man Portable Air Defense missiles and anti-aircraft artillery the JNIM insurgents used with great effect during the attacks in Gao and other places.

The flight leader, Commandant Élisabeth 'le Couguar' Garreau keyed her microphone.

"You awake there, *Magicien*?"

"*Oui*, Couguar. Wide awake despite the other night's activities."

Commandant Garreau laughed to herself. She watched *Sous-lieutenant* Roméo Arceneaux two nights ago down at the Sheraton Bamako Hotel's bar living up to his call sign as all his efforts to secure female company led to all the women around him disappearing. She, on the other hand, lived up to her call sign, bestowed on her by her American Navy colleagues at NATO headquarters, in finding a younger man with whom to spend her evening. The sound of her aircraft's threat receiver shook her back to reality.

"Roméo!"

"I have it too..."

"Evasive!"

The two Mirages banked right, dove, and fired chaff and flares in an attempt to escape the oncoming threat. However, their efforts were in vain as the four Russian-built S-400 surface-to-air missiles chased them down. The first aircraft stuck was Lieutenant Arceneaux's. The direct hit turned the aircraft into a fireball, killing the young lieutenant instantly.

Commandant Garreau dodged the first missile that targeted at her aircraft, its flares, and chaff seducing the missile away from her. Her luck ran out with the second one. It struck her starboard wing, forcing the aircraft into an irrecoverable flat spin. She fought valiantly to regain control, but the damage was too severe. As aerodynamic forces began to tear her aircraft apart, Élisabeth had one final thought.

How?

CHAPTER
TEN

Nimb Hotel
Copenhagen, Denmark

Morgan pulled the McLaren Artura up to the Nimb Hotel's front door and he stopped in front of a wide-eyed parking valet. He opened the car's dihedral doors as Motley Crue's 'Kick Start My Heart' came out the speakers. The bellman approached the front of the car as Morgan popped the front trunk and passenger side door. He grabbed his attaché case as the bellman removed his garment bag followed by the trolley case. As the bellman closed both the trunk and passenger door, Morgan passed the key fob and two 200 kroner bills to the valet.

"Keep her up front, please," Morgan said.

"A car like this deserves such a spot," the valet said.

"She does indeed."

Morgan followed the bellman to the hotel's front desk. The two passed a pair of white bicycles with the hotel's logo as they headed to the desk, staffed at the time by a young, dark- skinned man with the name 'Juma' on his nameplate.

"Good evening, Mr. Curry checking in," Morgan passed the

desk clerk his AMEX black card and his Agency provided passport.

"Good evening, Mr. Curry," Juma said. "Here's your card and passport back, and the room number is on the key card folder."

"Thank you. What time's breakfast?"

"07:00 up in the Brasserie."

"Perfect."

"Rooms are accessible via the elevators to your left."

After a quick elevator ride, Morgan and the bellman walked along a stylish corridor to Morgan's room. Morgan unlocked the door and entered. Placing the garment bag in the closet and the trolley bag on a luggage rack, the bellman showed Morgan around the executive suite.

"Here's your bathroom and water closet. The doors led out to your private balcony with a view of Tivoli Gardens. And here's your bar area."

As the bellman pointed it out, Morgan was happy to see a Nespresso machine with an assortment of pods sitting on the counter.

"By the way, I didn't catch your name," Morgan said.

"Arne, sir."

Morgan reached out to both shake Arne's hand and pass him a 500 kroner note. "Please keep an eye on things if you could."

Arne looked at the note with a subtle nod, "My pleasure, sir. Anything else?"

"No, thank you. Have a great evening."

"You too, sir."

Arne placed the key card in a slot by the door and departed.

Morgan opened the balcony and looked out over the now closed Tivoli Gardens. He pulled his phone out of his jacket pocket, opened his contacts and encryption app, and placed a call.

"Peters."

"Gargoyle, I am prepared to authenticate.

"Authenticate, Charlie Oscar One Five One."

"I authenticate Zulu Five Oscar."

"Authentication accepted, Bob. How was your flight?"

"Arrived safely if not totally securely."

"What happened?"

Morgan briefly described the potential tail from the airport into the city center.

"You think pulling into the other hotel threw them off?"

"Maybe, we'll see."

"Well, while you were relaxing over the Atlantic, we received some news from the DGSE. The French Air Force lost two Mirage 2000s over Mali. They were flying too high and too fast for MANPADs or Triple-A. It looks like a Russian S-400 SAM took them down."

Too high and fast for Man Portable Air Defense missiles and Anti-Aircraft Artillery and still shot down? Damn.

"That's not good."

"We need to expedite."

"The fund raiser is tomorrow night, my time. With what we donated, we'll get Rasmussen's attention."

"Hope so."

Morgan ended the call and opened the text window. He selected Ms. McCulloch's number and typed her a message that he'd arrived and mentioned the tail. He asked her to "check the seals."

Morgan hit send and headed into the spacious bathroom. He laid out his toiletries and splashed some water on his face. He looked at himself in the mirror. He needed a shave, but he still looked okay for a guy who's just crossed the Atlantic. He also looked at the prosthetic, still not used to his face's newfound symmetry. He briefly considered heading to bed, but the drive over keyed him up, so he decided to hit the hotel's bar for a drink. He went over to his attaché case and opened it, removing his Nano and holster. Changing into khaki pants, he slipped the holster and gun into the waistband. He pulled on a polo shirt and left it untucked to hide his weapon. He left the room with his key card after switching off the light.

Morgan found his way to the Nimb bar, located above the hotel lobby. He sat at the bar, picked up the Hans Christian Anderson-themed menu, and looked at the drink choices. Paging past the fairy tale-themed drinks in the front (with descriptions in both Danish and English), he found the classic cocktails section with one drink in particular catching his eye. He caught the bar tender's attention to place his order.

"Vesper martini please," Morgan said.

"God aften hr!" (Good evening, sir!) the bartender replied in Danish. "Shaken or stirred?" he asked switching to English.

Morgan gave the bartender a smirk. "I think we both know the answer to that."

The bartender laughed and began to mix the drink while Morgan looked around. The bar sat in a corner of a large lounge area filled with several sets of couches, chairs, coffee tables, and the ubiquitous piano. As the sound of ice in a cocktail shaker reached Morgan's left ear, a most pleasant British-accented female voice reached his right.

"May I join you?" asked the voice.

Morgan turned to his right and saw the source of the sensual sound.

One of the loveliest women he had seen in a long time stood at the bar stool on his right. Blond hair, amazing green eyes, and standing maybe 5 feet 2 inches at most. Her resemblance to the actor Vanessa Kirby was striking. She wore a smart green blouse and black paints combination with black leather flats. She gripped the barstool's backrest with one hand and her drink in another. Her accent was pure Received Pronunciation, or what non-British people consider a 'typical' British accent.

"Please do," Morgan replied. The bar tender placed his martini on the bar. "I'm Bob Curry by the way."

"Lily."

"A pleasure, Lily. Which part of the U.K are you from?"

"The Maidstone area, south east of London. American?"

"Yes, grew up in the mid-west but now live in Northern Virginia. You staying here?"

"Heavens no, couldn't afford it. Just checking out the area before tomorrow's fundraiser. You?"

Morgan hoped he hid his disappointment as he responded, "Yes, and I'm also here for the fundraiser."

"Excellent. By the way, I love your glasses. They suit you well."

"Thank you! I love your velvety smooth accent."

"Really?"

"Oh yeah, women with British accents get me every time. I have a great date in mind if I ever had the opportunity to meet someone with an accent like yours."

"Oh really? I'm intrigued. Please do tell." Lily looked Morgan directly in the eyes.

"Well, we'd go out for an amazing dinner somewhere local, no chains, or anything stupid like that. I'd be in my best bespoke suit, and she'd be in a cocktail dress which fits her just so."

"What color?"

"Basic black always works, but if she had your hair color, I'd go with dark green."

"Very nice, please continue."

"Afterwards we'd return to my place. I'd take off my jacket, kick off my shoes, loosen my tie, and unbutton my collar while she kicked off her attractive yet not too high heels before sitting on the corner of the couch. After turning on the appropriate lighting, I'd join her and place my head in her lap as she read to me."

"What would she read?"

"Wouldn't matter. It could be Ian Fleming, Harry Potter, or even the phone book if they still made those things. I would just want to hear the sound of her lovely voice as I relaxed."

"Sounds quite romantic."

"But I neither have time nor the opportunity for such things."

"That's unfortunate, but I do understand. Thank you for the company, but I have an early morning tomorrow. Good evening, Bob."

"Good evening, Lily. See you tomorrow night?"

"I guarantee it." Lily said with a smile as she turned to leave the bar.

The bar tender came back to collect Morgan's now empty drink glass.

"*Det er en meget attraktiv kvinde* (That's one attractive woman)."

Morgan, who didn't speak a word of Danish, still caught the jist. "Heh, you ain't kidding, my friend." Morgan said as he slipped the bar tender a 200 kroner note. "Keep it," he said with a friendly smirk as he headed back to his room for the night.

CHAPTER
ELEVEN

Morgan awoke the next morning and threw on one of the hotel's ultra-plush bathrobes. With a cup of coffee from the Nespresso machine he sat on the balcony with his phone. There were no further developments from either Clint Peters or Ms. McCulloch. There was nothing of note on his news feeds.

Morgan finished his coffee, showered, and dressed for the day. He slipped on a Sunspel navy blue polo shirt with khaki paints finished off with his black suede Sanders and Sanders boots. He collected his Agency issued laptop, Guardian II, and Smith & Wesson and locked them in the room's safe.

Not perfect, but it will slow someone down.

He slipped on his Kirkpatrick shoulder holster, slid in the Nano, and covered it with his new and expensive John Varvatos jacket before heading out for the morning.

He headed down to the restaurant to sample the breakfast buffet. When he entered the Brasserie, Morgan's eyes lit up. It was filled with fresh baked breads, buns, pastries, and other baked goods; heaven for a carb-craver like Morgan. Morgan sat and a waitress approached.

"Good morning, sir. Coffee or tea?"

"Coffee please, black, no sugar."

The waitress departed and returned with his coffee a few moments later. Morgan let it cool while he hit the buffet. Morgan's first stop was the bread table where he selected his usual croissant but also tried something new, a pistachio pastry with strawberry jam. When he passed the beverage table, he decided to grab some orange juice, but stopped short when he saw the open Champagne bottle.

A mimosa? Why not?

Sitting at his table, he ate his breakfast while reading one the hotel's complementary newspapers.

No mention of the Mirage shoot-down in Mali, the French must be keeping it under wraps.

A sudden cooing sound caught Morgan's attention and he turned towards the Brasserie's huge floor-to-ceiling windows. Peahens and peacocks strutted across the restaurant's terrace, feathered visitors from the Tivoli Gardens looking for a quick snack or some sucker tourist who would feed them.

Sorry guys, not today.

Finishing his breakfast, Morgan left the Brasserie with an appreciative nod towards his waitress who left him to enjoy his breakfast in peace. One thing he liked about Europe, the waiters and waitresses leave you alone, unlike those in the States. He stopped at the reception desk to obtain a wristband for the Tivoli Gardens Park, the venue for the evening's festivities. Sitting a moment in the lobby, Morgan pulled his phone to set up video recording from his prosthetic. He blinked his eyes three time quickly and looked down at his phone. He saw an image on the phone's screen matching his prosthetic's view. He moved his head back and forth with the screen view moving along with it. He blinked three times again, and the screen went back to the recording software's home screen. He pressed the play button and watched the recording.

Perfect.

He placed the phone back into his jacket pocket, left the hotel's lobby, and ventured out into the Tivoli Gardens. Looking back at the hotel, Morgan admired the hotel's Moorish style architecture. He turned back and looked over the gardens and fountains situated between the hotel and the amusement park areas of Tivoli Gardens. He blinked three times and began to scan the area looking for all entrances and exits. He didn't expect any trouble at a black-tie event, but you can't be too careful in this line of work.

He moved from the gardens and fountains towards the amusement park area, wandering between the rides, roller coasters, and other amusements with memories of summers spent at Cedar Point in Ohio going through his mind. Morgan watched as the staff prepared the park for day.

I wouldn't want their job, too many people.

Morgan shut off the recording and crossed the street and entered Copenhagen's main train station. He purchased an all-day pass and caught the A Metro towards Solrød Strand Street where he changed trains for his final destination. He arrived at Sluseholmen 2, 2450 København the headquarters of RDS Shipping, eight minutes later.

Morgan turned on his prosthetic's recording system and began to walk around the RDS building. A set of railroad tracks with a marina beyond was on his left while the headquarters building sat on his right. He walked northwest along Sjaellandsbroen Street where the bus had dropped him off, before rounding the corner onto Sluseholmen, just one pedestrian of many walking from point A to point B. So far, he had not noticed any security outside of the building. With any luck, he'd be inside at this time tomorrow.

After returning to his room, Morgan checked his luggage and room safe for any evidence of intrusion with negative results. He used his phone and one of the Agency's provided apps to sweep the room for any listening or video devices, again with negative results. He set up his laptop on the desk and reviewed the footage recorded by the prosthetic. The video showed a five story, L-shaped building with offices for several companies with an Arbejdernes Landsbank branch located on the, as the Euro-peans call it, ground floor. The front of the building had several company logos on it including, at the very top, RDS Shipping. The main entrance of the building sat on the opposite side of the bank with a revolving door. The main parking area sat nestled between to two arms of the L. A back entrance sat at the opposite side of the building from the revolving door right by the bus stop Morgan used earlier in the day. This looked promising for any late-night activities he may need to do, but he needed to see the inside to know for sure.

Time to get ready for the party. After another shower, and a quick trim of his moustache and Van Dyke beard, he put on his new tux. Looking at his reflection in the bathroom mirror, Morgan had one thought.

There are dinner jackets and Dinner Jackets; this is the latter indeed.

He gave himself a quick smirk and with the music of David Arnold going through his head, headed out the door.

CHAPTER
TWELVE

Tivoli Gardens
Copenhagen, Denmark

I hate parties.

Morgan walked around the fountains and gardens as the fundraiser guests arrived. The Nimb Hotel provided the food and drinks for the occasion with black-tied, white-gloved servers working the crowd. The only thing making the event bearable was the presence of several dogs, with leashes held by various animal rescue organization personnel, wearing pocketed vests with "Adopt Me!" printed in both English and Danish. Morgan noticed the pockets were stuffed with Kroners, Dollars, and Euros, proving beyond a shadow of a doubt that cuteness pays. Morgan found an adorable Golden Retriever mix and placed a 500 Kroner note in its vest before giving the dog a few scratches behind its ears and over the top of its 'smarty bump.' After a few minutes amongst the dogs and the elegantly dressed guests, Morgan headed for the Nimb's lobby to get away from the increasing crowd of people.

Morgan found an inconspicuous place to observe the guests' arrival. Never before had he seen so many Mercedes S-Class

ROBERT A. ADAMCIK

limousines, Maybachs, long wheel-based Jaguar XJs and BMW 7 series vehicles in one place. Watching a Jaguar disgorging yet another well-dressed couple, a very different car caught Morgan's eye. A gorgeous, brand new BMW Z4 M40i pulled up to the valet stand, its Frozen Grey Metallic paint shining under the hotel's lights. From his vantage point, the valet blocked his view of the driver. However, he did see a shapely foot wrapped in a black leather pump followed by simple gold chain ankle bracelet, and an equally shapely calf in black hosiery. But what caught his eye was the tattoo above the ankle, two paw prints in black ink, just dark enough to be seen through the stockings. The valet turned away and Morgan saw who exited the BMW. It was her! Lily, wearing a shimmering black cocktail dress that hugged all of her ample curves, arriving in style. Morgan moved quickly to avoid being seen by her too soon.

Maintaining a discreet distance, Morgan followed Lily as she checked in with the event's attractive hostess, something Morgan needed to do himself. After checking in, Morgan followed Lily outside to the gardens, grabbing two glasses of champagne from a passing server. Morgan moved behind Lily as she stopped at a table with several cats available for adoption.

"Good evening, Lily. If I had seen that tattoo last night, we would have had a lot more to talk about," Morgan said.

Lily turned around and smiled. "Good evening, Mr. Curry. Is that for me?"

"Yes, it is. If you'll join me." Morgan handed her a glass.

"What shall we drink to?"

"To dogs and cats! Better company than most people I know." Morgan raised his glass.

"I will gladly drink to that, cheers." Lily tapped his glass and took a drink.

"Tell me about the tattoo?"

"They are the front paws of one of my kitties. I placed her paws on a scanner, printed the picture, and had the artist trace the outline for the tattoo."

66

"Very nice! What's the kitty's name?"

"Miss Moneypenny. She's one of my calicoes. I have two of them and two tortoise shells."

"Moneypenny?" Morgan asked with a look of surprise. "Glad to see I'm not the only Bond fan here."

"So, you're a fan, are you?" Lily asked with a conspiratorial look in her eye. "Okay, who played Felix Leiter in 'Thunderball'?"

"What? Rik Van Nutter."

Lily choked slightly on her drink. "You actually know that!? My apologies, Mr. Curry, you are indeed a fan."

"Coming from one of His Majesty's subjects who knows enough to even ask the question, that is a high compliment indeed."

Lily was about to respond when a hush went over the crowd. Their attention turned to the center of the fountain area where three people stood. The first was a huge man who stood at least six foot six with impossibly broad shoulders and a fiery red beard, an ancient Viking warrior come to life. His obviously tailored suit barely concealed the bulge of a handgun under his jacket. The second was Mr. Edward Rasmussen, the party's host, standing proud like he owned the place. The final stood to Rasmussen's right, Lady Aurora. She was almost as tall as her father owing to both her Nordic heritage and her tall, high heel shoes. She wore a red gown slit up to her left hip, the color contrasting with the dark hair and dark complexion she inherited from her mother. The word striking did not begin to describe her beauty.

"*God aften, mine damer og herrer*! Good evening ladies and gentlemen!" Rasmussen began in both Danish and English. "Thank you for attending this evening's fund raiser for the Royal Society for the Prevention of Cruelty to Animals, Rescue Me! Of Denmark, and the Danish Centre for Animal Welfare. Together, we have raised over 62 million Kroner, over 10 million U.S. dollars, to help feed, shelter and find homes for the homeless dogs and cats of Denmark, the United Kingdom, and the rest of Europe!" A loud round of applause interrupted Rasmussen's speech. He continued, "All of you contributed very generously, but one contributor stands out. With a single contribution of one million U.S. dollars, we thank Mr. Robert Curry, Chief Operating Officer of Raptor Microsystems. Mr. Curry?" Applause began to swell amongst the crowd.

Morgan turned to Lily and whispered, "Aw, shit. Here we go." He turned to the crowd and waved.

Rasmussen continued, "All the homeless animals of the continent thank you. Now, please continue the party!" Rasmussen concluded. The trio of the Rasmussens and the man Morgan mentally christened The Great Dane strode over to Morgan and Lily.

"Mr. Curry, Edward Rasmussen." Rasmussen held out his hand.

"Bob Curry, sir. A pleasure."

Rasmussen turned to Lily. "And who are you, my dear?"

"Lily Matthews. I represent Four Paws UK. We greatly appreciate the support and patronage you and Lady Aurora have provided our organization over the years."

"You are most welcome, Ms. Matthews. My daughter and I believe strongly animals are the purest form of love on the planet, and it's our duty, our responsibility, to see to their welfare. Hopefully, by helping them, we can earn that love."

"Mr. Rasmussen," Morgan began.

"Edward, please." Rasmussen interrupted.

"Edward, I hate to mix business with all the incredible cuteness around us, but I was wondering if I could have a few moments of your time over the next day or two to discuss a business proposition."

"Of course! After such a generous donation to our cause, any time wouldn't be enough. Aurora, please make the arrangements." Rasmussen and his bodyguard turned towards the rest of the crowd, shaking several pairs of hands as he went.

Aurora looked him up and down in an appraising manner.

"Mr. Curry, will 9 a.m. tomorrow morning work for you?"

"Certainly, I'm a morning person."

"Excellent! Hopefully, I can see that in action someday."

Morgan arched his eyebrows and smirked, "I'll make a note."

Aurora turned and walked towards her father who was holding court on the other side of the garden.

"Careful with that one. 'She's deadly man, she could really rip your world apart,'" Lily said with venom as she stared at Aurora.

Morgan looked her straight in the eye, gave her a smirk, and asked, "She's a man eater?"

Lily smiled back. "Exactly."

"Into eighties music?"

"Oh, yes. To me, good music ended on the thirty-first of December 1989."

"Outstanding. Well, Ms. Matthews. Care to wander around the amusement park with me?" Morgan offered his left arm.

"Certainly, Mr. Curry." Lily replied as she wrapped her right arm around his left.

As the couple walked towards the Tivoli Garden's rides, the Rasmussens watched them from a distance.

"What do you think, Father?" Aurora asked.

"He could be the man our source in the CIA mentioned, but so could anyone here. Would you consider a more personal assessment, my dear?"

"Certainly, father," Aurora said with a cat-who-ate-the-canary smile. "He's handsome enough. He's wearing a Nimb hotel wrist band, I'll get into his room and see what I can find."

"Excellent. If he's CIA, we'll let Ivar deal with him and dump his body in the Kattegat."

CHAPTER
THIRTEEN

Morgan returned to the Nimb Hotel's lobby at about midnight after spending an amazing evening with Lily. He offered a nightcap up in his room, but she declined gently citing an early day. She did kiss him gently on the lips as they waited for her car at the valet stand. When it arrived, she climbed aboard, dropped the roadster's roof, and drove off with a wave of her hand and quick toot of her horn.

Morgan turned towards the elevators, but someone called out his name.

"Mr. Curry!" It was Arne the bellman.

"Good evening, Arne!" Morgan replied. "What's going on?"

"Just letting you know, sir, I let your 'friend' into your room," Arne said with an all too obvious wink.

Morgan pulled a 500 Kroner note from his tux jacket and slid it into Arne's hand.

"Thanks for the heads up," Morgan added with an equally overly exaggerated smirk.

Getting off the elevator, Morgan moved quickly and silently towards his room. He left his weapons in their hidden compartment inside his locked attaché case feeling he wouldn't need them at an animal welfare event, plus it would be quite out of character for his cover. A high-tech COO would not be carrying a small arsenal on his person after all.

Morgan opened the door to his executive suite slowly and silently and stepped inside. The sight he beheld as he closed the door stopped him dead in his tracks. Lady Aurora stood next to his bed, her long, jet black hair draped seductively over her shoulders. She wore a matching sheer red bra and panty set which left little to the imagination. Her legs were covered by thigh-high stockings in a matching red. A pair black stiletto heels rounded out the look.

"Good evening, Mr. Curry. Or do you prefer Robert?" Aurora said.

"Bob please, milady," Morgan said with an exaggerated bow. "To what do I owe the pleasure?"

"Well," Aurora said as she turned towards the room's honor bar showing Morgan her exquisite, sheer panty-clad tush. "I wanted to thank you personally for your generous donation. Drink?"

Morgan removed his tuxedo jacket and draped it over a nearby chair. "Please. I prefer the company of dogs and cats to most people I know, so it was the best million our company ever spent. Present company accepted, of course."

"Of course." Aurora poured two glasses of bourbon and handed one to Morgan. "Cheers."

"Cheers."

Aurora set her glass down and began to untie Morgan's bow tie.

"So, what's the best way to thank you for your generosity?"

"Oh, I can think of a few things."

Morgan kissed Aurora hard on the lips with their tongues exploring each other's mouths. He picked Aurora up and carried her to the suite's magnificent four-poster bed.

Morgan learned to sleep through most sounds while in the Navy. No sound, other than the General Quarters alarm or gunfire, could wake Morgan up. Light, however, was a different story. Whether it was the rising sun, or the harsh fluorescent light of the recruit barracks at Great Lakes, once light hit Morgan's eye, he would be wide awake.

When Lady Aurora woke up to use the bathroom, some light escaped the room and woke Morgan. He rolled over and looked over at the bathroom but continued to act asleep. He watched Aurora's shapely silhouette leave the bathroom and head over to his tuxedo jacket. She proceeded to search through his pockets. He smirked to himself.

Got you!

A perfectly executed Prop Trap. All his pocket trash showed his was his cover, nothing incriminating. Definitely not the behavior Morgan expected to see in an animal-loving philanthropist. He felt Aurora climbing back into bed and after feeling her arm drape over his chest, fell back to sleep.

A few hours later, the rays of the rising sun entered Morgan's suite, waking him immediately. He rolled over and found the other half of his king-sized bed empty. He climbed out of bed and found a handwritten note on hotel stationary sitting on his nightstand.

Bob,

> *Thank you for a lovely evening! See you at 9!*
> *Love,*
> *Lady A.*

Ah, the things I do for Old Glory.

He checked his luggage, room safe, and laptop. As expected, they showed signs of attempted entry or access, but the luggage and safe did not appear to be breached nor his laptop accessed. Aurora had time to try something, but she did not succeed. Unless she had an NSA-level decryption tool hiding in her lingerie, Morgan's laptop was still secure.

Morgan showered and dressed for breakfast and his morning meeting. He pulled the first of his two new suits from the closet. After he donned his navy-blue two-piece, single-breasted, double vented suit with a subtle light grey pinstripe, he added a white, presidential folded pocket square too his jacket. The final touch was his scarlet and grey regimental stripped tie around the collar of his bright, white, custom-fitted shirt. Looking in the room's full-length mirror, he admired his tailor's work, perfect despite the tight timeline.

Damn, Mark! Followed my directions to the letter. I look like a Kingsman. All I need is an umbrella.

Grabbing his attaché, Morgan headed downstairs for a quick run at the breakfast buffet. Afterwards, he headed to the parking valet stand. He handed his valet ticket over with a quick "McLaren Artura, please," to the young man behind the podium. As he waited, he swapped his Frost eye ware for his Matsuda sunglasses. Moments later, he heard the McLaren's twin-turbo V-6 shortly before it rounded the corner and stopped in front of him. The valet exited the vehicle with a look of awe.

"Beautiful car, sir." the valet said.

"Thank you. She's quite a beauty, isn't she?" Morgan slid a 200 Kroner note into the valet's hand.

Morgan set his attaché case behind his seat, climbed into the vehicle, closed the dihedral door, and took off towards RDS Shipping's offices. He adjusted the Artura's photo chromatic sunroof for maximum darkness as he reached the city streets.

Fifteen minutes later, Morgan arrived at his destination after a great drive through Copenhagen's City Center. Parking to the left of the main entrance, he pulled his attaché case from behind the seat and opened it. Being careful to keep what he was doing out of sight, he took his Nano and its extra magazine from the hidden compartment and placed them in one of the Artura's modified door storage pockets. He straightened out the papers in the attaché, blinked his eyes three times, switched to his Frost glasses, and headed to the lobby.

CHAPTER
FOURTEEN

RDS Shipping Offices
Sluseholmen 2, 2450 København
Copenhagen, Denmark

Morgan went through the building's revolving door, and headed to the reception desk, his head on a swivel as he did so. Seeing him approach, a lovely blonde behind the desk sat up.

"*Godmorgen hr. Hvordan kan jeg hjælpe dig*?" (Good morning, sir. How may I help you?)

Again, not understanding a word of Danish, but being fluent in the international language of offices around the world, Morgan replied in English.

"Good morning. I'm Mr. Bob Curry. I have a 9 A.M. appointment with Mr. Rasmussen at RDS Shipping."

"Ah, one moment please, sir," the receptionist said switching to English while picking up her phone.

Morgan took a second to look around the reception area. To his right there was a long corridor that ended in an exit door, probably the one he noted yesterday by the bus stop. To his left were the elevators and another corridor with the bank branch entrance. The sound of a telephone handset returning to its cradle directed his attention back to the receptionist.

"Someone will be down in a moment," the receptionist said with a smile.

"Thank you," Morgan headed towards the elevators unaware of the appreciative glance the receptionist gave him and his backside.

Morgan watched the elevator's floor display change from "4" to "G" as the car came down from the top floor. When it reached the ground floor, the elevator door opened, and a huge man exited the car. The Great Dane himself.

"Good morning, Hr. Curry. I am Ivar. This way please," Ivar spoke in heavily accented English.

"Will there be room for the two of us in there?"

Ivar gave Morgan a look that would have killed most people, but he just moved aside with a gesture towards the elevator.

Morgan and Ivar exited the elevator on the top floor and entered the lobby of RDS Shipping. A large reception desk sat in the lobby's center with pictures of the RDS fleet of ships hanging on the walls. Ivar gestured towards a corridor on the left. At the end of which stood a large glass wall with a door into another, smaller reception area. Morgan let Ivar open the door for him, and he was greeted by Rasmussen and his daughter.

"Mr. Curry! Welcome to RDS!" Rasmussen said as he reached out his hand.

"Thank you, Mr. Rasmussen." Morgan shook Rasmussen's hand.

"Like I said last night, Edward please. Of course, you remember my daughter, Aurora?"

"She's quite unforgettable," Morgan said. He gave Aurora a smirk and a slight tilt of his head.

"Good morning, Bob," Aurora said. "Sleep well?'

"Like a well-fed puppy."

"Excellent!" Edward said. "Let's get some coffee and talk in my office."

The pair entered Rasmussen's tastefully decorated inner office. It was obvious that Rasmussen took his role as the head of a large shipping company quite seriously. The room looked like the great cabins of U.S.S. *Constitution* or H.M.S. *Victory* with a lot of wood paneling and brass accessories on the walls. More pictures of RDS's ships added to the nautical theme.

Rasmussen pointed towards a chair in front of his desk as he sat down in another seat behind it. Aurora stood next to her father with coffee for the three of them.

"So, Bob. What can RDS do for you?"

"Raptor Microsystems recently landed a huge contract with the U.S. Space Force to provide the next generation GPS receiver cards for all branches of the Department of Defense for use in ships, aircraft, tanks, trucks, etc. As part of that contract, Raptor has exclusive rights to expand that next generation technology into the civilian sector. We're creating GPS receivers with accuracies that nearly equal present military-grade systems. We've lined up auto manufacturers ranging from BMW, Mercedes, and McLaren to Toyota, Honda, and Tesla to provide them receivers for their in-car navigation systems. We also have Apple and Google on board for smart phone receivers. What we need you for, is to ship all those new commercial-grade receivers from our facility in Malaysia to our customers around the world. If we don't line up solid, reliable transportation, our product is not going anywhere."

"Well, congratulations are in order! And I'm happy that you chose RDS to handle your shipping needs. Aurora, please call Elias Svane and have him meet us in the conference room."

"Yes, father." Aurora reached for her phone.

"Elias is my operations director. He can get you started."

"By the way, thanks for the great coffee. Most offices only serve dregs to their employees."

"A company, like any ship, lives on coffee. The better the coffee, the more productive the crew."

A tall, blond, very Nordic man entered the office.

"Ah, Elias! Meet Mr. Bob Curry from Raptor Microsystems. He has some business for us. Let's head to the conference room."

The four went into the main conference room that had floor-to-ceiling windows and a single, long table. Morgan and Elias set up at the head of the table that had access to the company's computer network. Once Elias and Morgan began to work, Rasmussen and Aurora stood by the conference room door.

"Gentlemen, Aurora and I have other business to attend to, so I'll leave you two to continue working."

Morgan stood and offered Rasmussen his hand.

"Thank you again for your time and hospitality, Edward. If you are ever in the States, please visit us at our Crystal City headquarters in Arlington, Virginia. Our CEO, Matt McClellen, would love to meet you."

"Thank you for the invitation, but don't worry. I'm sure we'll be seeing each other again very soon."

Rasmussen and Aurora turned and left the conference room while Morgan and Elias continued working with Morgan's prosthetic recording everything he saw.

Rasmussen and Aurora entered Rasmussen's office, and he sat behind his desk.

"Did you discover anything last night, darling daughter?"

"Other than he has two pop culture tattoos and a thing for thigh high stockings, no. His laptop had both encryption and biometric protections, and I couldn't get past his luggage's locks without obvious damage."

"A little too robust for a simple corporate COO?"

"Yes, father," Aurora said. She moved behind Rasmussen and began to massage his shoulders.

"Ah, thank you, dear. Thought so. After much persuasion, our contact at CIA finally sent a picture of the agent we've been expecting," Rasmussen opened an image file on his computer.

"That's him!" Aurora exclaimed. "But what's with the eye patch? Mr. Curry has two very attractive hazel eyes."

"His real name is James Robert Morgan, a reserve U.S. Navy

Lieutenant Commander, and that left eye is some sort of pros-thetic. Elias will keep him busy this afternoon, and we'll have a surprise waiting for him if he returns this evening."

CHAPTER
FIFTEEN

Nimb Hotel
Copenhagen, Denmark

Morgan spent several hours with Rasmussen's operations director arranging shipments of fictional GPS receivers while his prosthetic recorded every key stroke and screen display Elias Svane performed during their time together. Their conversation went no further than the job at hand, despite Morgan's attempts to elicit some details about RDS operations beyond his fictitious requirements. Once they were finished, Morgan took his leave and drove back to his hotel. After passing the Artura to the parking valet, returning to his room, and changing out of his suit and into more casual attire, Morgan called back to Langley.

"Peters."

"This is Gargoyle. I am prepared to authenticate."

"Authenticate Quebec Sierra Five Zero Two."

"I authenticate Delta Foxtrot Lima Four Four Seven."

"Authentication accepted. Hey, Bob."

"Successfully contacted Rasmussen and Lady Aurora last night. Met with them and the company's operations director this morning. I have enough information to pay the RDS office a visit after working hours tonight."

"Good to hear. I'll pass your update on to General Bailey. Anything else?"

"Not right now."

"Okay, be careful tonight."

"Roger, will do. Gargoyle out."

Morgan ended the call and sent two texts. One went to Ms. McCulloch with the same update he discussed with Clint Peters. The second went to Susan, his aircraft's co-pilot.

Susan,

Expecting to leave sometime around midnight for Langley. See you then!

Bob

Morgan received a quick response.

Bob,

Looking forward to it! ;-)

Susan

Morgan smirked as he read Susan's text.

Man, sometimes I love my job!

His thoughts turned to Lily. Try as he might, and despite the delightful ministrations of Lady Aurora, he could not get her out of his mind.

What the hell was I thinking? I left her last night without getting her contact information. Really bright, Bob.

Morgan opened his laptop to review the video streamed earlier by his prosthetic. Starting with the ground floor lobby, he looked for any security cameras or personnel he may not have noticed himself. Finding nothing of note, he let the video run until he saw the fire evacuation diagram by the elevator. He didn't notice it while he was there since Ivar took up most of his attention, but now he could focus on it. According to the diagram, there was a set of stairs inside the door at the right-hand wing of the building. Perfect! He had the tools Chop provided to make short work of the lock and any surveillance cameras in the area.

Morgan fast forwarded the video until he found the footage of him and Elias working in the conference room. He hit play to watch as Elias accessed the room's computer. It appeared that Elias used both a Personal Identification Number and a card similar to his CIA issued Common Access Card. Despite Elias's speed on the keyboard, Morgan noted the PIN and with a CAC emulator in his bag of tricks, he knew how to access RDS's network.

With his ingress and information collection plan well in hand, Morgan turned to a much baser need, food. He missed lunch while working at RDS, and since he did not know when he'd be able to eat again after tonight, headed to the hotel's brasserie for an early dinner. He ordered a sparkling water with lime (or a *mousserende vand med kalk*), an appetizer of toasted brioche with the mushrooms and cream, a steak frites with salad and sauce béarnaise for his main course, and a crème brûlée with Polynesian vanilla for dessert. The sumptuous meal didn't do his diet any favors, but he was on travel, so why not?

Returning to his room, Morgan prepared for the night. He packed his new tuxedo and suits back into his garment bag, set both his laptop and phone for remote recording before placing the laptop in the attaché case, and packed his toiletries and other personal items in the trolley bag after removing the special kit bag Chop put together for him from the trolley's hidden compartment. He went to room's safe and pulled out his Smith & Wesson 6904 and its shoulder holster. Once all the items he needed were laid out, he hung the 'do not disturb' sign on his door and took what he called in the service, a 'battle nap' to ensure he was ready for a potentially long night's work.

CHAPTER
SIXTEEN

Kalvebod Brygge Road
Copenhagen, Denmark
2330 hours

Morgan drove the McLaren Artura along the Kalvebod Brygge Road, paralleling the Sydlhavnen River. The purr of car's three-liter, twin-turbo V-6 hybrid engine competed with its Bowers & Wilkins stereo system as it played John Barry's theme from 'On Her Majesty's Secret Service.'

He arrived at the RDS headquarters building, but instead of making the left-hand turn onto Sluseholmen as he did earlier in the day, he continued down Sjaellandsbroen, making a U-turn just past the bridge over the river. Morgan placed the Artura in all-electric mode and parked the car silently under a tree in a parking lot adjacent to the RDS building, which sat lower than street level, keeping him, and the car out of sight from his target.

Morgan climbed out of the Artura and moved towards the small hill that concealed him from the building. He crawled up the hill and stopped next to a tree. He pulled the first of Chop's toys from his jacket pocket, a night vision/thermal imaging scope no larger than a cigar tube. He scanned the area around the building's back door and did not see anyone lurking. He did see a camera watching the door. Tightening the image, Morgan saw that the camera was cordless and probably connected to the building's security system via a Wi-Fi connection.

Perfect!

Morgan pulled on a balaclava along with his Gatorz Magnum tactical glasses and moved towards the door, being careful to stay out of the camera's field of view. Morgan reached the building and flattened himself against the wall to the right of the door. He pulled out his next piece of equipment, a Wi-Fi jammer that would make the camera appear to lose its Wi-Fi connection. He activated the jammer and moved towards the door. Looking through the door, he saw a uniformed security guard sitting where the receptionist sat earlier with his face buried in a smartphone. Morgan pulled a lock-pick tool from his jacket and made short work of the door's simple mechanical lock. He opened the door swiftly, locked the door behind him, and dove towards the stairwell. Taking a moment to catch his breath, Morgan looked around and saw no one in the stairwell. He shut off the Wi-Fi jammer and headed quietly towards the top floor.

Morgan carefully opened the door to the top floor and used a small, stick-mounted mirror to check the corridor. He saw the back of a tall man standing a few feet from the door.

Ah shit! Where did he come from?

He pulled the mirror back inside the stairwell, opened the door a bit wider, and moved quietly behind the man. Morgan took his left hand and tapped the man on the left shoulder. As the man turned towards the tap, Morgan crouched in the Keysi Fighting Method's 'Pensador' position and dropped the guard with a vicious right cross to the jaw. He dragged the guard back into the stairwell and immobilized him with the guard's own shoelaces. He searched the guard and found a couple of items that may come in handy. One was a collapsible assault baton that Morgan tucked into his belt, and the second was a nasty PP-2000 submachine gun under the guard's jacket. Morgan unclipped the PP-2000's strap, wrapped it around his arm, and tucked the weapon under his own jacket.

Well, guess I can get souvenirs in this job.

Morgan checked the corridor again. All clear. He moved carefully, keeping his back against the wall. He used his mirror again and saw the lobby and entrance to the conference room apparently empty. Pulling the baton, he moved towards the conference room and caught some movement to his left via the prosthetic. Another guard? He expanded the baton and struck the target in the knee and neck dropping him immediately. Morgan dragged him into a doorway and entered the conference room.

Morgan moved swiftly to the conference room's computer. He turned the computer on and waited for the log on screen. Once the CPU finished starting, Morgan pulled two more items Chop provided. First was a high-capacity thumb drive, and the second was the CAC emulator. Morgan inserted the CAC into the computer's card reader and watched it work its magic. The card emulator read the certificates used in the past 24 hours and listed the users on the screen. Morgan selected Elias Svane's certificate and using the PIN he recoded earlier gained access to RDS's entire network.

So much for two factor authentication.

Morgan inserted the thumb drive into a USB socket, sat back, and enjoyed the show. The thumb drive was the latest from the fine folks at the National Security Agency, Fort Meade, Maryland. It contained the software necessary to crack most encryption programs and download the contents of the network's share drives. An amazing hacking tool made for people like Morgan who can't even spell cyber security let alone understand it. After a few, agonizingly long minutes, the thumb drive finished its work. He pulled it from the computer, placed it in his inside jacket pocket, and moved quickly towards the door.

Glancing out into the corridor, the way out appeared clear, so Morgan began to leave. Before he made it to the lobby, something, or someone, stuck him in the legs knocking him to the floor. He rolled and rose to his feet quickly just in time to dodge a fist heading towards his skull. He saw a hooded figure in all black, like him, assume a familiar fighting stance.

Krav Maga? This guy's serious.

The opponents moved around each other, each waiting for the other to make the first move. Whoever this was, they were not very big, but size doesn't matter much to a Krav Maga practitioner.

Finally, Morgan's opponent made a move with a high kick towards the head. Morgan moved from the 'Pensador' position, blocked the kick, and delivered a blow to the abdomen. As his opponent collapsed towards the floor, Morgan grabbed the hood and tore it off. Much to his surprise, Morgan saw a mess of long, blonde hair spill out from under hood.

"Lily?"

Lily struck with blinding speed striking Morgan hard in the left jaw. She stood back and resumed her fighting stance.

"Lilly! It's Bob!" Morgan said as he removed his balaclava.

Lilly looked back at him with a great deal of surprise.

"Bob? What are you doing here?"

The sound of approaching feet caught their attention.

"No time for explanations now. I think we've worn out our welcome."

Lily headed towards the center stairwell as a group of men move towards them from the right. Automatic weapons fire made the pair duck and head for the stairs. Morgan drew his Smith & Wesson and returned fire before closing the door while Lily headed down the stairs.

"Lily! Slow down!"

Morgan caught up as the pair reached the ground floor while the gunmen entered the stairwell. They entered the now empty lobby and moved towards the back door. They looked out the door and paused.

ROBERT A. ADAMCIK

"Ah, bugger all," Lily said as they saw a group of four armed men surrounding her Z4 in the building's back parking lot.

"This is going to break my heart."

She pushed Morgan back behind the door jam, pulled a small remote control from her pocket, and pushed a button. The BMW roadster exploded in a large orange fireball taking out the men and shattering the glass door. A piece of glass shot under Morgan's tactical glasses and struck near his left eye.

"Ah, fuck!" Morgan cried out.

"You alright?"

"I'm fine. Follow me!"

CHAPTER
SEVENTEEN

Copenhagen, Denmark
0030 hours

Morgan and Lily moved past the burning wreck of Lily's car and headed for Morgan's Artura. The pair leapt down the hill towards the sunken parking lot as automatic weapons fire struck the top of the rise. Morgan hit the Artura's remote to open the doors and the pair jumped in the car. He pressed the engine start button, put the car in gear, and tore out of the parking lot.

Heading for the airport, Morgan turned left onto the Ved Stigbordene followed quickly by another left onto Sluseholmen. As they drove around the RDS building Morgan saw several cars heading out the front parking lot.

"Heads up! We're about to have company," Morgan said.

"Not a problem. I'm always dressed for company." Lily replied as she pulled a Walther PPK from a holster behind her back.

Morgan pushed the Android Auto phone interface button on the Artura's center console as he performed a left-hand drift onto Sjaellandsbroen.

"Dial Sierra Hotel!"

"Dialing Sierra Hotel," the Artura's in-car voice responded.

After a couple of rings, the phone on the other end picked up. "Hello?"

"Susan! This is Morgan! I'm on the way and I coming in hot!"

"We'll be ready."

"Out!" Morgan said as he ended the call.

"Sierra hotel?" Lily asked.

"U.S. Navy aviator speak for 'shit hot.' Susan is my aircraft's first officer."

Morgan went into the Artura's sound system and hit the random button for his Galaxy's Driving Tunes playlist.

"Is that really necessary?"

"It helps me concentrate while driving."

As Alien Ant Farm's cover of Michael Jackson's 'Smooth Criminal' pumped out the Bowers & Wilkins speakers, three Mercedes sedans pursued the Artura towards the E20 highway. One of the Mercedes' windows opened and a gunman leaned out with a PP-2000 and opened fire. The nine-millimeter rounds struck the Artura's back window with its protective film preventing any damage.

"Modern safety glass?" Lily asked as she racked a round into the Walther.

"You could say that," Morgan replied with a knowing smirk.

Lily lowered her window, leaned out, and returned fire. Her rounds found the front windshield and struck the driver in the head. As the driver's head exploded like a popped balloon, and the Mercedes began to swerve and crashed into a roadside ditch.

"One down!" Lily shouted. "But I'm out!"

Morgan reached the Artura's driver's side door storage area and pulled out the Nano and an extra magazine.

"Eight rounds ready to go, seven rounds on your lap!"

Lily grabbed the Nano and fired at the two remaining Mercedes who hung further back after the loss of their compatriot. As she continued to fire, she noted a change in the music.

"John Williams, 'The Empire Strikes Back'?" she asked.

"Oh yeah! Ten points if you can name the track."

"The Asteroid Field."

"Very good. Great music for dodging traffic, bullets, or the odd floating space rock."

The Artura roared along the E20 motorway, its 671-horsepower hybrid twin turbo V-6 keeping the two pursuing Mercedes far behind. Morgan saw that it was only two kilometers to the exit of the E20, so he decided that he needed to end this. He moved over to the left lane and slowed.

"What are you doing?!" Lily asked.

"Reach inside the right side of my jacket, there's a PP-2000. Pull it out."

Lily felt under Morgan's jacket, unclipped the strap, pulled out the sub-machine gun, and extended the stock. She then lowered her window.

"Ready!"

Morgan saw the exit and swiftly accelerated back ahead of the lead Mercedes. He began a right-hand drift that took the Artura in front of the Mercedes.

"Now!" Morgan shouted.

Lily tucked the PP-2000 into her shoulder and opened fire. At the Artura skidded right, Lily's bullets struck the driver's side front tire, window, and windshield. The Mercedes's right-front fender whispered by the rear of the Artura and continued uncontrolled down the motorway.

Talk about crossing the 'T!'

The Artura made the exit and entered the airport grounds. Morgan thought that this would end the pursuit, but he was quite mistaken.

Morgan saw the Cessna on the tarmac and headed towards it. He skidded under the aircraft's left wing pointing the passenger side door towards the aircraft's ladder. He unlocked the doors and reached for his attaché case.

"Go!" Morgan shouted.

Lily grabbed her PPK and ran headlong into the aircraft.

89

Morgan grabbed his attaché as the last Mercedes reached them. The Mercedes's occupants began to fire at the Cessna and the Artura, and Morgan saw Susan come out from behind the front landing gear.

"Introduce them to your little friend!"

Susan smiled a sweet little smile and raised her M4 carbine with an underslung M203 40-millimeter grenade launcher. While bullets struck both the Artura and the ground around her, Susan took careful aim and fired a grenade towards the Mercedes. The grenade flew true and shattered the driver's side window before exploding. The car came to an immediate stop and burst into flames. She emptied the M4's magazine into the burning wreckage just to make sure the job was done. Before anyone else showed up, Susan ran up the ladder and closed the door.

"Captain! Get us out of here!"

The Cessna lurched forward as the Captain applied power to the engines, and it moved quickly down the taxi way. It reached the end of the runway, turned, and the Captain increased the throttles to full. At a ground speed of 200 knots, he pulled back on the control yoke and the Cessna launched skyward. Back in the passenger cabin, Lily and Morgan strapped themselves into their seats. Lilly looked over at Morgan and smiled.

"I've forgotten how much I hate air travel!" Lily shouted over the roar of the jet engines.

Back at the airport, a fourth Mercedes stopped near the burning wreckage that was the third car. Ivar climbed out of the passenger's seat and muttered to himself. *"Hvis du vil have noget gjort rigtigt.* (If you want something done right...)" He reached into his jacket and pulled out his phone.

CHAPTER
EIGHTEEN

Once the Cessna reached cruising altitude, Morgan rubbed his still sore jaw and turned towards Lily.

"So, seeing your choice of weapons and your mad Krav Maga skills, I take it your name is not Lily Matthews and you don't work for an animal charity."

"Correct, my name is Catherine Roberts, Cat to my friends. I work for His Majesty's Government. And I take it you are not a tech start-up COO named Bob Curry?"

"Yes ma'am. My name is Morgan, James Morgan, but my friends do call me Bob."

"Bob?"

"Middle name."

"Okay, Bob."

Morgan looked Cat straight in the eyes and actually presented her a slight, shy smile.

"Actually, I think I'd like it better if you call me James."

Cat returned the smile. "James it is then."

Morgan heard someone clearing their throat behind him.

"I hate to break this up," Susan said, "but we have a problem."

"What's going on?" Morgan asked.

"The gunfire punctured some of our fuel tanks. We won't make it back to the States."

"How far can we go?"

"We have maybe two hours of flight time. We need to decide where to go."

"Okay, judging by the reception we received, one of us was compromised. Cat, did anyone follow you when you arrived in Copenhagen?"

"No, nothing. Even ran a surveillance detection route when I drove to my hotel."

"Okay, odds are then that the problem is on my side. Susan, can we make Salzburg?"

"Yes, we're about an hour out from Austria."

"Good, go ahead and head there please. By the way, great shooting! That M4 suits you."

"No well-dressed woman should be without one." Susan smiled and headed back to the cockpit.

"What do you have in mind, James?" Cat asked.

"Two things. One, set a trap for whomever my leak is. And two, figure out what's next."

Morgan grabbed the plane's satellite telephone. He picked it up and dialed Clint Peters.

"Peters."

"Just took off from Copenhagen under a hail of bullets. Rasmussen had a small army waiting for me, but I retrieved what I needed. The aircraft took some damage, so we're heading for Berlin."

"Copy all, Gargoyle. We'll take someone meet you there."

"I'll let you know what I dig up from the RDS computer files."

Morgan ended the call and selected the satellite phone's text application.

One trap down, one to go.

He quickly drafted a text to Ms. McCulloch:

Ms. McCulloch,

Had a warm reception this evening at RDS, too warm. Grabbed what I needed but left in a big hurry. Please apologize to Chop for me, the Artura took a few bullets that the car's protective film did not stop. The aircraft took some damage, so we're heading to Munich for repairs. If possible, please have someone from Global Services meet me there to re-equip/re-arm. Thank you, ma'am!!!!!

Gargoyle

Morgan pulled his Agency issued cell phone out of his jacket pocket, shut it off, and pulled the battery and the sim card, then snapped it in two.

Whoever the leak is, they won't be tracking this phone.

He turned to Cat.

"The only two people who knew everything about my mission were Clint Peters, my handler, and Ms. McCulloch, the Agency's Assistant Deputy Director of Operations. We'll see what happens at those two locations as we head to Austria. Now, let's see what sort of goodies I grabbed from the RDS network."

Morgan pulled his laptop from his attaché case and started it up. He slid the thumb drive into a USB port and let it go to work. He turned to Cat.

"So, was the story about your tattoo part of your cover?"

"Oh no, that is all true. Ms. Moneypenny is one of my four cats. My other calico is named Miso, and my two torties are Calisto and Nebula."

"Nebula? Astronomy fan?"

"'Guardians of the Galaxy'."

She's an 80s music, Marvel, Bond, and Star Wars fan? Oh man, she's a keeper if we ever get out of this.

"Outstanding. Love the Marvel films," Morgan replied.

"How about you, James? Anyone or anything at home?"

"Nope, neither two-legged nor four-legged family await me at home. With my travel schedule, pets are a non-starter. Growing up in Cleveland, I had one of each, a Siamese cat named Opal, and a Golden Retriever mix named Hunter. They taught me that animals are worth far more than people. Left them with my parents when I enlisted in the Navy, broke my heart to do so."

Morgan stared at the laptop. Looking though the downloaded files, one name stood out from the rest, 'hantu'. He clicked on it, and saw that it was password protected, the only file with additional security measures.

"Well, we'll just see about that," Morgan muttered to himself.

Morgan accessed the password-cracking app on his laptop and allowed it to do the work. While waiting for the file to open, he turned again to Cat.

"What brought RDS Shipping to the attention of MI-6?"

"We were investigating an arms smuggling operation that fed some nasty weaponry to the Real IRA. As things progressed, we discovered that arms were not the only things smuggled by the Rasmussens. They've been dealing in human trafficking for the past two years. Hundreds of refugees, sex workers, and domestic help, all taken away from their homes and families via RDS container ships."

"That explains it. When we ran RDS's financials, we noticed that the company was not doing well until recently when it started running consistently in the black. Too consistently. We believed it was from gun running, but human trafficking is a far more lucrative enterprise."

"150 billion U.S. dollars a year lucrative, three times as much as dealing in weapons."

"Even a one percent cut of that would aid the bottom line quite nicely."

The cut under Morgan's eye began to bleed, catching Cat's attention.

"James, your left eye is bleeding again."

"Ah, shit. Hold on a moment."

Morgan felt the blood under his left eye. He then removed his tactical glasses, pulled out his prosthetic, place it in its case, and placed an eye patch over his left eye. Cat looked on with surprise and concern.

"What happened?" Cat reached out to wipe the blood from Morgan's cut before cleaning the wound with supplies from the aircraft's first aid kit.

"Ambush while on mission. My Global Services guy hooked me up with the prosthetic for this trip."

"He did a marvelous job. I could not see a difference. It matches your wonderful hazel eyes." Cat smiled as she finished treating his wound.

"Thank you. The prosthetic has more going for it than looks."

Morgan looked down at his laptop.

"Okay, the file is open. Come take a look."

Cat came around the coffee table where Morgan had set his laptop, sat to his left on the leather couch, and wrapped her right arm around his left, much to Morgan's surprise and delight.

"See here, we have names of ships, ports, and cargoes." He pointing to a spread sheet on the screen. "But this column has some alpha-numeric designations with specific quantities in the next column. To anyone else, these letters and numbers are gibberish, more shipping speak. But to folks like us, they tell a story that ends with a lot of dead French soldiers in Mali, or dead policemen in Northern Ireland."

Cat pointed to one row in particular.

"Is that what I think it is?"

Morgan looked where she was pointing.

"Yes, that's the PCL191, the Chinese domestic version of their less-powerful AR3 multiple launch rocket system they export all over the world. This shows that there are five PCL191 MLRSs sitting in Singapore awaiting transport to Mali on board the M/V *Aurora Express*, a feedermax-class container ship. Shit, this is very bad. Whoever is funding all this has some serious pull. The Chinese don't export the PCL191, just the less capable AR3. The PCL191 has eight, 370-millimeter, satellite guided rockets with a 350-kilometer range, and it only requires three people to operate it. The French forces in Mali will be in a world of shit if the insurgents get a hold of this."

"What's our next move, James?"

"I have something in mind that would aid both our missions, but we need to get to Singapore. Cat, can you have some of your assets meet us in Salzburg?"

"Maybe. May I borrow your satellite phone?"

"Be my guest."

Cat picked up the phone and dialed a few numbers. A few moments later, she spoke.

"Finn, this is Calico..." she then stood up and walked towards the rear of the aircraft.

Morgan smirked to himself as he watched Cat speaking on the phone.

Calico? She does love her cats. Perfect call sign!

Ten minutes later, after some furious scribbling on her part, Cat rejoined Morgan on the couch.

"James, we may be in some luck..."

CHAPTER
NINETEEN

Wolfgang Amadeus Mozart Airport
Salzburg, Austria

The Cessna Longitude landed at Salzburg's W.A. Mozart airport after declaring an emergency, while using the aircraft's U.S. State Department clearance, to keep the local Austrian officials at bay.

The Cessna taxied to a private aircraft hangar to await repairs. Morgan and Cat gathered their equipment, including the satellite phone, Susan caught Morgan's attention as Cat descended the ladder.

"She's a lucky girl," Susan whispered.

"Is it that obvious?"

Susan smiled and nodded her head.

Under the looming shape that was the famous Untersberg, Morgan and Cat entered the airport's executive terminal. Finding an empty meeting room, Cat began to lay out their next move.

"My boss at Vauxhall Cross says we have a ride to Singapore."

"Oh?"

"Yes, a C-17 Globemaster from 24 Squadron R.A.F., on a

training flight from RAF Brize Norton to Singapore, is being diverted here to pick us up. My people added some equipment to their cargo prior to take-off to help us out. We'll arrive in Singapore at noon local time the day after tomorrow."

"Outstanding! What about transportation and accommodations?"

"We have reservations at the InterContinental Singapore hotel, and an appropriate vehicle will be waiting for us at the airport."

"Perfect," Morgan said. "Now, I need to get some needed help out there."

Morgan picked up his satellite phone and place a call.

"Lieutenant Kroll," the voice on the other end said.

"Doug! It's Lieutenant Commander Morgan. Can you talk?"

"Yes, sir! What can I do for you?"

"Where are you and your team right now?"

"Guam, wishing I was anywhere else."

"Could you make it to Singapore in the next day or two?"

"Let me think about that a minute, yes!"

"I have an off the books mission for my other employer, and I could use your help."

"What will I need?"

"I'll text you the details. If you feel you need to add anyone please do so, but only if you can trust their discretion. I'm keeping this close to the chest."

"Roger. I do have someone in mind."

"Talk to you later."

Morgan hung up the call and drafted the text outlining his requirements and schedule. After hitting send, he noticed Cat's surprised expression.

"*Leftenant* Commander?"

"Yes, U.S. Navy Reserve. I'm an Intelligence Officer by trade, recruited to the Agency from the active duty ranks."

"Oh, Dad would just love you. He's a retired Royal Marine colonel."

"Indeed. But I wouldn't like to meet him looking like this, definitely wouldn't pass inspection. Besides, I'm a bit stinky."

"We have a safe house across the street from the British consulate. We have a few hours before the Globemaster arrives so can get cleaned up before our flight."

"Outstanding."

As the couple stepped out of the terminal, Morgan noticed the mountains in the distance. They reminded him of his late mother's love of the film, 'The Sound of Music.' Morgan turned to Cat.

"Cat, while we're in Salzburg, just promise me one thing."

"Yes, James?"

"No 'Climb Every Mountain'."

"Aw!" Cat replied with a sexy pout. "'Edelweiss'?"

"No."

"'Do Ra Mi?'"

"No," Morgan replied with a smirk.

"'16 Going on 17'?"

"Definitely no!" said Morgan barely holding in a laugh.

Cat paused for a moment. "'Maria'?"

"AH!"

Morgan and Cat took a taxi from the airport to the MI-6 safehouse. Located on Johann-Wolf Strasse, the apartment shared space with a local veterinarian. They exited the cab a few blocks away and arrived on foot. Cat reached into the specimen box hanging off the door. She felt around the tubes of cat blood and containers of dog urine and pulled out a set of keys.

"Perfect place to hide these," Cat said holding up the keys. "No one wants to reach in something that may be filled with dog vomit and cat poop."

The pair went around the back of the building to a set of stairs. Climbing up, Cat opened the door and they carefully walked inside. After checking all the rooms, they set their things down in the living room. Morgan looked around and noticed the Nespresso maker in the kitchen.

"Ah, civilization at last," he said. He turned to Cat. "Do you want to shower first?"

"No, go ahead. You need it more than I do," she said with a sniff and a smile.

"Gee, thanks."

Morgan stripped down and entered the shower in the surprisingly spacious bathroom. While waiting for the water to get hot, he pulled his prosthetic out its case, rinsed it off, and dried it carefully before placing it on the sink ledge. He climbed in the shower and began to scrub off his accumulated sweat and stink. A few moments later, he felt a cool breeze on his back.

"Room for one more, sailor?"

Morgan tuned around and saw a naked Cat standing in the shower. She wrapped her arms around his neck and kissed the surprised look right off his face.

A few hours later, and feeling considerably better, the pair left the safehouse, dropped the keys back into the specimen box, and took a cab back to the airport. As they approached the executive terminal, they spotted a huge Boeing C-17 Globemaster in RAF livery.

"Ah, our ride is here," Cat said.

They walked straight through the terminal, onto the tarmac, and towards a RAF officer standing by the open rear ramp.

"Calico? I'm Squadron Leader Sebastian Williams, and I bring greetings and some gifts from your Uncle Freddy."

"Thank you, Squadron Leader. My dear uncle certainly knows how to take care of his favorite niece. How soon can you take off?"

"As soon as you're ready, ma'am. I have an aircraft full of student pilots eager to get some flight time in this grand lady."

"Good. This is my associate, Commander Teach. He'll be joining us for this flight."

"Welcome aboard, Commander. This way please." Williams pointed towards the ramp. As they walked aboard, Morgan whispered in Cat's ear.

"Commander Teach? As in Blackbeard?"

"Well James, between your beard and eye patch, you do look a bit like a pirate."

Morgan began to respond, but his witty reply was forever lost in the sounds of the closing ramp and the revving of jet engines.

CHAPTER
TWENTY

Royal Air Force C-17
35,000 feet above the Adriatic Sea
Course: 150 degrees true

Once airborne, Cat and Morgan took a look at the material provided by Cat's employer.

"Uncle Freddy?" Morgan asked. "Your boss at Six?"

"No, he's my real uncle. My mother's brother. He heads the service's Science and Technology Branch. He was quite happy that his favorite niece decided to join the family business."

"So, what did dear Uncle Freddy send us?

Cat opened the pelican case lashed to the deck and smiled. Morgan looked over her shoulder and whistled appreciatively.

"Merry Christmas."

"Uncle Freddy always knows what to get me."

Inside the pelican case were two C8 carbines, two Sig Sauer P226 nine-millimeter handguns, a Remington 12 gauge shot gun, several flash-bang and smoke grenades, five sets of communications equipment including whisper microphones and ear pieces, two empty duffle bags, and ammunition. Under the foam padding protecting the weapons were two sets of tactical clothing, boots, and body armor. There was also an envelope with Cat's name on the front. She took it out and opened it.

Cat,

As requested, here is the equipment for your trip to Singapore courtesy of the SAS. Please be careful dear niece, we'd miss you terribly around the holidays. Love and Cheers!
Uncle Freddy

P.S. The Colonel added one last thing for you. It's at the bottom of the case.

Cat found what her uncle mentioned under the body armor. It was a long thin box about the length of her forearm. She opened it and saw a vision in black, a Fairbairn–Sykes commando fighting knife. Made famous by the British Commandos in World War II, the Fairbairn–Sykes knife was also used by the U.S. Office of Strategic Services, precursor to the CIA, several of the Allied forces on D-Day, and the Royal Marines. This one resided in a leather arm sheath and looked sleek and deadly.

"Thanks, Daddy!" Cat said aloud.

As the pair began to organize their equipment and pack the two duffle bags, footsteps approached from the direction of the flight deck.

"You two look like kids in the sweets shop," Squadron Leader Williams said.

"You have no idea," Morgan replied.

"Squadron Leader," Cat began. "Commander Teach and I can be assured of your and your crew's discretion regarding our presence here?"

"Yes, ma'am. I flew C-130s with 47 Squadron before transitioning to the C-17, and I flew several SAS and SBS teams several times into and out of theater, so I know how to keep my mouth shut. As far as my students are concerned, you two were never here."

With that, Morgan and Cat finished packing their equipment into the duffle bags. They retreated to two of the aircraft's jump seats and settled in for the remainder of the fifteen-hour flight to Singapore. Morgan fell sleep almost immediately with Cat looking on with a mixture of affection and envy.

How the hell can he fall asleep so easily? Lucky bastard.

Cat snuggled up next to the handsome American and eventually fell asleep herself.

Morgan woke with a start, forgetting for a moment where he was, which occurred often when he slept deeply. Looking down, he saw Cat sleeping peacefully next to him.

I could get used to this view.

He looked at his Omega and saw that they should be landing in a couple of hours. He gently moved a lock of her hair away from her eyes and shook her arm.

"Good morning," Morgan said.

"Good morning. Where are we?" Cat asked as she stretched her sleep stiffened limbs.

"Judging by the time, we should be somewhere over the Indian Ocean approaching the Straits of Malacca."

"Okay, there is coffee in the galley. Get us some while I head up to the flight deck?"

"Sure, how do you take it?"

"Black, no sugar, please."

"A woman after my own heart," Morgan said with friendly smirk. "Learned from your father?"

"It's the only way we drank it growing up."

Cat headed towards the ladder leading to the flight deck while Morgan went to the galley via the aircraft's lavatory.

Morgan finished pouring two cups of what the RAF considers coffee when Cat joined him in the galley.

"How's the coffee?" she asked.

"Swill, but any port in a storm." Morgan handed her a cup. "The Royal Navy could teach these guys a thing or two about how to brew a cup of coffee. A Royal Navy officer I served with made an amazing cup despite the low quality of the U.S. Navy coffee he had to work with."

Cat took a sip, "I've had worse, but I've also had a lot better. Anyway, we'll be landing at 13:00 hours local time. I checked my phone, and our man in Singapore will meet us at the airport."

"Great, he's read in?"

"He is, as you Americans say, 'In the loop'.'"

Two hours later, the massive Globemaster landed at Singapore's Changi airport and taxied to a Republic of Singapore Air Force hangar. The pair grabbed their duffle bags and headed down the rear cargo ramp. When they reached the tarmac, they were greeted with an impressive sight. To their left, by the hangar doors, stood a current generation Honda, or Acura as Morgan knew it, NSX in Source Silver Metallic. A tall, black-haired, male-model handsome, and dapper gentleman in an off-white tropical weight suit stood next to the car. He offered a friendly wave.

"Cat!" the man shouted as the pair approached.

"Hello, Bertie!" Cat said. They exchanged a quick hug and Cat turned to Morgan.

"James, this is Bertie Scott, head of Station 'S' and our man here. Bertie, please meet Lieutenant Commander James Robert Morgan, United States Navy Reserve and CIA. Bertie and I joined the Service at the same time."

"Please call me Bob," Morgan said as he shook Bertie's offered hand. He could not help noticing that Bertie bore a passing resemblance to the late actor Christopher Reeve with identical jet-black hair and square jaw.

"Welcome Bob," Bertie said. "Cat, I hope you approve of our

choice of vehicle. I remembered your love of high-performance automobiles. Here's the key fob."

"It's perfect, thanks Bertie. Any word on our target?"

"She's still in port, sitting at the Pasir Panjang 2 container terminal, berth seven."

"Good, you have eyes on?"

"I have a full surveillance detail at piers and in the port operations office. So far nothing unusual."

"My guess is that they'll load any contraband just prior to getting underway," Morgan added. "Still scheduled for tomorrow night?"

"According to the harbor master, yes. 22:00 hours. Also, I have all the paperwork you and your team need to get into the terminal sitting in the car."

"Perfect, my team arrives tonight. Cat, ready to go?"

"Absolutely, lunch and the hotel's shower are calling to me."

Cat used the fob to open the NSX's rear hatch. They loaded the duffle bags into the back and moved to get inside. Morgan walked to the left side of the car and took a look through the window.

"Well shit," he said with the disappointment dripping from his voice as he saw the passenger seat instead of the expected steering wheel and driver's seat. "I guess you're driving."

"Can't let you have all the fun, James," Cat said with a smile she sat behind the wheel. Morgan shrugged and climbed into the passenger seat before Cat started the twin turbo charged, six-cylinder hybrid engine. She spun the tires, and took off away from her startled countryman.

CHAPTER
TWENTY-ONE

Hotel Intercontinental
Singapore

Morgan remembered why he didn't mind Cat driving, left side of the road traffic. He never drove anywhere where cars were on the left, and he believed that if he ever was trapped in a round-a-bout, he would end up curled up in a ball, crying, and looking for his happy place. Cat, however, was in her element. She dodged easily the thickening traffic on the East Coast Parkway, better known as the ECP, as she listened to 1980s era hair metal music streaming from her phone. As Def Leopard's 'Pour Some Sugar on Me' came on, he looked over to her.

"So, you going to break out the stripper pole?"

"Excuse me?"

"Sorry. In the States, this song is known as the strippers' anthem as it's played in pretty much every gentlemen's club in the country."

"Ah, I see. Maybe later?" she said with a smile.

"It's a date," Morgan replied with a smirk.

As the song changed to Mötley Crüe's 'Girls, Girls, Girls,' Morgan looked over at Cat who had begun shaking her head in time with the music, her blond hair moving in a cloud around her skull.

"So, were you and Bertie an item during training?"

Cat looked at him incredulously, "Why? Are you jealous?"

"Maybe, he's a handsome guy. Makes me feel downright ugly."

"You never have to worry about being ugly," Cat said with a brilliant smile. "To me, Bertie was the little brother I never had growing up. Besides, you're more his type than I could ever be."

Morgan looked at Cat with some confusion, then her meaning hit him.

"Oh," Morgan said quietly with a look of understanding crossing his features.

"Aw! You're cute when you are confused. Yes, he is gay. Many of my female classmates lamented Bertie's sexual orientation, but he's a great guy and an even better operative. He and his partner, Jéred, have been together for the past ten years now."

"Jéred?"

"Um hm. He's Catalonian, and they first met in Barcelona when Bertie worked out of Station 'M' Madrid."

Cat left the ECP and turned onto Rochor Road before finally turning left onto Victoria Street and arrived at the Hotel Inter-Continental. She pulled up to the parking valet and handed over the key fob. A porter began to pull the bags out the back, Morgan interrupted him, and, after passing him a 50 Singapore dollar tip for the effort, took the bags himself. He caught up with Cat at the hotel's front desk.

"We're in the Heritage wing, James," Cat said as she handed him a key card.

"Sounds good to me, these damned bags are getting heavy. Maybe I should have accepted the porter's help."

"With what we have in those bags, not a wise idea."

"Tell that to my back."

The pair made their way through the hotel's Heritage wing,

where the architecture and décor reflected Singapore's colonial past. They arrived at their room, opened the door, and stood in absolute awe.

"Well done, Bertie," Cat said quietly.

Looking down the hallway, they saw the suite's coffee and tea making facility featuring Morgan's preferred Nespresso machine. They walked through the living room and took a quick look out the window of the private balcony, which overlooked the Bugis Junction indoor shopping mall. Passing a bathroom that was larger than Cat's Maidstone flat, they stowed the duffle bags in the walk-in closet, and they collapsed on the huge, king size bed.

"Eat first or shower?" Morgan asked.

"Eat, as much as I need a shower, I need food more."

"Okay, I'm texting home on the satellite phone to let them know I'm still alive."

Morgan grabbed the satellite phone and headed to the balcony. He sat in a chair and texted both Clint Peters and Ms. McCulloch in a group text while watching the shoppers.

Folks,

Despite rumors to the contrary, I'm quite alive! My phone is off and the battery removed, so don't bother trying it. Working a lead, will update you when I can.

Gargoyle

He returned to the bedroom and saw Cat standing there with a peculiar expression on her face.

"Ready to go?" she asked.

"Let me grab an accessory and we'll be on our way."

Morgan opened his attaché and pulled out his Nano and its shoulder holster. He slipped the weapon under his left arm and put on his jacket.

"Now I'm ready."

"Excellent," Cat said as she grabbed Morgan's left arm. "I'm starving."

After a quick stop at the Concierge desk for a recommendation, Morgan and Cat ended up at the Third and Sixth Bistro Bar. Located about a half kilometer from the hotel, the Third and Sixth specialized in monster sized hamburgers, perfect for the two starving agents. After Morgan consumed a Number 36, and Cat, despite her normally pescatarian diet, the Naked Joe, along with a pair of beers to wash them down, they made the walk back to the hotel. When they returned to the suite, Morgan noticed something different. All the lights were off, and several candles provided the only illumination. Morgan turned to Cat and saw her moving towards the bathroom while taking off her top.

"Join me for a bath?" She looked back over her shoulder.

Morgan smirked and began to strip off his clothes.

So, this is why she had that peculiar look on her face. I almost caught her arranging all this.

Later, they sat together in the soap-filled, oversized tub, with Cat between Morgan's legs and her back up against his chest, Cat turned her head towards Morgan.

"Tell me about your life James, before you got into all this."

Morgan told her about his rather ordinary life growing up in Cleveland, his late parents and three siblings, his time in high school, and his leaving for the Navy.

"You enlisted so young, why did you do that?"

"Two reasons, I guess. I was a bit impatient to get my Navy career started since it was my hobby growing up, and I wanted to get away from the assholes I grew up with. I graduated high school a year early, so I took advantage of that and left Cleveland for good. Haven't been back except for my parents' funerals."

"Sounds familiar, I didn't have many friends going up either with a father in the Royal Marines and all the moving that entailed. Guess that's why we are how we are. Introverts who prefer the company of our animals to most other people."

"Exactly. I had a few good friends, especially one guy, Jerry. He managed to keep me sane through our high school years. We later went to university together, and he became a U.S. Marine

Corps officer while I continued my Navy career. He was killed a couple of weeks ago by weapons provided by the Rasmussens while working as a military contractor in Mali. The rest of those sons of bitches back home, I wouldn't give the time of day. How about you, Cat? Any siblings?"

Cat gave Morgan a hug and a gentle kiss before answering, "Three older half siblings from my mother's side. Their father was a friend of my uncle's and while working for MI-5, died in Northern Ireland during the Troubles. My father met my mother after he returned from the Falklands where he served as commander, K Company, in 42 Commando. After that harrowing experience, he decided to settle down, met my mother, and they had me. My elder siblings did not take to my father's regimented way of doing things and left as soon as they could, so I grew up virtually an only child. Since I didn't make many friends, I threw myself into my studies, passed my A-Levels, and read history and linguistics at Oxford.

"Linguistics?"

"Yes. It turned out that I'm a bit of a polyglot."

"Really? How many languages can you speak?"

"Fluently? I'm up to ten."

"Ten? That's impressive."

"Thank you, and that's what Uncle Freddy thought. He encouraged me to join the SIS, and, in my own bit of rebellion, joined him in entering the service."

"Rebellion?"

"Yes, Daddy didn't like me joining MI-6. He's a tad old fashioned when it comes to women, and a career in intelligence, he felt, wasn't 'lady-like.' However, as I progressed in the service, his attitude began to soften to the point of being just as proud of me as any parent could be. Daddy knows of my love of fighting knives I developed over the years, so he sent me the Fairbairn–Sykes for this mission…"

A loud knock on the door interrupted the conversation.

"Expecting anyone?" Morgan asked.

"No," Cat said as she left the bath.

"Oh shit, here we go."

Morgan stood up, put on one of the hotel's bathrobes, pulled his Nano from its holster, and headed towards the door. He moved carefully by the door handle and held up the Nano.

"Yes?"

"Commander Morgan? It's Doug and Dallas."

Recognizing the voice, Morgan looked carefully out the door's peephole, not something he would normally do while on mission. He saw his two teammates standing in the hallway and, while standing off towards one side, opened the door. LT Kroll and Chief Shaw came in dragging two large cases behind them. At that point, Cat came out of the bathroom clad only in the other bathrobe, Walther PPK in hand, covering Morgan and the door. Morgan held up his hand behind him.

"It's okay, Cat. Gentlemen, please meet Ms. Catherine Roberts, MI-6. Cat, this is Chief Petty Officer Michael Shaw, call sign Dallas, and *Leftenant* Douglas Kroll, call sign Doug."

After shaking hands, the group moved to the living room. Cat looked over at LT Kroll.

"So, no catchy call sign like Dallas or Gargoyle?"

"No, ma'am. Waste of time."

LT Kroll then noticed what Morgan and Cat were wearing.

"Sir, did we interrupt something?"

"Yes, but it's okay. You're just here earlier than I expected."

"We caught an earlier flight, any chance to get out of Guam sooner rather than later."

"Good point. What do you have?"

Dallas opened the first case showing off two sets of diving gear for the two of them. Then he opened the second.

"As you requested, sir, two limpet GPS tracking systems. They have a 60-day battery life with world-wide tracking capability."

"Perfect, even if the *Aurora Express* shuts off her AIS transceiver, we'll still have her. Okay, here's what I have in mind."

Morgan outlined his plan to the three of them. When he was finished, he turned to the team.

"Questions? Anything I missed?"

"Just one, why not sink it?" Chief Shaw asked.

"Two reasons. One, we need to trace the weapons to their eventual destination in Mali so the French can cap the pipeline at that end. And two, there might be human trafficking cargo involved. That's why Cat and Six are involved. If there is a container filled with women and children, the ship needs to stay afloat. Anything else?"

LT Kroll and Chief Shaw had nothing further, so they stood up to take their leave.

"We'll meet back here tomorrow night before heading to the port. Do you have transportation?"

"We have a mini-van, not exactly glamorous, but needed for our gear."

"Good, see you tomorrow night. Enjoy Singapore."

The pair left their dive gear and trackers with Morgan and left the suite. He walked up to Cat and lifted her up out of her living room chair. He gave her a kiss as he untied her bathrobe.

"So, where were we before we were so rudely interrupted?" he asked then led her to the bedroom.

CHAPTER
TWENTY-TWO

Pasir Panjang 2 Container Terminal
Singapore

Morgan laid atop a four high container stack with an unobstructed view of the *Aurora Express*, the ship's black hull, white superstructure, and RDS Shipping logo quite visible on the ship's exhaust stack under the bright illumination provided by the port's huge pier-side lights. Two rows of containers away, Cat laid in her hide with a pair of binoculars focused on the *Aurora Express*'s brow.

"Doug to Gargoyle," Morgan heard in his earpiece. "Dallas and I are heading to the water."

Morgan tapped his throat mike twice to acknowledge Doug's report. So far so good. Morgan activated the prosthetic's recorder and looked towards ship. Five large trucks approached the ship's brow. As they came to a stop, two figures came across the gangway and stepped onto the quay.

Well, well, Edward and Aurora. This shipment is getting a top flight send off.

As the Rasmussens greeted the truck drivers, Morgan's prosthetic caught movement to his left. A sixth truck pulled up. This arrival caught Aurora's attention and she turned towards the new arrival.

"Calico, Gargoyle. Human cargo?" Morgan asked. Cat replied with two taps of her throat mike.

Yes.

He looked back over to the first five trucks. He saw Edward talking with an Asian gentleman who looked official in his well-tailored suit.

Chinese Ministry of State Security? People's Liberation Army?

Morgan took a long look at this person for later examination. He saw one of the truck drivers pull the tarp on the lead truck open. Underneath he saw the business end of one of the PCL191s. He'd now seen enough, time to get the hell out of there and report.

Before he had the chance to move, he felt someone grab his neck and pick him up off the top of the container. He was turned completely around and looked into the eyes of a large, angry man.

"Ivar!" Morgan shouted before being knocked unconscious.

CHAPTER
TWENTY-THREE

Morgan awoke in a kneeling position with his hands bound behind his back. Looking around, he saw that he was on the quay a few feet away from the *Aurora Express*'s brow, and his weapons and equipment were lined up neatly nearby. He also saw two armed guards at the end of the gangway and three additional guards on the quay. The quay itself was now empty, both the MLRS trailers and human cargo-filled container had already been loaded on board the ship. He felt a hand grab his right shoulder from behind.

"Good evening, Mr. Curry. Or is it Commander Morgan? I think I prefer your naval rank. Something you earned, yes?"

"Hello, Edward. Fancy meeting you here," Morgan said as Edward moved in front of him.

"Indeed. Considering the mess you made in Copenhagen, you should have expected to see me. You and your little British bitch cost me a lot of people and material, and I'm going to take it out on you. Well, actually I'm not. He is. I abhor violence."

Morgan gasped as Ivar grabbed him by the front of his tactical jacket and dragged him to his feet. He planted a punch to Morgan's gut, two to the ribs, and one across the left side of face knocking him back to the ground.

"Many of the men you killed served with Ivar in the Danish armed forces. They were like brothers to him. Ivar and his men had a pleasant reception waiting for you in Berlin, and he was quite disappointed when you didn't show up. I must say that I do pity you, Morgan. Your death will be most unpleasant."

Berlin? Aw shit.

Morgan showed no emotion at the revelation. He looked up at Rasmussen.

"Can't be any worse than dealing with you, Edward. You need stronger mouth wash."

Rasmussen slapped Morgan across the face. He grabbed him by his hair and came even closer.

"You have no idea who, or what, you're dealing with, and you'll die never knowing. We're searching for Ms. Roberts now. Yes, we know who she is, and when we find her, your last romantic moments together will be laying on the ground watching each other bleed out."

"Don't give him to Ivar yet, father. I'd like to say good-bye first," Aurora said as she joined her father.

"Oh, very well, dear daughter. I could never say no to you."

Aurora knelt down to Morgan's level, caressed his face sensually and blew lightly in his right ear.

"You were one of my favorites, Bob. I'll be sad to see you go. But I have to know, what does that fragile little English tart have that I don't?"

"A soul?"

Aurora stood up and punched him square in the jaw, drawing a bit of blood.

"She hits harder that you, Edward." Morgan spat some blood out of his mouth. "Now, I'm not the greatest fan of people, but I draw the line at selling them."

"People are nothing more than commodities. Whether we place them in various industries around the world or reduce the surplus population with the weapons we deliver to our customers, it results in fewer people in the world. Something I'm sure you appreciate as well."

"Sorry you feel that way. You two are real pieces of work. Misanthropy incarnate. You two truly deserve each other."

Aurora moved next to her father, "You have no idea, Bob."

Aurora kissed her father on the cheek.

"Good bye, Bob."

With a quick, flippant salute, Aurora walked up the gangway and stepped onto the deck of her namesake. As she opened a door to head inside the ship's superstructure, Edward called out.

"Aurora dear, please ensure we don't have any visitors below."

"Of course, father," Aurora replied with a look that gave Morgan a cold shiver. She blew a kiss to her father and entered the ship.

"Now then, I have a plane to catch. Good bye, Commander. Please give my regards to Davey Jones."

Rasmussen and three of the armed men walked away. The remaining two climbed the gangway just before crew members pulled it up off the quay. The deck hands began to take in all lines as the ship began to get underway. Morgan heard the ship's screw turning in the water and hoped against hope that Doug and Dallas finished their mission before the screws started moving.

As the ship moved away from the quay, Morgan was now alone with Ivar. The giant grabbed Morgan by the scruff of his neck and dragged him into the rows of containers. He threw Morgan against a container and delivered two quick blows to his ribs.

"I'm going to enjoy this, Morgan, and I'm going to take this slow," Ivar said in English as he delivered another blow, this time to side of Morgan's head.

"Love you too, Ivar," Morgan said drunkenly.

CHAPTER
TWENTY-FOUR

Cat laid atop her perch observing Lady Aurora and her men opening the newly arrived container. Inside, she saw at least twenty people huddled by the opening trying to take in as much fresh air as they could while the doors were open. Her men pushed the people back into the container using the butts of their sub-machine guns if someone did not move fast enough. She saw Aurora attempt to sooth the fears of her human cargo, appearing to be what the Americans call 'the good cop' to her men's 'bad cop.'

"Manky scrubber," she whispered to herself.

She turned her attention to Morgan's hiding place just in time to see four men scramble up the side and head for him. One of them was huge, so it had to be Ivar.

"James!" she shouted into her whisper mike, but it was too late. She saw Ivar grab Morgan and knock him cold. She figured that she had seconds at most before someone came for her, so she immediately left her hiding spot and climbed off the container stack. When she hit the ground, she pulled her dagger from its forearm sheath and moved quickly towards Morgan's container. Cat kept her Walther holstered, figuring that she didn't want a gunfight to attract the attention of either Rasmussen's men or the port's security force.

As she came around a corner, she smelled something quite strong, aftershave. She ducked as an assault baton passed over her head. Any slower, and it would have caught her in the temple. She sprung back up and assumed a fighting stance. The goon swung his baton again and Cat dodged it easily. She delivered a round-house kick that caught him in the ribs, the sound of them cracking resounded in the area between containers. As he bent over to protect his mid-section, Cat grabbed him by the hair, pulled his head back, and drove the dagger's seven-inch blade in the back of his neck, severing his spinal cord. She already began to move to get away as she pulled the knife from her victim.

She encountered a second member of Rasmussen's security detail, and she dispatched him quickly and quietly from behind with a thrust of her knife into right side of the man's throat. He collapsed to the ground with a surprised expression forever frozen on his face as she pushed her blade forward through his trachea. She crouched in the shadows and watched as the illicit cargo of weapons and people was loaded on board the ship. She saw the still unconscious form of Morgan laying on the quay wall, his hands zip tied behind his back. She also saw Morgan's weapons and other equipment lying a few yards from him.

She looked on with a sense of relief when Morgan regained consciousness, but that was short lived when both Edward and Aurora began to assault him. Finally, Ivar grabbed Morgan and dragged him behind a stack of containers. She moved out from her hiding place and headed towards Morgan's equipment, staying in the shadows as much as possible so she wouldn't be seen by the ship's deck hands. With one last look around, she sprinted to the pile of equipment and grabbed it on the fly while heading in the direction Ivar dragged Morgan.

CHAPTER
TWENTY-FIVE

20 Meters Down
Pasir Panjang 2 Container Terminal
Singapore

Doug and Dallas both heard the two clicks from Morgan's throat mike and immediately went into action. They donned their 'Twin 80s' air tanks along with the rest of their gear and moved towards a ladder leading down the quay wall and into the water. Once in the water, they took one last look around, took a bearing to their target, and dove under the surface. They swam as close to the harbor's bottom as they dared, the trash presenting a danger if they came to close.

Thirty minutes later, the pair arrived at the target ship and split up. Dallas swam towards the bow while Doug moved to the stern. Dallas reached the bow and attached his tracker as far down the hull as possible. It wouldn't be good if the tracker was visible when the ship was at its lightest when sailing in ballast. Once the tracker was in place, Dallas moved towards the rendezvous point. He swam a somewhat circuitous route away from the target before making his turn so that he would not be spotted from the surface too close to the target.

Back aft, Doug arrived at his intended attachment point with no difficulty. As he turned to leave, however, he felt something tugging at him. He twisted his body and his eyes shot open in horror. The one of the ship's two screws was turning, and its suction began to drag Doug towards it. He began to try to swim away, but his strokes made no progress against the propeller's increasing pull. Doug's body slapped the hull, and he tried to find a handhold as he slid closer and closer to the churning water. However, in the end, despite his panicked movements, he could not overcome the screw's pull and he said a quick, final prayer just before the first blade struck his body.

Back on the quay, Morgan continued to be beaten by Ivar. The Danish giant picked him up off his feet to deliver another blow when he shouted, dropped Morgan, and backed away in obvious pain.

Cat!

Ivar, grabbing his injured knee, turned away from Morgan to face the new threat. After kicking Ivar's knee, Cat backed away from him, pulled something from her belt, and tossed it past Ivar and right to Morgan.

"James! Guardian!" Cat shouted.

She drew her commando dagger and moved toward Ivar. She slashed at him, but he was surprisingly quick for such a large man. He moved away from the blade while reaching for Cat with his right hand. He slapped the dagger out of her grasp and grabbed her by the throat. He lifted her up off her feet and, while giving her a broad smile began choking the life out of her.

As Ivar and Cat squared off, Morgan leaped up, moved his hands from behind his back to his front, and grabbed the Guardian knife Cat tossed to him. He pulled the knife from its sheath with his teeth and cut the wire ties holding his wrists together. Once free, he moved to help Cat with Ivar, but he knew that his Guardian knife would only piss Ivar off even more, so he needed to do something bold to save Cat's life. It was time to go feral.

Morgan ran towards Ivar and with a cry that sounded like a dog's growl, he jumped on Ivar's back. He wrapped his arms around Ivar's neck and while hanging on for dear life, plunged his oversized canine teeth into Ivar's right cheek. Ivar dropped Cat immediately, screamed in pain, and began to try to shake Morgan off his neck. The harder Ivar shook, the tighter Morgan's grip around his neck and on his cheek became. Morgan also began to shake his head back and forth like a dog with a prey animal in its teeth.

After Ivar dropped her to deal with Morgan, Cat hit the ground with a resounding thud. She shook off the impact, caught her breath, and found her dropped commando dagger. She grabbed it and drove the blade up and through Ivar's right knee slicing though skin, ligaments, and cartilage. She pulled the now bloody blade out and plunged it the same way through Ivar's left knee.

Ivar howled in pain and began to fall to the ground. As Ivar fell, Morgan's teeth ripped a piece of Ivar's cheek right off his face, exposing his teeth and lower jawbone. Morgan looked at the prostrate Ivar and bared his teeth in a full on, malevolent smile, the piece of bloody skin still hanging from his teeth.

"Hmm, looks like you need some dental work." Morgan said as he looked into Ivar's open wound.

Morgan drew his Guardian II, pulled Ivar's head back, and plunged his blade through Ivar's left eye and into his brain. He pulled the knife out of the now dead skull and wiped the blade off on Ivar's shirt.

"Cheeky bastard," Cat said.

Morgan spat out the bloody piece of skin, which landed next to Ivar's corpse.

"Not anymore."

Cat then grabbed Morgan and hugged him like there was no tomorrow.

"Thank you, James," Cat while snuggled up against Morgan's chest.

"Come on, we have to meet up with Doug and Dallas."

The pair gather their weapons and headed back to the NSX.

Morgan and Cat arrived at the rendezvous and saw Chief Shaw sitting by himself by the rental mini-van looking out over the harbor. They exited the NSX and walk over to him.

"Dallas!" Morgan called out.

The Chief looked up at the approaching pair and waved them over.

"Chief, where's Doug?" Morgan asked.

"He's not with you? He wasn't at the rendezvous point when I arrived here after planting the tracker. I hoped he'd be with you."

"No, Cat and I had a fun time entertaining Rasmussen's number one goon. We didn't see Doug. We need to find him."

The trio drove back to the quay where the Aurora Express had been berthed. Chief Shaw entered the water and began to search. Ten minutes later, he surfaced holding a bloody, dented Twin 80 air tank.

"Found this on the bottom, sir. Nothing else," Dallas reported.

"That fucking bitch! She had the captain turn the ship's propellers suspecting a diver may be in the water. Damn it!" Morgan took several deep breaths, calmed himself, and turned to Dallas.

"Well, we can make damned sure Doug did not die in vain. Chief, you have the trackers' laptop with you?"

"Yes, sir."

"Okay, let's bring it up and see if both trackers are working. If we have both signals, we'll know that Doug succeeded before he died."

Dallas pulled out a ruggedized laptop computer, attached an external antenna, and turned it on. The screen showed a map of the waters surrounding Singapore and two, closely spaced dots.

"We're receiving data from both trackers," Dallas said. "It looks like ship is in the Malacca Strait, on course 300 degrees, speed 15 knots. They're passing Batu Pahat on their starboard side."

"Bless you, Lieutenant. Okay Dallas, get back to Guam and report what happened to LT Kroll. Cat, alert Bertie and his cleaners, and ask him to drop an anonymous tip to the Singapore police about an incident in the harbor. Hopefully, they can recover Doug's remains. We can spin a story about a diving accident."

"Aye, aye, sir," Chief Shaw replied before departing in the mini-van. Morgan then sat on the quay wall and stared out over the water. Cat sat next to him and put her arm around her shoulder.

"Hey, it's not your fault," she said.

"I know, Cat," Morgan grasped her hand. "It's just I never lost anyone under my command before."

"We don't have time to mourn him right now, James. We have to get moving, or his death will truly be in vain."

Morgan looked at Cat and gave her hand a quick squeeze and stood up. They climbed into the NSX and took off out of the port.

CHAPTER
TWENTY-SIX

Lady Aurora stood on *Aurora Express'* port bridge-wing looking at the containers stacked on the cargo deck below. She didn't like being there, but the presence of Morgan and that little British bitch in Singapore made it imperative that this shipment make it to West Africa unmolested. If CIA and MI-6 were on to them, who knows who else may interfere. Both the weaponry and the human cargoes were worth millions to her, her father, and their benefactors. As far as Morgan and that English Sheep Dog were concerned, Aurora was sure that Ivar dumped them both into the Malacca Strait.

In her younger years, Aurora attended university in London, Paris, and Zurich, and cultivated a very public stable of lovers. Once she earned her degrees in finance and economics, she pursued the disgusting, and recently widowed, Sir Ian Essen-high, not for his love, but for his substantial wealth. Father engineered the introduction between the British knight and his daughter, 40 years his junior. She used her feminine wiles to convince him to propose, and after they were married, convinced him to dis-inherit his worthless son and daughter. Once the ink was dry on the new will that named Aurora sole beneficiary, she ensured her dear husband enjoyed his favorite daily cocktail, a Scotch and Soda. This one digitalis laced. Once the probate ended, Sir Ian's children were destitute, and the Lady Aurora now controlled a vast fortune valued in the hundreds of millions of Pounds Sterling.

Aurora used her newly acquired wealth to help her father's ailing shipping company. Utilizing her skills in finance, both light and dark, she brought RDS Shipping from the brink of bankruptcy to solid financial solvency. She also became her father's partner in the running of the company. With her father handling the day-to-day operations, Aurora concentrated on cultivating new clients, both legitimate and not-so. She charmed her way into the shadow worlds of high-end weapons and human trafficking, using her work on animal-friendly charities as cover. Now, RDS Shipping moved, by her conservative esti-mates, twenty percent of the world's illicit weapons and thirty percent of the world's human cargo. This, plus legitimate cargoes, brought the company, and her family, hundreds of millions annually. Additionally, she used her financial skills to launder the illicit cash, making it all squeaky clean.

Now, she oversaw this shipment, ensuring that the cash kept flowing. She also ensured that the very dangerous organization who provided the contacts that furnished the high-end weaponry, most of which were not normally exported from their countries of origin, was kept happy. She did not know what their plans were, but they were powerful people, and she did not want to cross them by failing to deliver their cargoes.

"Lady Aurora," the *Aurora Express'* master said coming up behind her.

"Yes, Captain?"

"Some of our…guests are causing a ruckus down on the cargo deck. I was hoping you could…reassure them?"

"Certainly Captain, a little visit from Auntie Aurora fixes everything."

"Thank you, milady."

Aurora made her way to the cargo deck, ignoring the stares of the crew members she passed on the way. She only allowed the Captain to speak to her directly, everyone else did not dare speak to her unless spoken to. Still, some of them were hand-some enough. She may dirty her cabin's sheets with one of them at some point. It was a long trip to West Africa.

CHAPTER
TWENTY-SEVEN

United States Naval Station,
Rota, Spain

The two weeks following the *Aurora Express'* departure from Singapore, were a whirlwind of activity for both Morgan and Cat. First, Bertie and his cleaners took care of the bodies Cat and Morgan left behind. Ivar's remains were particularly challenging and required two body bags to hold them. Bertie also arranged off the books medical attention for the two of them with Cat's throat injuries being minor compared to Morgan's cracked ribs. The anonymous tip to the Singapore police also led to the recovery of LT Kroll's remains. The local Singapore medical examiner listed his cause of death as accidental, the U.S. Embassy collected the body, and it was returned to his family in Yorktown, Virginia.

Once they were well enough to travel, Cat and Morgan flew under new MI-6 provided snap cover identities first to London to debrief Cat's bosses at MI-6, and, with Cat staying behind to arrange things on her end, on to the Unites States. While en route to Virginia, Morgan arranged an off-site debriefing with only General Bailey in attendance. He also placed a phone call to a couple of old friends. Once in the US, Morgan stopped briefly at his condo to pick up a few items and met with the DDI at a mutually agreeable location, the United States Marine Corps Museum, Quantico, Virginia. The General met Morgan on a bench on the Semper Fidelis Memorial Park's grounds.

"You okay, Bob?" General Bailey asked as he sat down.

"Not bad considering, sir."

"You certainly left a bit of a mess behind in Copenhagen, the Chief of Station is none too happy, especially about the car. He and his cleaners had a hell of a time scrapping the bodies off the motorway and airport tarmac."

"Sorry about that, but bullet holes do tend to appear in things when you're getting shot at. As far as the bodies go, better them than me, right?"

"True." The General reached into his jacket and pulled out a black, rectangular object. He handed it to Morgan.

"Here, a new phone with the video app for your prosthetic. It's clean. So, not that I mind getting out of the office to immerse myself of the history of my beloved Marine Corps, but why meet here?"

"We have a leak, and I know who it is."

"Who?"

"Not yet, sir. I want to finish this first. The best play is to let everyone believe I'm either dead or still in Singapore. We're tracking a ship with five Chinese-made MLRSs bound for Mali and at least one container of trafficked people. With your concurrence, I'd like to engage some Navy assets to track the MLRSs to their destination in Mali once they leave the ship so the French can seal the pipeline from that end, take the ship down secure the human cargo, and secure the human cargo. While I was on my active duty period, I heard about a NATO brigade-level amphibious exercise about to get underway in the western Mediterranean. The exercise is being run by the commander of Expeditionary Strike Group Two, our mutual friend, Rear Admiral Allard. I made some calls, and he and his staff are willing to help. We may also have additional help from the British Special Boat Service since RDS Shipping is also gun running into Northern Ireland. All I need is your go ahead."

"You have it, Bob. I'll contact my opposite number in the DGSE and get the French on board. Take those sons of bitches down, Gargoyle, and I'll provide any top cover you may need in the Agency or the Department of Defense. I'll also put Chop on arranging supplies along your route. And, if I can, I'll hook you up with an old acquaintance of mine who lives in that neck of the woods."

"Thank you, sir," Morgan said as he stood up. General Bailey also stood and offered his hand.

"Good luck, Commander. Please pass my regards to Marty Allard when you see him and be careful out there."

The next morning, after a red eye military flight from Naval Air Station, Norfolk, Morgan stood on the flight line at Naval Station, Rota, Spain watching a U.S. Marine Corps MV-22 Osprey come in for a landing. The tilt-rotor aircraft taxied towards a nearby hangar, and Morgan watched its cargo ramp lower to the tarmac. Two figures, one in a flight suit, one in a U.S. Navy working uniform (popularly known as 'Guacoflage') walked off the aircraft and headed over to Morgan. The sailor executed a very sharp salute and spoke first.

"Commander Morgan? I'm Lieutenant Arthur Read, Admiral Allard's flag lieutenant." He pointed to the aviator. "And this is Captain Elias Luna, the Osprey's aircraft commander. I bring compliments from the Admiral, and we're ready to head out when you are."

"Thank you, Lieutenant. Let's go."

The trio headed into the Osprey with Captain Luna continuing on into the cockpit. After donning a U.S. Navy Mark 1 life jacket, commonly called a 'float coat', Morgan and LT Read strapped themselves into a pair of jump seats, and donned cranial head protectors with built-in communications headsets. The Osprey taxied a short distance and took-off in full vertical mode. The aircraft quickly transitioned into horizontal flight and went to full speed towards the Atlantic.

"Show off!" Morgan yelled into the headset.

As the flight continued, Morgan turned towards the Lieutenant.

"So, what call sign did the Admiral give you? He called me 'Gargoyle' because of my taste in eyewear."

"Simple, sir. Book."

Morgan's laughter was drowned out by the sound of the Osprey's engines.

CHAPTER
TWENTY-EIGHT

U.S.S. *Kearsarge* **(LHD 3)**
Position: 35°53'50" North by 009°26'48" West
Course: 250° True
Speed: 10 Knots
Time: 0800 Local

After two hours on the Osprey, Morgan looked out the aircraft's window and was greeted by an awesome sight. Arrayed below him were the ships of the NATO amphibious task force. In front of the formation was the Royal Navy's large amphibious ship, the H.M.S. *Albion* with the Duke-class frigate H.M.S. *Iron Duke* off *Albion*'s stern. Two American amphibious ships, the San Antonio-class U.S.S. *Arlington* and the Whidbey Island-class U.S.S. *Fort McHenry* rode on the formation's flanks. The French Mistral-class amphibious assault helicopter carrier, F.S. *Tonnerre* sat in the rear of the formation. The ship at the formation's center was his destination, the Wasp-class amphibious assault ship U.S.S. *Kearsarge*, Admiral Allard's flag ship. The guided missile cruiser U.S.S. *Gettysburg* sat in plane guard station 1,000 yards astern of the *Kearsarge*.

The Osprey circled the 50,000-ton assault ship and

approached her from her port side. The tilt-rotor aircraft transitioned to vertical flight and landed on one of *Kearsarge*'s amidships landing spots. Morgan saw the Landing Signalman signal to the two Chock-and-Chainmen, who secured the aircraft to the ship's flight deck. Captain Luna opened the rear cargo ramp and the Osprey's aircrewman led Morgan and Read out of the aircraft. The pair were picked up by one of the flight deck crew and shepherded into the ship's superstructure. Once inside, they removed their life jackets and cranials. Morgan looked up and saw a dark haired, somewhat petite, Hispanic woman in the 'Guacoflage' uniform with a Surface Warfare emblem over her left pocket, a Command at Sea pin on her left pocket flap, and a silver eagle rank emblem on the center tab.

"Permission to come aboard, ma'am," Morgan said.

"Granted, Commander Morgan. I'm Captain Jasmin Torres, Admiral Allard's Chief of Staff. Welcome aboard. The Admiral will see you as soon as you're settled. I have to say, your phone call certainly set off a flurry of activity thorough out the Strike Group. In the past 24 hours, a British Special Forces team embarked *Albion*, and *Tonnerre* received a mysterious visitor. A SEAL platoon along with your SWCC team with their supporting boats and aircraft arrived on board *Arlington* earlier this morning. Care to let me in on what's going on?"

"Not yet, ma'am, and certainly not out in an open passageway. I'll explain everything in the Admiral's cabin as soon as I'm more presentable."

"Very well, Commander. See you then," Captain Torres turned and walked down the passageway.

After making his way down to the ship's O-2 level, Morgan opened the door to his assigned stateroom up in forward officer's country and tossed his bag on the bunk. He pulled out the dress khaki uniform he brought over from his condo and changed out of his civilian clothes. After ensuring that his ribbons and warfare pins were straight and his hair just so, he left his stateroom and headed aft to the ship's flag cabin. He stopped at the cabin's door, knocked three times, and heard a deep voiced "Enter." Morgan then opened the door.

Walking in, he saw Captain Torres standing of to one side of a large desk with a tall gentleman in a U.S. Navy flight suit standing behind it, Rear Admiral Martin 'Mallard' Allard, United States Navy. Admiral Allard stood about six feet, four inches tall with thinning brown hair. His flight suit (which he referred to as his 'zoom bag') had his two-star rank emblem embroidered on the shoulders, an Expeditionary Strike Group Two patch on the right front side, an Amphibious Squadron Eight patch on the right shoulder, an American flag on the left shoulder, and a leather patch on the left front embossed with his gold Naval Aviator wings and his name and call sign. Seeing Morgan enter the room, he walked out from behind the desk, smiled a huge smile, and offered his hand.

"Gargoyle! How the hell are you, son?" the Admiral asked in his somewhat thick Southern accent.

"Not too bad, sir. General Bailey sends his regards," Morgan shook the Admiral's offered hand. It was at this point Morgan remembered that the Admiral had a way about him that made people want to follow him wherever he led them, even if it's to Hell and back.

"You're working for Ron Bailey over at Langley? Sierra Hotel! He's good people. If the CIA was going to steal you away from my staff, at least I know you are working for the best. So, what's exactly going on? There are a lot of snake eaters and black-bag types running around my ships."

The Admiral directed Morgan and Captain Torres to join him around his cabin's dinning/conference table. Once seated, Morgan briefed both officers on the situation starting with the attacks in and over Mali, the DGSE's request for assistance, to the recent actions in Copenhagen and Singapore.

"So that's where we stand Admiral, Captain," Morgan said as he nodded to each officer. "The *Aurora Express*' AIS position has her rounding the Cape of Good Hope on course for the coast of

The Gambia which matches the position provided by our trackers. If they follow their usual pattern, they'll shut off their AIS transceiver to 'disappear' two days before arriving on station. Our trackers will cover that gap and cue us to their location so we can get surveillance assets in the area."

"Sounds like you've been busy. What else do you need from us?"

"I have a plan for following the weapons up the Gambia River and into Senegal, but I'd like to run it by you for a sanity check."

"Sure," the Admiral replied with a smile. "COS." He pronounced it 'COZ'. "Please clear my schedule for the next couple of hours. If it doesn't involve an actual emergency or war, please take care of it."

"Aye, aye sir," Captain Torres headed for the cabin's door.

"So, Gargoyle, what do you have in mind?"

CHAPTER
TWENTY-NINE

U.S.S. *Kearsarge*
Time: 1000 Local the Following Day

Morgan and Admiral Allard spent the remainder of the preceding day either huddled in his cabin or working closely with Captain Torres and Commander Kieran Martin, the Strike Group's Operations Officer, known as the N3, in *Kearsarge*'s Flag Plot working out the details. Now, the next morning, Morgan stood on the O-6 level weather deck just aft of the bridge, watching the various players in what the N3 now called Operation: Eclipse.

First to arrive was a French Navy AS532 Cougar helicopter flown over from the *Tonnerre*. Once secured to the deck, Morgan saw a tall, formidable looking gentleman with dark hair and an olive complexion debark the aircraft.

Must be the guy from the DGSE.

Next a U.S. Navy MH-60 Seahawk with 'U.S.S. KEARSARGE' emblazoned on its tail boom landed on the flight deck, one of the ship's search and rescue helicopters. He saw the side door slide open and four men climbed out, three were Morgan's Dirty Boat crew while the fourth was a U.S. Navy lieutenant he did not recognize.

Finally, came a Royal Navy Merlin Mk 3 helicopter from the *Albion*. When the large aircraft touched down, Morgan heard four bells ring from the ship's announcing system.

"*Albion*, arriving," the Boatswain Mate of the Watch added after the bells sounded.

Albion's C.O.? What's he doing here?

He saw a Royal Navy captain leave the Merlin along with a second officer and a blond-haired woman.

Cat!

Morgan walked quickly to the nearest ladder and headed down to the O-3 level. He entered Flight Deck Triage, a space designed to handle combat casualties that arrive via aircraft, which doubled as the ship's V.I.P. reception area, and came to a halt. He first saw Cat looking amazing in combat boots, black tactical pants, white t-shirt, and navy-blue wooly pully-style sweater. He then saw the Royal Navy captain standing next to her, and a surprised look of recognition crossed his face.

"Mags!" Morgan offered his hand. "What the hell are you doing here?"

Captain Magnus Carr, RN, commanding officer of the *Albion* grabbed the outstretched hand and pulled Morgan into a bear hug.

"DCA! How the hell are you? And what happed to your eye? You had two good ones on *Churchill*."

"Occupational hazard," Morgan replied sardonically. "Captain?"

"Yes, I have the privilege of commanding *Albion*. When Calico here said you'd be onboard, I had to come aboard for your briefing."

"Outstanding! And congratulations on command, sir. You certainly deserve it." Morgan then turned to a smiling Cat. "Captain Carr and I served together on *Winston S. Churchill*. He was the Navigator when I was the Damage Control Assistant. He was the RN officer I mentioned during our flight to Singapore. Anything he's told you about our time serving together is a lie, unless it's not," Morgan added with a smirk.

Morgan noticed another Royal Navy officer standing behind Cat and Captain Carr. The officer stood a head taller than the Captain, but had a thinner, runner's type of physique. He wore the Royal Navy number 4-dress uniform along with a green beret of the Royal Marine commandos that had a unique cap badge. The badge had two, blue waves bisected by a sword with a scroll underneath that read 'By Strength and Guile' against a black background, the emblem of the British Special Boat Service. He extended his hand again.

"Gargoyle."

"Leftenant Commander Montgomery Hunter," the gentleman shook Morgan's hand.

"Monty here is the officer commanding X-Ray Squadron SBS, our Maritime Counter Terrorism force," Captain Carr added.

"Excellent! Welcome Commander." Morgan saw LT Read enter the space and waved him over.

"Book, do we have staterooms ready for everyone?"

"Yes, sir. Most of our guests have already headed that way. Captain Carr and his party are our last arrivals. Ms. Calico's room is in troop officer berthing, right next yours, per her request."

"Excellent. Calico, may I escort you to your room, ma'am?" Morgan offered her his left arm.

"Certainly, Gargoyle." Cat took his arm with a smile. The pair exited Flight Deck Triage to the looks of amazement, and outright admiration, of both Royal Navy officers and LT Book.

Morgan led Cat to her stateroom via *Kearsarge*'s command and control spaces, all of which were located on the ship's O-2 level, one deck beneath the flight deck. Using the knowledge from his deployment on *Kearsarge*'s sister ship, the U.S.S. *Bataan*, Morgan took her first to the Landing Force Operations Center, or LFOC, where the U.S. Marine command elements operated, then on to Flag Plot, where Admiral Allard's staff worked, to the Joint Intelligence Center, or JIC, where he had worked on *Bataan*, ending finally in the ship's Combat Information Center, or CIC, where *Kearsarge*'s crew fought their ship. Reaching the stateroom, Morgan opened the door for Cat as he put her bags inside. Cat closed the door behind her, jumped into Morgan's arms, and kissed him passionately. Morgan kissed her back but winced in obvious pain.

"Whoa, not so tight! The ribs are still a bit tender," Morgan eased himself from her embrace.

"Sorry James, but I've missed you terribly."

"Missed you too, Cat. I am a bit surprised, pleasantly surprised, but surprised nonetheless that you're here. How'd you pull it off?"

"Oh, a bit of blackmail, a bit of pouting, a few favors called in, and a threat to leave the service if I didn't go. There was no way I was going to miss bringing that bitch Aurora down, not after what happened to you, and what I saw, in Singapore."

"Don't worry, we'll have our chance. Now I'm hungry, lunch is being served in the wardroom. Join me?"

"Absolutely."

They entered *Kearsarge*'s wardroom where a good many of her 70 or so officers were seated for lunch. They grabbed their trays and walked through the serving line. It was a Wednesday, so they were in luck. Slider day! Morgan had a double cheeseburger with bacon while Cat had a single cheeseburger made with an Impossible beef-substitute patty. They found a seat in the corner of the wardroom where they could talk and eat in near privacy. Before he could sit, however, he had one final task to perform. He walked over to the forward portion of the wardroom towards a single, long table. There, the ship's Executive Officer, or XO, sat along with her department heads. He stood by the XO's chair and cleared his throat to catch her attention.

"Permission to join the mess, ma'am?" Morgan asked.

The XO looked up and smiled.

"Permission granted, Commander, and may I add a belated welcome aboard."

"Thank you, ma'am on both counts. It's a pleasure to be on board the Special 'K'."

Morgan returned to his table and much to Cat's amusement and delight, began to dig into his burger.

CHAPTER
THIRTY

After indulging in the Navy's Slider Day tradition, Morgan took Cat around the rest of the ship, starting on the bridge where he showed her what he used to do for a living when he first became an officer. They visited Debark Control, where the ship's XO controlled surface launched landing craft, specifically the Air Cushioned Landing Craft or LCAC, during amphibious operations, followed by the Primary Flight control space commonly known as 'Pri-Fly'. They wandered down to the hangar bay where they marveled at the new F-35 Lightning II Short Take-Off/Vertical Landing fighters as well as the somewhat clever call signs for the Marines who fly them stenciled on the aircraft.

Captain Megan 'Stormy' Weathers? Major Jim 'Doctor' Scholl? Really? And I thought my jokes were bad.

At 13:30, a boatswain's pipe sounded 'attention' and the Boatswain's Mate of the Watch passed the word:

"An operations brief will be held in the Flag Briefing Room at 14:00."

Morgan looked at Cat, "That's our cue. Let's go."

The pair headed back up to the O-2 level and entered the Flag Briefing Room where all the briefing participants, except for Admiral Allard, waited. Looking around, he saw the three members of his SWCC team with a new SEAL lieutenant. He also noticed the French contingent, the DGSE's Action Division representative he noticed earlier on the flight deck. Standing along the briefing room bulkhead, Morgan saw an African-American U.S. Marine Corps Major wearing both a Marine woodland camouflage uniform and a *Kearsarge* ball cap.

Ship's Air Operations Officer.

A few moments later, LT Read entered the briefing room.

"Attention on deck!" the flag aide shouted as Admiral Allard and Captain Torres entered the room.

Sitting down and pulling out a pair of reading glasses, Admiral Allard turned to Morgan.

"Okay, Gargoyle. Hit it!"

"Thank you, sir. Good afternoon Admiral, Captain Torres, ladies, and gentlemen. I'm Gargoyle, and I represent a certain U.S. government agency." This drew a few laughs and smiles from the room. "I know a few of you, but there are several new people here that I haven't had the pleasure of meeting. Could we please go around the room and introduce yourselves and whom you represent? Let's start on my right," Morgan said as he turned to Cat.

"I'm Calico, and I work for His Majesty's Government," she said with a knowing smile. The introductions continued.

"Captain Magnus Carr, Royal Navy, commanding officer, H.M.S. *Albion*."

"Leftenant Commander Montgomery Hunter, Royal Navy, X-Squadron, SBS."

"Major Paul Manzer, U.S. Marine Corps, *Kearsarge* Air Operations Officer."

"Monsieur Edouard Hachette, French government."

"Lieutenant Paul Coslick, U.S. Navy, First Platoon comman-der, SEAL Team 4."

"Chief Special Boat Operator Michael Shaw, call sign 'Dallas', Special Boat Team 20 supporting LT Coslick,"

"Special Boat Operator First Class Martin Haugen, call sign 'The Judge,' Special Boat Team 20."

"Special Boat Operator Second Class Jose Hernandez, call sign 'Fantasma,' Special Boat Team 20."

With introductions complete, Morgan looked over at the SEAL lieutenant, "LT Coslick, you're LT Kroll's replacement."

"Yes, sir," he answered.

"How do you want to be called, Lieutenant?"

"Galahad, sir."

"King Arthur fan?"

"No sir, Kingsman."

"Outstanding," Morgan replied with a smirk.

With introductions out of the way, Morgan began the briefing in earnest.

"Ladies and gentlemen, welcome to Operation: Eclipse. Our objectives are three-fold. First, secure the M/V *Aurora Express* and her human trafficking cargo. Second, track a shipment of Chinese-made MLRSs up the Gambia River to their destination in Mali and pass that information on to French forces. Three, capture Lady Aurora Essenhigh for delivery to U.K. law enforce-ment." Morgan pointed to an image taken from his prosthetic's video recording on the briefing room's screen "Don't let her beauty fool you, she's as deadly as they come, and she is directly responsible for the death of a U.S. Navy SEAL officer." Morgan looked over at Dallas who had the look of grim determination on his face. Morgan brought up a second picture on the screen.

"This is Zheng Yuhan, former Chinese Ministry of State Secu-rity and now working for Thundergate Industries, a wholly owned subsidiary of the Chinese Communist Party and manu-facturer of the PCL191 MLRS. We don't know if he's on board

Aurora Express, but if he is, we'd really like to talk to him." Morgan paused a moment to let the room express a laugh. He continued.

"Our forces will be deployed on the *Albion* and *Arlington* with Captain Torres acting as officer in tactical command once detached from the rest of the task force. The *Iron Duke* will serve as escort for our ad-hoc squadron. *Albion* with Calico and Commander Hunter's SBS team will be tasked with taking down the *Aurora Express* via airborne insertion after the MLRSs are offloaded. They will secure the ship, the human cargo, and our targets of interest. When ready, a prize crew provided by Captain Carr will take command of the *Aurora Express* and continue her journey, minus her contraband. They'll re-activate the ship's AIS transponder so that anyone watching will believe all is well."

"*Arlington* will host myself, M. Hachette, Chief Shaw's two SOC-R riverine operations boats, courtesy of Special Boat Team 22, and LT Coslick's SEALs. *Arlington* already has the task force's two Fire Scout Unmanned Aerial Vehicles embarked, and we'll use them to keep an eye on our target and as cueing assets for our attack. Once the lighterage with the MLRSs sails over the horizon from the *Aurora Express*, the two Army MH-47s from the 160th Special Operations Aviation Regiment will transport the boats from *Arlington* to a position about 30 miles or so behind the lighterage. We will follow them up the Gambia River. Galahad, do you and Dallas have the civilian clothing and camouflage for you and the boats?"

"Yes, sir. We're ready. We've already begun painting the boats in their new color schemes."

"Good, no sense in getting the Gambians or Senegalese involved in all this if we can help it."

A hand went up and Morgan looked over and saw that Major Manzer had a question.

"Yes, Major?"

"Why use the boats and SEALs at all? Just follow the barge with a drone and attack it when it reaches its destination?"

"Fair question. Let's just say there are other factors at play that precludes us from 'nuking the entire site from orbit,' including the possibility of more human trafficking victims. We need human eyes on target to ensure all mission objectives are met."

The USMC Major nodded his head in understanding as Morgan continued.

"Once we observe the offload of the MLRSs, their location will be passed by M. Hachette to French forces in Mali for further action. If all goes well, these actions will seal this pipeline permanently. Admiral, pending your questions sir, this concludes my briefing."

Admiral Allard removed his reading glasses and stood up. "Thank you, Gargoyle. I'm glad to see your time away from my staff hasn't dulled your briefing skills. Folks, we came out here for an exercise, and this real-world operation fell in our laps. This is a great opportunity to show the capability a NATO amphibious task force brings to the table, aid an ally in their fight against Islamic terrorism, and rescue people whose only crime is wanting a better life for themselves. All that's left to do is wait until our prey shows up. Now, we all have work to do. Let's get busy. Good luck. Dismissed."

With that, the seated participants rose and Admiral Allard and CAPT Torres left the briefing room. The pair walked to the Flag Cabin where Admiral Allard sat at his desk while his Chief of Staff took a seat.

"So, COS, what do you think?"

"It's crazy enough to work, Admiral. You seem pretty keen on this Gargoyle gentleman."

"He was my N2 when I was PHIBON 8. During our deployment on *Bataan*, we conducted a non-combatant evacuation from Sierra Leone, and his work identifying safe and defendable landing zones for our V-22s saved a lot of lives. One of those saved was the CIA Deputy Chief of Station. She was impressed with his work during the operation and recruited him right out from under me," Allard said with a smile. "He's a prior enlisted SWCC guy, so he went into the Agency's Special Activities Center's Maritime Branch. That's how he lost the eye. Gargoyle's one tough hombre, he'll get the job done."

CHAPTER
THIRTY-ONE

U.S.S. *Arlington*
Position: 13°53'48" North by 019°20'44" West
140 miles West Southwest of Dakar, Senegal
Course: 180° True
Speed: 10 Knots
Time: 2200 Local

Morgan stood on the starboard bridge wing of the U.S.S. *Arlington* enjoying a quiet evening at sea. Named for the Pentagon's Virginia location, and site of the crash of American Airlines Flight 77 on September 11th 2001, the *Arlington* was a 25,000-ton San Antonio-class landing platform dock commissioned in February, 2013. Built with steel salvaged from the Pentagon after the attacks of 9/11, she carried two air-cushioned landing craft in her well deck and she could operate up to four of the large U.S. Marine Corps CH-53 helicopters on her flight deck, though only the two slightly smaller U.S. Army MH-47s two sat there now. Looking out over both the calm Atlantic waters and the H.M.S. *Albion* sailing 4,000 yards off *Arlington*'s starboard beam, looking close enough to touch, Morgan reflected on the past few days.

. . .

Morgan, Cat, and the rest of the planning team spent a few days on board *Kearsarge* finalizing plans, except for Captain Carr who returned to his ship directly after Morgan's brief. Despite their desires to the contrary, the pair kept their hands to themselves in deference to their hosts. They did, however, work out together in *Kearsarge*'s vast gym located on the O-2 level forward of their staterooms in troop officer berthing, preparing their bodies for the fight to come.

Some of the embarked Marines saw the pair sparring on the gym's mats and were curious as to the fighting styles they used, so they ended up teaching an impromptu class on Krav Maga and the Keysi Fighting Method. At one point, Morgan stood off to the side and looked on with affection and pride as Cat easily took down Marines over twice her size while most of their fellow Marines stared at her with unbridled awe. However, one Marine was not impressed.

"What a bunch of candy-asses letting some little English thing like her take you down. She sounds like someone's auntie."

Morgan and Cat looked to see who spoke. The Marine stood six feet five inches tall, weighed over 250 pounds, and was built like a football linebacker. Morgan began to say something, but Cat stopped him.

"Hold on, James. I'll handle this."

Morgan looked at her, shrugged his shoulders, and moved back out of her way.

"Do you think you can do better…?" Cat began.

"Staff Sargent Lambert, sweetheart. And yes, I can." The sergeant took of his uniform top and tossed it on the deck.

Sweetheart? Cat's going to kick his ass.

The two began to circle each other around the exercise mat. Staff Sergeant grew bored and frustrated and made the first move, exactly as Cat hoped. He swung at her with his massive right arm that Cat easily blocked with her left forearm. Cat responded with three vicious palm strikes, two to the nose and one to the throat. She then grabbed his shoulder and neck, bent him at the waist, and delivered two kicks to the groin. As the sergeant fell forward, Cat grabbed his right arm by the hand and wrist, squeezed it between her legs at the knee, and began to sit up. The pressure exerted by the maneuver nearly caused the sergeant's shoulder to dislocate. The sergeant screamed in pain as Cat increased the pressure. She then stood up while keeping a grip on his hand and bent the arm behind the sergeant's back. She placed her left knee on the sergeant's neck and drew her commando dagger from her right boot. She the caressed the sergeant's right cheek with the razor-sharp blade as blood dripped on the deck from his now broken nose.

"Care for a kiss from your old, English auntie, dearie?" Cat said with sweet venom dripping from her voice.

Morgan came over to admire Cat's handiwork with a satisfied smirk.

"Staff Sergeant Lambert, I'm Lieutenant Commander Morgan and the lady with your life in her hands is a guest on board this ship. I highly recommend that you apologize for your rude comments, or I'll have you up on charges of conduct unbecoming a United States Marine. Decide quickly, she looks really angry."

"I'm sorry, ma'am. I meant no disrespect," Staff Sergeant Lambert stammered as best he could with a knee on his throat.

"I don't know," Morgan began. "He doesn't sound very sincere. What do you think, Calico?"

"I think he needs a scar to remind him of his ill-mannered behavior."

"Maybe next time."

Cat rose up off the sergeant and pushed him over to the side with her boot.

"Fucking wanker," she added with a snarl.

She sheathed her dagger as she looked around the gym space with an expression that said, 'who's next?'

"Anyone else care to try their luck?" Morgan asked. After no one came forward, Morgan continued.

"Didn't think so. Carry on, Marines."

"Aye, aye, sir!" they shouted in unison.

Finally, after a week on board the 'Big 3,' Morgan received a call in his stateroom. Morgan picked up the stateroom phone, "Commander Morgan."

"Sir, this is Ensign Tilly Williamson, the JIC Watch Officer. The AIS position of the *Aurora Express* has disappeared."

"Thank you, Ensign. On my way."

Morgan knocked on Cat's stateroom door before heading down the passageway. She peered out the now open door.

"Hey, Cat. *Aurora Express*'s AIS track disappeared. It's time."

"Right," she replied as only a British subject could.

Cat joined Morgan in the passageway. They arrived in the JIC a few moments later and after buzzing-in, entered the hub of *Kearsarge*'s intelligence activities. As they came in, they saw Chief Shaw sitting at a table with an open laptop computer, a young Ensign standing over his shoulder.

"Ensign Williamson, I presume?" Morgan asked.

'Yes sir, ma'am," the Ensign said acknowledging Cat's presence. "Chief Shaw and I are looking at the *Aurora Express*'s position transmitted by the trackers he planted."

"Very good. Dallas, what do you have?"

"She's still on course for that spot off the coast of Serrekunda you uncovered at Langley. She'll be there in another five days, present speed."

"She shut off her AIS transponder earlier than expected, but as long as she's heading to that rendezvous point, we'll be in good shape. Ensign, I'll need someone watching this display 24/7 for any deviation in our target's course and speed."

"Yes, sir. I'll make the arrangements with the Intelligence Officer."

"Thank you. Calico, it's time to debark."

A few hours later, two helicopters sat on *Kearsarge*'s spots 5 and 6, both aircrafts' rotors spinning. One was *Kearsarge*'s own SAR aircraft while the other was a Royal Navy Merlin. Morgan and Cat stood together in flight deck triage, their bags sitting on the deck at their feet. On the other side of the space stood Captain Torres, Leftenant Commander Hunter, M. Hachette, Chief Shaw, and Petty Officers Haugen and Hernandez who also awaiting boarding. A flight deck crewman wearing a white cranial and float coat came in from the flight line.

"Everyone heading to *Albion*, your aircraft is ready for boarding."

Leftenant Commander Hunter grabbed his bags and headed to the door. Cat turned to Morgan and kissed him deeply and passionately. She held Morgan's face in her hands and looked directly in his eye.

"I love you, James Robert Morgan. Please do be careful and come back to me," Cat said quietly.

"I love you too, Catherine...you know, I don't know your middle name," Morgan replied somewhat apologetically.

"Sarah."

"I love you too, Catherine Sarah Roberts. I'll be damned careful now that I have someone to come back to, and you be careful as well. Please pass my warm regards to Aurora."

They kissed one more time and Cat grabbed her bags, donned her cranial and float coat, and headed out the door and into the waiting Merlin. Morgan looked on as Cat's helicopter lifted off the flight deck en route to *Albion*. He saw Dallas and The Judge looking over at him. The Judge gave him a thumbs up gesture while Dallas said "Congratulations, sir."

"Thank you, gentlemen," Morgan replied. "Let's get this done so we can all go home."

At that moment, an aircrewman in a green flight suit and white flight helmet came into the space.

"Okay folks," the aircrewman said. "We're ready to leave for the *Arlington.*"

Morgan, Captain Torres, and the rest of the party grabbed their bags and headed for the Seahawk.

That was three days ago. Now Morgan stood on *Arlington*'s bridge wing, anxious to get the operation underway. A young, female African-American Lieutenant Junior Grade came out from the bridge, the unique pentagon-shaped emblem on the side of her U.S.S. *Arlington* ball cap quite visible even in the dark.

"Sir, the Fire Scout is holding *Aurora Express* on its cameras. Your presence is requested in CIC.

"Thank you, Lieutenant. Quiet watch so far?"

"Yes, sir. It's my first watch after qualifying as a SWO."

"Congratulations and enjoy. Nothing better than having the watch on a night like this."

Morgan took one last look around then headed below.

CHAPTER
THIRTY-TWO

U.S.S. *Arlington*
Time: 2300 Local

Morgan entered *Arlington*'s Combat Information Center and saw Chief Shaw and Captain Torres standing behind the Fire Scout operator. The Chief of Staff waived him forward.

"Good evening, Commander. Come take a look at this," Captain Torres said. Morgan peered over the operator's shoulder.

Morgan saw the light grey image of the *Aurora Express*'s stern in the forward looking infra-red display monitor. Reading Morgan's thoughts, the operator zoomed in to the ship's transom where her name was quite visible.

"That's her all right," Morgan said. "Could you move the Fire Scout higher for a view of her cargo deck?"

"Yes, sir. That's super easy, barely an inconvenience," the operator said with a look of pride on her face.

The image on the monitor changed as the RPV gained altitude. A few minutes later, the Fire Scout reached an altitude of 10,000 feet, and a view of the entire cargo deck filled the monitor. Morgan pointed at the display.

"Look, here between the rows of containers. Those are the MLRS trucks and trailers, all five of them," he said. He noticed a group of heat signatures in one of the containers.

"See these?" he asked Captain Torres.

"People?"

"Yes, ma'am. The human cargo Calico and I saw in Singapore. I'm seeing at least twenty unique heat signatures."

"Indeed. What's next?"

"We pass this info on to Calico, Commander Hunter, and his SBS team. They'll need to know the location of the human cargo." Morgan turned to the Fire Scout operator. "Can we transmit this video to *Albion*?"

"Yes, sir."

"Excellent, please do so. Dallas, how far away are they from their expected rendezvous point?"

"They are a day out, present course and speed."

"Perfect, looks like tomorrow night's the night. Pass the word to the boat crews and SEALS that we'll meet tomorrow morning in the hangar bay for our final briefing."

"Aye, aye, sir."

Morgan grabbed a red-colored handset mounted next to the Fire Scout operator, the secure radio connection to *Albion*.

"*Albion, Arlington*, over," Morgan passed over the radio.

"This is *Albion*, roger, over," Morgan heard over the speaker. The female voice had an accent Morgan would describe as UK midlands.

"Request to speak with UK government representative Calico or SBS X-ray Squadron actual, over."

"Roger, wait one."

A few minutes later, Morgan heard a familiar voice come over the radio.

"*Arlington, Albion*, Calico here."

"This is Gargoyle. Are you receiving the Fire Scout video? Over."

"Yes, we are. We've marked the containers with the cargo of

interest. We also spotted the MLRS trailers. What is H-Hour? Over."

"Looking at H-Hour at approximately 23:00 hours tomorrow depending on target actions. Target expected at rendezvous point at that time. Over."

"Copy all, Gargoyle. The candles are lit. Over."

"Copy that, Calico and concur, out." Morgan said as he finished the conversation.

"'The candles are lit?'" Captain Torres asked.

"Inside message, ma'am," Morgan answered with a shy smile.

Morgan took that opportunity to leave CIC and head to his stateroom.

CHAPTER
THIRTY-THREE

U.S.S. *Arlington*
Time: 1000 Local the Following Day

Morgan gathered his team in the hangar bay at 10:00 hours, four hours after the Fire Scout landed. Along with LT Coslick, ENS Luca Patel, the SEAL platoon's XO, the rest of the platoon's 16 SEALS, Chief Shaw, and Petty Officers Haugen and Hernandez were Special Boat Operator Third Class Emilio Sharpe, Chief Shaw's fourth crew member, and Chief Special Boat Operator 'Marvelous' Marvin Hurd from Special Boat Group 22 and overall officer in charge of the two SOC-R boats along with his three boat crew members. U.S. Army Captains Callum Jenkins and Giana Mejia, the two senior MH-47 pilots joined the group along with their aircrafts' crew chiefs while M. Hachette stood along the hangar's bulkhead, there yet not. Seeing that he had everyone, Morgan started the mission brief.

"Good morning ladies and gentlemen, last night our target ship came within range of our Fire Scout UAV. Its cameras confirmed that both the MLRS and human cargoes are still on board. As of this morning, the ship is 225 nautical miles from us and 195 nautical miles from her rendezvous point. We anticipate she'll begin offload of the MLRS at about 23:00, which should mean a completion a few hours before sunrise. The Fire Scout will track both the lighterage as it heads towards the Gambia River and our boats so we can maintain a discreet distance as we enter the river. At that point, we'll be on our own."

Chief Hurd raised his hand, "Sir, how about fuel? We have additional cans in the boats, but that still won't get us into Senegal."

"Great question, Chief. Let's say that my primary employer has made all necessary arrangements for fuel and other supplies," Morgan replied with a knowing smirk.

Chief Hurd seemed satisfied with that answer. Morgan continued, "Stealth will be the order of the day. If the lighterage crew spot us, it's game over. Everyone, dirty boat guys, and SEALs will be in civilian clothing, and the boats weapons will be stowed or covered until needed. Once the MLRS are offloaded, our French associate will pass the location of the MLRS drop off to his government for further action. Questions?"

No one had any additional questions or comments. Morgan wrapped things up, "Okay, I've wasted enough of our time. Let's get moving."

The boat crews continued preparing their craft, which sat on a two-tier trailer on the flight deck, while the SEALs worked on their weapons. Morgan examined the boats' new paint scheme. Instead of the standard green and black camouflage, the boats now sported a colorful paint job that mirrored the local craft seen along the Gambia River. It should, in theory, keep the boats from being looked at too closely by either the Gambians or the Senegalese. Add the civilian clothing, and the team should pass muster.

The Special Operations Craft-Riverine, or SOC-R boats, the team would use for this mission were ten meters long, three meters wide and weighed ten tons. Each SOC-R carried a crew of four and could hold up to eight additional personnel, as they would be for this mission. The boats armament consisted of two, GAU-17, six barreled, 7.62 millimeter mini-guns; two, M240B 7.62-millimeter belt-fed light machine guns; two, MK 19 40-millimeter grenade launchers; and a single M2 50 caliber machine gun mounted aft. The boat crew and engines were protected by Kevlar armor that could stop small arms up to 7.62 millimeter. The boats had two, 440 horse power diesel engines that moved the boats' V-shaped hull at a speed of 40 knots via waterjet propulsion. They also carried state of the art electronics including a GPS-based electronic navigation system, Forward Looking Infra-Red optics, and a full suite of VHF, UHF, HF, and satellite communications gear. They were smart, sleek, fast, and lethal.

As day moved into night, the team cleared the flight deck after flight quarters sounded for the launch of one of the two Fire Scouts. Once airborne, the Fire Scout soon found the *Aurora Express* exactly where she was supposed to be. It monitored the ship and the approach of a crane-equipped barge under the control of a pusher-type boat with a draft shallow enough for a transit up the Gambia. Once the barge was alongside the ship, both the ship's crane and the barge's crane began to lift the MLRS vehicles off the cargo deck and on to the barge, all under the watchful eye of the Fire Scout and, by extension, Morgan's team. Once the last vehicle touched down on the barge, the first Fire Scout reached the limits of its loitering time and headed back to *Arlington*, training its cameras behind it to watch the barge pull away from the *Aurora Express* and head for the Gambia River. With that, the flight deck crew began preparations to launch the second Fire Scout to relieve its partner.

Once the second Fire Scout launched, the two MH-47 began to spin their rotors for takeoff. Morgan, dress out in his battle gear and wearing his prosthetic along with his Gatorz tactical eye ware inspected his team in the hangar bay.

"Absolute bad asses!" he said doing his best *Aliens* impression. "Galahad, Dallas, Marvelous Marvin, get the team on board as soon as the flight crew says go. I'm heading to CIC."

Morgan entered *Arlington*'s CIC and walked over to Captain Torres who stood in front of one of the CIC's large screen displays along with *Arlington*'s commanding officer, Captain Jon "Bo" Dachos, USN. Mounted on the bulkhead above the Tactical Action Officer, or TAO, station, the screen showed *Arlington* in the center with circles representing *Albion* and *Iron Duke* to starboard. At the extreme edge of the display's field of view was a diamond shaped symbol with the tag AUR EXP along with a square shaped symbol with the tag BARGE. Between the two groups of surface contacts, two semi-circular symbols, looking like the upper portion of a whole circle marked the position of the two Fire Scouts as they headed to their destinations. A television monitor next to the large screen display showed the *Albion* with two Merlin helicopters sitting on her flight deck.

"Captain Torres, Captain Dachos," Morgan said acknowledging both senior officers. Captain Torres looked up and a confused expression crossed her face as she noticed Morgan's slightly altered appearance.

"It's my prosthetic," Morgan continued. "Ma'am, we're ready to go. Any word from *Albion*?"

"Nothing official yet, though they seem to be preparing their aircraft." Captain Torres reached for a bulkhead-mounted radio handset.

"*Albion*, Lima Bravo, over," Captain Torres said using her Composite Warfare Commander call sign.

"Lima Bravo, this is *Albion* actual, over," the voice over the radio said. Using the term '*Albion* actual' meant that Captain Carr himself was on the other end of the conversation.

"What's your status? Over."

"We're ready and awaiting your word. Over."

"Roger, stand by. Okay Gargoyle, get to your aircraft. It's time to go. Good luck."

"Aye, aye, ma'am! Thank you."

Captain Torres brought the radio handset back up to her ear and squeezed the transmit button.

"All units Bravo, this is Lima Bravo. Land the landing force!"

CHAPTER
THIRTY-FOUR

H.M.S. *Albion*

"Land the landing force!" said the voice of Captain Torres over the Operations Room's speakers. Captain Carr, sitting in his designated OPS Room seat reached for the intercom to speak with the bridge.

"Officer of the Watch, Captain. Green deck."

The rotating light up on the flight deck changed colors from amber to green. The first of the two Merlins lifted off the flight deck followed quickly by the second. On board the first Merlin, Cat sat next to Commander Hunter facing aft, both wearing headsets connected to the helicopter's cockpit. In front of them sat members of Hunter's SBS team, each checking their weapons one last time before they saw action. One SBS operator held a L96A1 sniper rifle on his lap, ready to act as an airborne over watch. The heliborne element would take the ship and secure any persons of interest as well the ship's human cargo. A Royal Navy Wildcat helicopter from the *Iron Duke* provided armed escort of both Merlins. The rest of the team would follow up via Ridged Hull Inflatable Boats, or RHIBs, to provide security for the transfer of trafficked personnel to *Albion* for medical screening and eventual return to their countries of origin.

Cat and Commander Hunter heard their pilot over their headphones.

"One minute to target."

Commander Hunter passed the word to the rest of the team via their throat mics and hand signals. Cat double checked her silenced Walther, now in a holster strapped across her chest, her commando dagger in its forearm sheath strapped to her left arm, and pulled a black balaclava over her long, blond hair. A moment later, the Merlin pulled into a hover and its door slid open.

"Go, go, go!" Commander Hunter shouted and the team began to exit the aircraft. The fast-roping operators hit the deck on the *Aurora Express*'s superstructure aft of the bridge with Cat and Commander Hunter being last out of the aircraft. The Merlin gained altitude, utilized a series of flashing lights to disorientate the bridge watch team while the SBS operator with the snipper rifle sat on the edge of the doorway watching for any threats.

Cat and Hunter headed for the pilot house's port-side entrance with two other operators approaching the starboard-side entrance. The second Merlin off loaded it operators over the bow. The starboard group opened the door and tossed in a flash-bang grenade at which point all four entered the space. The team's silenced L119A2 carbines and Cat's equally silenced Walther made short work of the bridge watch standers. The operation lasted no more than 30 seconds from the time the team hit the deck until the bridge was secured.

One deck down from the bridge, Corporal Archie Cole and Lance Corporal Angus Baker moved quickly and silently down the passageway. They came in the first Merlin with their C.O. and that very fit SIS bird with the goal of finding the ship's communications room. They found a sign that read 'radio room' on a door in the center of the passageway. They took positions on either side of the door, exchanged a look, and kicked the door in. They found the radio room operator fast asleep in in a chair with his feet propped up on a desk, dead to the world. The two SBS operators made sure he stayed that way with two rounds from their silenced carbines into his sleepy head. They then left the radio room to commence the search for the two targets of interest.

On the cargo deck, four SBS operators, led by Colour Sergeant Rufus Watts moved from their landing zone on the bow and moved swiftly down and aft towards the containers. They came across three guards watching a stack of containers. The four made short work of the guards then opened one of the containers. Colour Sergeant Watts shined his torch inside, and what he saw made his jaw drop. He saw stack upon stack of U.S. produced Desert Tech Micro Dynamic Rifles, a next generation, Bullpup-style assault weapon. By his quick count, Watts determined that there were enough MDRs to outfit an entire regiment.

"Fuck me," Watts whispered to himself.

After assigning one of his men to guard the container, Watts moved on to search for any additional crew members.

A few minutes after securing the bridge, Cat began to hear updates from the rest of the operators in the first aircraft and those from the second.

"Cargo deck secure, three tangoes down."

"Engine room secure, two tangoes down."

"Radio room secure, one tango down. Caught him napping, literally. Searching for people of interest."

Commander Hunter responded, "Roger, copy all. Continue your sweeps for any additional personnel."

"Monty, I'm going to find the container with the human cargo."

"Aye, ma'am. Careful. There may be some crew members we missed."

Cat left the bridge and headed to the cargo deck using the superstructure's external ladders. Once on the cargo deck, she preceded forward when she felt the air waft over her head, like someone took a swing at her skull and missed. She instinctively dropped and rolled and came up with her dagger in hand. In front of her stood a large Asian gentleman, probably Malaysian, holding a length of metal pipe commonly used to firmly close the latches on water-tight doors and hatches. The nautical term was 'dogging wrench.'

"*Anda mati, jalang!* (*You're dead, bitch!*)"

Cat replied in perfect Malay, "*Kita akan melihatnya (We'll see about that).*"

The two began to square off, each one of them circling the other looking for an opening. Finally, the Malaysian became impatient and took another swing at Cat's head. She easily ducked the dogging wrench while at the same time bringing up her dagger and sliced the forearm that held it, cutting through tendons and arteries. Her cut turned the Malaysian's hand and upper arm into a useless lump of flesh. He immediately dropped the dogging wrench, held his now bleeding, immobilized arm, and looked up at Cat with a mixture of hate and abject horror.

"Fuck you!" he shouted.

"Language!" Cat shouted back as she planted one of her metric size 36 combat boots swiftly and firmly against his genitals.

The Malaysian crumpled to the deck with a groan as he covered his now ruptured testicles. Cat moved behind him, grabbed him by the hair, exposing his throat. Placing her now bloody dagger against his carotid artery, she whispered in his ear.

"Where are the people?"

The Malaysian pointed to a container that stood by itself on the cargo deck.

"Thank you."

Cat plunged her dagger though the Malaysian's throat. She left him to bleed out while she moved to the container. She then saw a shadow moving along a container.

You have to be kidding me. Another one?

She crouched down and waited to pounce on her prey. Before she could pounce, however she recognized the shadow as belonging to one of the SBS operators assigned to clear the cargo deck. Colour Sergeant Watts.

"You missed one, Sergeant," Cat told him with an evil smile as she pointed to the body behind her.

"Right, sorry about that, ma'am. Give you much trouble, did he?"

"Not a bit. Come with me, the container with the human cargo is right over here."

The pair approached the container with caution. Cat, looking up noticed a series of holes drilled along the container's upper edge.

Air holes.

They found the door and saw that it was locked. Sergeant Watts drew his expandable baton and used it to pry the lock open and watched as the pieces of the snapped lock dropped to the deck with a resounding clank. They lifted the handle and slowly opened the door.

"Hello?" Cat called out as she shined her torch into the container.

"Bloody hell," the sergeant whispered as they took in the scene.

Inside there were at least 50 people, men, women, and children, crammed into the container under squalid conditions. The horrendous smell of sweat, urine, and feces reached them quickly, and Sergeant Watts did all he could not to wretch. Opening the container fully, Cat looked around and spoke to the group.

"Hello, does anyone speak English?" she asked in English. She repeated her question in Mandarin Chinese and Malaysian.

One young lady raised her hand cautiously. "I do."

"Good evening, what's your name and where are you from?"

"Tan Bao. I'm from China."

"Are most of the people in here from China?"

"Most of us, some from the Philippines, Korea, Indonesia…"

"Could you translate for me?"

"Yes."

"Please tell everyone that we're from the British government, and we're here to get you home."

Tan translated Cat's words, and the people in the container began to weep quietly when they realized that their long nightmare was over. Cat heard Commander Hunter's voice over her ear piece.

"Calico, Hunter."

"Go."

"The sweep is complete, and we have one of our persons of interest up on the bridge."

"Very well, Commander. I'm on my way up. Also, contact *Albion* and let them know that we're looking at 50 or so people and to send over the boats."

"Aye, ma'am."

Cat turned to Tan, "Are you aware of anymore containers like yours?"

"No. There may be more, but we haven't seen anyone else."

"Okay, I'm going to leave you for a few minutes, but I'll be right back. Let everyone know that boats from a British ship are on their way to get you out of here."

Tan translated the message, and the people began to stand taller showing that they were more than ready to leave.

Cat headed up to the bridge, and when she arrived, she saw a familiar Chinese man on his knees with his hands on his head flanked by Corporal Cole and Lance Corporal Baker.

"Zheng Yuhan, I presume?" Cat asked.

The gentleman attempted to hide his surprise in hearing his name but failed miserably.

"My name is Lei Chen. I'm a Chinese diplomat," he said with an air of authority.

Commander Hunter handed Cat a black passport issued by

the People's Republic of China with the name 'Lei Chen,' the man's picture, and several entry and exit visas from various countries. A cover identity, probably, provided by his old employer, the Chinese MSS.

"Mr. Chen, if that's your actual name, you have been discovered on a ship with trafficked persons in international waters. We also have pictures of you with not only the human cargo in Singapore, but also with non-export, Chinese-made heavy weapons outside of China. Caught you bang to rights in both human and weapons trafficking. So please, spare us the diplomatic immunity codswallop. Commander, if you would."

Hunter took his cue and plunged a hypodermic needle into Zheng's neck. The Chinese weapons dealer fell to the deck and was carried off by the two corporals. Cat turned to Hunter.

"Any sign of our other person of interest?" she asked.

"Nothing yet, but we may have found where she was staying."

"Show me."

The pair climbed down a series of ladders to what was the Captain's Cabin. Hunter opened the door, and the pair entered the room. A tangle of sheets and blankets covered the bunk, and a quick look inside a nearby trashcan showed at least two used condoms.

"Well, someone had a right jolly old time," Cat said with sarcastic venom dripping from her voice.

"We also found some discarded women's underwear and toiletries in the head." Hunter pointed out the door to the Captain's private bathroom.

"But no sign of the target?"

"No, ma'am."

"She must be with the barge heading for Gambia. Wonder why she's going along? No matter, I'll let Gargoyle and his team know to expect her. Let's see to our guests, shall we?"

The pair headed to the cargo deck where, looking out to sea, saw the *Albion* launching several RHIBs from her well deck.

They saw a pilot's ladder rigged to starboard and witnessed the first operators of Hunter's second team climbing on board. Colour Sergeant Watts began to direct the newcomers to their positions around the ship. Two of the newcomers, however, were not SBS. They wore white armbands with red crosses, *Albion*'s medical officer, and one of her medical technicians. Cat approached the pair.

"Good morning, ladies," Cat said. "One of the victims, a Miss Tan Bao, speaks English and has been my translator today. Follow me and I'll introduce you."

They walked to the container and found Tan Bao tending to her people. Cat introduced her to the two medical practicioners.

"Tan, these ladies will be seeing to your and your people's medical needs. They will accompany you to our ship for the journey to a friendly port. I have to leave now, but you are in very capable hands."

"Thank you. What happened to the ship's crew? Many are afraid that they will come back."

"Please pass on that the crew will never hurt them, or anyone else, ever again. Ever."

"And that horrible woman? She dragged some of our young boys and girls up to her room. They never returned."

"Don't worry about her either. We'll take care of her the same way as we took care of the crew."

Tan look at Cat with a brief look of surprise then one of understanding. Nodding once, she turned to the two medics and began to spread the word to all her people. Cat took that moment to slip away and head back to the bridge. When she arrived, she saw two Royal Navy officers and a pair of ratings taking positions on the bridge by the ship's navigation display and the helm console. She saw Commander Hunter standing off to the side.

"The prize crew?" she asked.

"Aye, there are two Engineering Technicians down in the engine room preparing the ship to get back underway."

"Good, and the AIS transponder?"

"They'll turn it back on once everyone is back on board *Albion*."

"Very good. Not a bad night's work all in all. Are all your operators accounted for?"

"Aye, and in good health."

"Good. Is there anything else we need to account for?"

"Colour Sergeant Watts found a heavily guarded container filled with next generation assault rifles, enough to outfit a regiment. Hopefully, the documentation we seized will tell us where they were heading."

"More importantly, Monty. We need to know for whom they were intended. I've been working on gun running operation to the Real IRA. If they are meant for them…"

"Things could get very ugly very fast, a real threat to the Good Friday Agreements. One more thing, Calico. It would be an honor if you'd join the lads and me for a post-mission tradition."

"Oh?"

"When the SBS conducts a mission like this, we gather the team by one of the target's life rings for a picture. Sort of proof that we captured the ship. We'd like you to join us for that picture."

"Commander, it would be an honor."

The pair left the bridge and headed for the fantail where the SBS team awaited their arrival. The team took positions on either side of a deck railing-mounted, international orange life ring inscribed with 'M/V AURORA EXPRESS' across the top and 'COPENHAGEN' along the bottom. As they posed for the picture, Cat thoughts turned to Morgan.

Good luck, my dearest James. Your mission has become a bit more challenging.

CHAPTER
THIRTY-FIVE

U.S.S. *Arlington*

Morgan double timed from CIC to the flight deck when he heard the voice of *Arlington*'s TAO over the ship's announcing system.

"Land the landing force!"

Morgan arrived at the flight deck as the last of his team boarded the MH-47s. As the twin-rotor aircraft spun on the deck, Morgan boarded his, placed a communications headset on his head, and strapped into his jump seat. Within seconds of his boarding, the Chock-and-Chainmen removed the aircraft's restraints and with the raising of the Landing Signalman's arms, Morgan's Chinook lifted off the deck followed quickly by its partner. Morgan's aircraft circled back and hovered over the first of the two SOC-R patrol craft staged on the flight deck. Once in position, Chief Shaw and his crew, using a system known as the Maritime External Air Transportation System, or MEATS, connected their boat to the underside of the Chinook. Once the boat's connections were secure, the crew entered the still hovering helicopter via a rope ladder though the aircraft's open belly hatch. The Chinook increased speed and lifted the SOC-R clear of the flight deck. With the air space clear, Chief Hurd's crew secured their boat to the second Chinook and once the boat crew climbed aboard, the second MH-47 followed its partner to the drop off point.

Morgan looked on with satisfaction as both boats and aircraft safely cleared *Arlington*. Over the radio, he heard *Arlington*'s air controller pass bearing and range to the boat's drop point, 25 miles behind the weapons carrying barge on a bearing reciprocal to the barge's course towards the Gambia River. With the barge a moving target, the air controller adjusted the aircrafts' course to ensure a precise rendezvous.

Morgan heard the voice of Captain Mejia, his aircraft's commander, over his headset.

"Two minutes to drop!"

Morgan, Chief Shaw, the boat crew, and half of LT Coslick's SEALs stood up and prepared for deployment. Chief Shaw led his crew back down the rope ladder into the SOC-R. The Chinook descended to an altitude a few feet above the water where, once in position, the SOC-R was detached and landed with a gentle thud. The aircraft moved in front of the boat where Morgan and the SEALs ran out the back of the Chinook's open cargo ramp and into the water. They swam to the boat and climbed aboard.

"How we doing Dallas?" Morgan asked once on board.

"Good, sir. The Judge got the engines started."

"We up on comms yet?"

"Not yet. El Fantasma's working on it."

"Very good."

Morgan opened a small storage locker and pulled out a small signal lamp. He slid a red filter over the front and pointed it at the other boat. He switched it on and began to send a flashing light signal to Chief Hurd's crew.

Can't hack a flashing light.

MARVELOUS DE GARGOYLE INT SATUS K. (Marvelous this is Gargoyle. What's your status? Over.)

Morgan saw a response come over from the other boat.

GARGOYLE DE GALAHAD, MARVELOUS BUSY WITH ENG CASUALTY. ALL PERSONNEL OK. BT INT COMMS. HAVING ISUES WITH SATHICOM K (Gargoyle this is Galahad, Chief Hurd is busy with an engineering casualty. Break, what is your communications status? We are having issues with the satellite high communications channel. Over.)

DE GARGOYLE, RGR ALL. COMMS IN PROGRESS. RPT WHEN UP SATHICOM AND WHEN ABLE TO GET UW. K. (This is Gargoyle, roger all. Report when up on satellite high communications channel and when able to get underway. Out.)

Morgan turned to Chief Shaw, who was at the boat's control station assisting Petty Officer Hernandez with the radios.

"How's it going, Dallas?"

"We're ready to try a radio check on satellite."

"Good. Marvelous is having engine issues, let's close and see if we can help."

"Aye, aye, sir."

Chief Shaw took the boat's wheel and closed Chief Hurd's boat. As they moved, Petty Officer Hernandez picked up the satellite radio's handset.

"*Arlington*, this is Fantasma. Radio check, over."

A voice came over the radio's speaker, "This is *Arlington*. Roger, over."

"This is Fantasma, roger, out. Sir, we're up on satellite."

"Outstanding. What was the issue?"

"Had to re-load the crypto, the initial load didn't take."

"It's always something. We're approaching the other boat, let's pass that along."

"Aye, sir."

Morgan's boat came along side Chief Hurd's and between the two crews, that boat also came up on satellite communications and started its engines after clearing saltwater intrusion into the fuel lines. After a quick conversation between the two craft masters and Galahad, Morgan decided they were ready to go. He picked up the satellite radio handset.

"*Arlington* this is Gargoyle, bearing and range to target, over."

"This is *Arlington*, target bearing 045 degrees, range 30 nautical miles. Target on course 055, speed 12 knots. Fire Scout has good track on target. Break. Message from Calico, *Aurora Express* and secondary person of interest secure. Primary person of interest not on board, say again, primary person of interest not on board. Suspect believed to be on board barge. Over."

Morgan looked over at Dallas with surprise. He replied, "Roger, copy all. Thanks for the update, out."

He looked over to Galahad, Dallas, and Marvelous.

"Well that's interesting. Guess we'll have a crack at Aurora ourselves. Any thoughts on why she's with the barge?"

"Ensuring delivery? Those MLRS are a major expense," Marvelous said.

"Maybe, though there is another possibility."

"You don't think...," Dallas began.

'Yeah, I am. Like what we saw in Singapore, she's probably there to pick up an additional cargo of people. Wonderful. Well that complicates things. Okay, we'll worry about that later. Let's get going, close the target until we get it on our radar, and slow to match its speed. Have your crews and SEALs go ahead and change into civilian garb and cover the heavy weapons, the sun will be rising soon."

The two boats increased speed to 15 knots, a crawl compared to the SOC-R's 40 knot maximum speed. Using Fire Scout information, the boats closed the barge until it appeared on the boat's commercial-grade surface search radar. They slowed to a matching speed of 12 knots keeping the barge at the extreme edge of radar range. As the sun rose in front of them, the boat crews began to see the lights of the Gambian coast appear on the horizon.

CHAPTER
THIRTY-SIX

Banjul-Registered Tow Boat *Gold Coast*
Position: 13°28'7" North by 016°33'26" West
5,000 yards North East from Banjul
Course: 120° True
Speed: 12 Knots
Time: 0900

Aurora felt like hell as she stood on the deck of the tow boat. Despite the calm conditions, the trip from the *Aurora Express* to the mouth to the Gambia River still did a number on her stomach. Her dear father was going to pay for this, and she thought of some quite delicious ways she can collect. The transfer of the cargo went smoothly the night before, so smoothly that Zheng Yuhan believed he could stay behind, satisfied that the cargo would arrive at its destination safely. Lucky him, missing the trip up the river. She, on the other hand, made the trip not just to deliver the weapons, but to pick up another load of people. More cogs for the great machines of the leisure and textile industries that chewed up and spat out humans with an unending hunger. This load was awaiting at the rendezvous point, where the weapons cargo would be dropped off and the other cargo picked up.

Still, this trip hadn't been a total loss. She had her fun with some of the crew, especially that hunky Malaysian. He satisfied her like no one in recent memory, well maybe except Morgan, but he would soon be dead once father found him, especially after he killed Ivar. And when she pulled some of the teenagers from the rabble in the container, mmmmmmmm that was a whole new level of fun.

Aurora moved into the tow boat's pilot house. She watched as the boat's master and a local pilot navigated the barge into the Gambia. She was impressed with the quiet professionalism of the Master and the crew; her father certainly knew how to hire the right people. After a few minutes, she grew impatient and walked over to the Master.

"How much longer till we get to our destination?" Aurora asked with an air of authority.

"We're 35 hours out, Lady Aurora. We'll be right at the edge of the navigable portion of the river."

"Good, the sooner the better."

She turned and left the pilot house. Aurora walked to what the Master called a 'guest cabin.' More like guest bathroom. She entered the cabin and pulled a bottle of bourbon from her bag, poured a glass full, and downed it in one swallow. *If I can't get laid, I might as well get drunk.*

Morgan and his two boats slowed to match the barge's speed as it entered the Gambia River. They took the opportunity to blend in with the local boat traffic. The colorful paint they used to blend in with the local boats worked like a champ. The other boats paid them no mind as they slowly approached the river's entrance. Add in the clothes the boat crew and SEALs wore, and they were good to go. The satellite radio speaker came to life.

"Gargoyle, *Arlington*, over."

"Gargoyle, over."

"Fire Scout holds target 10 miles into the Gambia River. We're at the point where we can no longer track the target without violating Gambian airspace, Fire Scout is RTB. Good luck and good hunting. Mallard sends. Over."

"Roger, copy all. My complements to the Admiral. Out."

Morgan turned to Chief Shaw and M. Hachette, who appeared seemingly out of nowhere, and passed on the message.

"We're on our own now, gentlemen. No over watch from here on out."

"No assets from your other employer?" Dallas asked.

"Negative, Chief. Too many ears on too many walls at Langley at present. That's why I stuck with mostly Navy assets for this operation. Unless your employer can assist, Monsieur."

"Let me see what I can do." M. Hachette reached for his satellite phone.

As the French agent spoke on his phone, Morgan's satellite phone buzzed in his pocket. He picked it up and saw a text message from Cat with an attached image.

Well this could be interesting!

Ensuring no one could see what he was looking at, Morgan opened the message.

Dearest James, you missed all the fun! Please delete the picture once you see it. XOXOXOXOXOX! Your Cat.

The attached image was of her and the SBS team by the *Aurora Express*'s life ring. Not exactly the picture he expected to receive from his girlfriend, but still exciting none the less.

That's a picture for the ages. Not many opportunities to work with the SBS on a ship take down.

He quickly deleted the text and the picture since it showed the faces of the SBS team, something not releasable to the public at large. When he looked up from the phone, he saw The Judge giving him a peculiar look.

"Oh, just a text from Calico with a picture of her and the SBS guys after the take-down," Morgan said.

Petty Officer Haugen looked at him with some level of skepticism, "Uh huh, sure it was."

"Seriously! No 'not safe for work' pictures."

"Uh huh, what's that expression about protesting too much?" The Judge said with a slight smile before he moved aft towards his engines.

Morgan sighed and shook his head. He moved to the boat's wheel where Dallas steered the boat towards the river entrance.

"How's it going Chief?"

"Not bad, sir. The slow speed is saving gas, but we will need to re-fuel eventually."

"Taken care of. How far to the town of Tendaba?"

Dallas checked the boat's navigation system, "About 150 nautical miles, 15 hours, or so if we maintain ten knots."

"Can we make it on fuel?"

"Yes, sir. We'll have about 50 miles range remaining at that point if we keep to these slower speeds."

"Good. Let's pull alongside the other boat so we can pass the word."

Dallas increased the boat's speed and pulled alongside Chief Hurd's boat. After a quick conversation, Chief Hurd pulled away and took the lead. Chief Shaw slowed his boat and moved off several yards from his partner. The two boats entered the river and Gambian territorial waters.

CHAPTER
THIRTY-SEVEN

CIA Headquarters,
Langley, Virginia
Time: 0530

Clint Peters dragged himself into the cafeteria at CIA Headquarters after spending a long night working an operation in Hungary, supporting an extraction team targeting an ISIS terror cell. With Morgan missing or dead, he no longer had a source for good coffee, so he had to settle for the swill they served here. Sitting at a corner table, Peters sipped at his coffee. Looking around, he saw Joe Acevedo from the Global Services division looking even more haggard than he was. He picked up his coffee and walked over to the supply guy's table.

"Hey Joe, join you?" Peters asked.

"Sure, have a seat," Acevedo replied.

"Man, you look just how I feel. What's going on?"

"You know, Clint, the usual. The time difference between here and there is going to kill me. I'm too old to be up at this ungodly hour. It's giving me Navy flashbacks."

"I know how you feel. Working a European operation?"

"No, West Africa, just as bad. Especially with General Bailey asking for status reports every five minutes."

"Heh, quite," Peters replied with a tired yet neutral expression despite the news.

West Africa! It couldn't be. Shit.

"Hate to commiserate and run, but I have to get back to my desk," Peters said. "Go get some sleep."

"Will do, when this operation is over."

Peters stood up and after tossing his coffee cup in the trash exited the cafeteria. Instead of heading to his desk, he headed out the building and towards the parking lot. Due to the still early hour, he found his car easily in the huge lot. He unlocked the door of his Audi SUV and climbed inside. He left his personal cell phone in the car's wireless charging pad and pulled a burner phone from the glove box. He selected the only number in its contacts list and pressed the call button. After a few rings, the other party picked up.

"It's Peters. We have a problem…"

Several hours later, and several thousand miles away, the two SOC-R boats approached the small village Tendaba, Gambia after a voyage that, to Morgan, looked a lot like a scene from 'Apocalypse Now.'

Only without the Wagner, mangoes, or the fucking tiger.

Still, Morgan couldn't help but admire the scenery along the banks of the Gambia. Its flat, savannah terrain sat between the lush rainforests of South America he had operated in with the CIA, and the stark Iraqi desert along the Tigris and Euphrates rivers he sailed as a teenager with the special boat units. Stunningly beautiful.

For the past few hours, the boats played a game of leap frog with one boat staying close to the barge while the other drifted in the river appearing, to the casual observer, to be fishing or doing anything other than tracking a barge pusher boat. Their job was made easier by M. Hachette coming through with DGSE provided, real-time over watch via a US-built MQ-9 Reaper RPV, controlled by the French Air Force, from Niamey air base, Niger. The French Reaper, like its US counterparts could be armed with Hellfire air-to-surface missiles, but for right now it was unarmed to allow additional loitering time.

As the sun set, the fuel levels on the boats began to get a bit too low for the two craftmasters' comfort. Morgan directed the two boats to hug the riverbank and slowed to five knots to save as much gas as possible as they approached their destination. Finally, the boats came around a right-hand bend in the river and the team saw lights along the shore, the village of Tendaba. Morgan had both boats pull up to a small inlet along the river bank and idle their engines. He gathered Dallas, Marvelous Marvin, and Galahad to pass on his plan.

"Marvelous and I are going ashore. There is a road 10 yards inland that we're going to follow into the village. When I give you the word, get the boats underway. There is a pier a little more than half a kilometer ahead. That's where we'll refuel the boats. Questions? Okay, let's go."

Morgan and Chief Hurd jumped off the boats and waded ashore. They left all but their side arms back on the boat with Morgan using his more concealable Smith & Wesson 6904 under his civilian clothing rather than his Navy-issue Sig Sauer. Once they were used to walking on land again, the pair move quickly towards the village.

"Uh, sir," Marvelous began. "Where are we going?"

Morgan replied a little too merrily for the Chief's taste, "To get a drink, and maybe meet a new friend. Just follow my lead and watch our backs. I do tend to stand out a bit in this part of the world after all."

They walked about a third of a mile from where they came ashore. They passed a small hotel called the Tendaba Camp, which, by its appearance had seen better days, and probably existed only to serve as a base camp for eco-tourists exploring the nearby Kiang West National Park and the Bao Bolong Wetland Reserve. Once past the hotel, they arrived at the rendezvous location Morgan was briefed about by General Bailey before leaving the States, the Bambo Bar. They walked up the walkway towards the bar's entrance where a hand painted sign reading 'Welcome to the New Bambo Bar' with a crocodile pointing the way in, welcomed guests. They passed a second, hand painted sign that read 'One million mosquitoes cannot be wrong, Bambo Bar is fabulous'.

Morgan read the sign and said, "Well this doesn't bode well. Glad I wore bug repellant."

Turns out Morgan feared standing out needlessly as there were several groups of white people at the establishment eating, drinking, and dancing poorly to the music provided by a local DJ.

Tourists, obnoxious everywhere in the world.

Looking around at the bar, whose décor could only be described as neo-Indiana Jones with giant wire rope spools serving as low slung tables, and colorful paintings of crocodiles and other local fauna adorning the walls, Morgan spotted his contact standing by the bartender.

The gentleman was tall, at least six feet three inches, with some of the darkest skin Morgan had ever seen on a West African. He wore shorts, sandals, collared shirt, and was fanning himself with a wide brimmed hat. On the other side of a low wall painted with a picture of a man about to have his hand bitten off by a crocodile, the bartender stood preparing drinks for the larger-than-normal crowd. Morgan walked over to him while Chief Hurd found an empty table.

"Excuse me, sir," Morgan began. "Do they serve pork chops here?"

The gentleman answered in English with a wonderfully rich West African accent, "No, sir they do not. They only serve halal foods here."

"Oh, sorry, my mistake. No offense meant. May I buy you a drink as an apology?"

"Certainly, sir, or if I may, Mister Gargoyle."

Morgan cocked his head in acknowledgement.

"I am Abdou Fatty, welcome to Gambia."

"Thank you, glad to be here," Morgan replied as he extended his hand.

Abdou shook his hand and continued, "Please come with me, I have what you need over at the jetty."

Morgan gave a signal to Chief Hurd and the trio headed out into the night. After exchanging introductions, they followed a dirt path to a surprising large jetty that extended out into the river. Morgan asked about it.

"The jetty serves the tourist boats that cross the river and into the Duntu Malang Bolon waterway and the wetlands beyond."

"Very cool. But I have to ask, 'Fatty'? Either your parents had an interesting sense of humor or someone had a great sense of irony when selecting your nick-name."

"Oh no, Fatty is not an ironic nick-name. It's a common surname in the Mandinka language, my native tongue. English is taught and spoken here as a holdover from British colonial days."

"Okay, outstanding. Learned something new today. So how do you know Ron Bailey?"

"We met years ago when he was assigned to the US Embassy security detail. He intervened in a street fight, saved my life that day. We've kept in touch over the years as he moved up the military ranks and into his new, unique career. Ah, we are here."

The three men arrived at the jetty. Several boxes and fuel cans sat on the end. Chief Hurd pulled a test kit from his pocket and drew a sample from one of the fuel cans. After checking the fuel for water and sediments, he turned to Morgan.

"Looks good, sir. This will get us where we need to be and then some."

"Excellent, Chief. Call them in."

Marvelous Marvin pulled a hand-held radio from his belt and spoke into it.

"Dallas, Marvelous, we're good to go here. Bring the boats."

Back over at the river bend, Chief Shaw answered the radio.

"Roger. On our way."

Dallas whistled to the other boat's engineer while twirling his right index finger over his head. The engineer waved back and both boats pulled away from the river bank.

Séverin Delaunay danced with the hot, American blonde on the Bambo Bar's dance floor. The tall, blonde Frenchman was dressed in khaki shirt and shorts, projecting the 'great white hunter' image he fostered as a tour guide at Kiang West National Park. He also worked as the eyes and ears of some of the local criminal gangs as a means to supplement his meager income. He received word to be on the lookout for two, unusual boats. Not the fishing boats common on the river, but something bigger and much more modern.

As he held on to the blonde, Delaunay's ears picked up on an unusual sound coming up over the music, the sound of diesel engines. He bent down to speak with his partner.

"Would you like another beer?" he asked while shouting over the music.

"Sure!" his partner shouted back.

Delaunay moved off the dance floor and walked towards the bar. On the way over, he looked out over the river and saw two boats moving towards the tourist boat jetty.

That has to be them.

He pulled his cell phone out of his pocket and dialed a number from memory.

"*C'est Delaunay. Deux bateaux se dirigent vers la jetée.*" (This is Delaunay. Two boats are heading towards the jetty.)

Delaunay ended the call and returned his phone to his shirt pocket, then picked up two beers from the bar tender. He returned to his date and noticed that her dancing began to become more provocative. He handed her the sweaty beer bottle. She kissed him on the mouth sloppily.

"Thank you, baby!" she said.

Well, this is going to be a very interesting evening.

The two boats glided quietly from around the small peninsula where the hotel and Bambo Bar sat and arrived at the jetty. Galahad deployed his SEALs to the foot of the jetty to provide security as the boats re-fueled and re-supplied. The Judge and his counterpart on Chief Hurd's boat took the jerry cans of fuel over to their respective boats and began emptying them into their fuel tanks. Morgan and Dallas took the time to examine the other supplies on the pier. Dallas knelt to examine a pelican case.

"Trackers? Though they look more advanced than what we use."

Morgan took a look.

"They're from my current employer. Specifically, a gentleman named Chop."

"Former Navy supply guy?"

"Of course."

Morgan found a note in the case.

Gargoyle,

Something for your friend with the DGSE at their request. Good luck!

Chop

Morgan called M. Hachette over.

"A present for you, *Monsieur*. A token of Franco-American friendship," Morgan said with a smirk.

The DGSE operative took a look inside the case and smiled.

"Ah *merci, mon ami*! I've been expecting this. Chop came through as always."

"You know him?"

"*Oui*! He has helped my agency in the past. He's quite the genius, no?"

"Yes, he is. I have him to thank for my prosthetic eye."

M. Hachette grabbed the case and headed to his boat while the other crew members took some boxes on board.

"Fresh food!" El Fantasma said with an excited grin. "Beats the MREs we brought."

"There is a farmer's market to the east." Abdou pointed in that direction. "Quite convenient."

Morgan heard a voice in his ear.

"Gargoyle, Galahad."

"Gargoyle, go."

"Sir, there is movement around the building closest to the jetty."

"Roger, stand by." Morgan turned to Abdou and pointed to a series of single-story white buildings with two towers at the center. "What's that building?"

"That's the Tendaba mosque. The two towers at the centers are the minarets"

"Ah, shit. Galahad, Gargoyle, that's the local mosque. Hold fire unless directly fired upon."

"Aye, sir."

Morgan gathered Marvelous and Dallas.

"We may have company, get this wrapped up and everyone back on the boats."

The two craft masters tended to their boats and Morgan turned to Abdou.

"Any insurgent activity around here?"

"No, most activity is in the north of Senegal…"

Abdou's voice ended abruptly as his head exploded in a spray of blood, brain matter, and bone. As the man's body fell to the ground, Morgan took cover behind some boxes.

"Sniper! Galahad, do you see him?"

"Got him, he's hiding in the mosque, up in the minaret."

"Take him."

Galahad's team sniper took aim with his MK 13 Mod 5 .300 caliber bolt-action rifle. The target stood out like a sore thumb in the sniper's night scope. He squeezed the trigger, and Abdou's death had been avenged. An explosive response came from the grounds around the mosque as automatic weapons fire rained down on the jetty.

Morgan shouted, "Covering fire! Get back to the boats!"

LT Coslick and his team began to return fire, being careful not to shoot directly at the building. The SEALs fell back by the numbers back to the boats. El Fantasma and his counterpart had uncovered the boats' GAU-17 7.62 millimeter six-barreled electrically-driven Gatling guns. Firing at rate of 6,000 rounds per minute, the mini-guns laid down suppressing fire to either side of the mosque, covering the SEAL's return to the boats. Once all hands were on board, the two craft masters cut the mooring lines and pulled away from the jetty at boats' full speed of 40 knots. They maintained maximum speed until navigating a right-hand bend in the river putting a large chunk of land between them and the threat.

Once around the river bend, the two boats drew next to each other. Morgan spoke with Chief Shaw, and everyone on his boat were safe and accounted for. Morgan called over to Chief Hurd and LT Coslick.

"Everyone alright?"

"All members of my team are accounted for," LT Coslick said. Chief Hurd added, "My boat's okay. We finished re-fueling before the attack."

"Outstanding. M. Hachette, please find out if the target is still heading up the river. If it is, we'll continue to close until we get close enough for visual confirmation, then pull back."

"Who the hell attacked us? Insurgents?" LT Coslick asked.

"Maybe," Morgan began. "Or our mission may have been compromised to our targets."

"Do we continue?"

"Yes, we've gone this far. We just need to be prepared for further attacks. M. Hachette, any word from the Reaper?"

"*Oui*, the target is still moving at ten knots and is about 20 miles ahead of us."

"Perfect. Let's get underway."

With that, the two boats continued down the river and deeper into the Gambian jungle. Judge walked up and stood alongside Morgan.

"Sir, this evening's frivolities are yet another reminder of my overall philosophy on life."

"What's that, Judge?"

"Never get off the boat."

CHAPTER
THIRTY-EIGHT

Gambia River, west of the village of Gouloubou, Senegal
12 Hours Later

Chief Shaw looked at his boat's navigation system and the satellite imagery provided by Commander Morgan. Moving his finger along the intended track along the river and matching what the electronic chart showed versus what the terrain actually looked like. Frowning to himself, he looked up to see Morgan on the bow.

"Gargoyle! Could you come over, please?"

Morgan moved aft, stepping over a couple of napping SEALs to the boat's wheel where Chief Shaw stood.

"Hey, Dallas. What do you have?"

"I have an idea about where the transfer will take place."

"Oh?"

"West of the village of Gouloubou, Senegal there is a bridge across the river that allows the N6 highway to continue from the south. The height of the bridge listed on the chart is too low for that tow boat to pass under, so they can't go any further. Looking at the satellite imagery your other employer provided, there is a clearing on the northern bank just to the west of the bridge that would be perfect to offload those trucks and trailers. There is a dirt road connecting that clearing to the N6 which connects to the N1 at Tabacounda, then heads into western Mali."

Morgan looked at the charts and imagery and gave Dallas a look of sheer admiration.

"Well shit, Dallas, you should have my job. That's absolutely brilliant. I should have seen that myself. Close the other boat so we can pass the word."

"Aye, sir," Dallas turned the boat's helm towards its sister.

Once alongside, Morgan briefed Galahad and Marvelous Marvin on the plan. Once everyone understood what would happen, the two SOC-Rs continued along the river. As the jungle moved by, Morgan reflected on the past 12 hours.

After the ambush and subsequent escape, Morgan called General Bailey directly over the satellite phone.

"General, this is Gargoyle. I am prepared to authenticate."

"Okay, authenticate Romeo Alpha Alpha 67."

"I authenticate Kilo Sierra Alpha 73."

"Okay, good evening Bob."

"Good evening, General. I'm calling with some sad news." Morgan went on to update the General on the re-supply stop, the ambush, and the death of his friend.

General Bailey's anger and sadness was evident in his voice, even over the phone, "Someone over here told tales out of school. And when I find out who, I'll see to it they spent the rest of their lives in a Supermax prison."

"Yes, sir. Judging by the force that ambushed us, it looked like someone sold tickets. And using the mosque as cover, brilliant. If they had hit a few minutes sooner, we would have aborted the mission due to lack of fuel. The boats crews finished the refueling in record time. It's lucky we got out of there with our lives let alone still fully mission capable."

"Any idea on how much longer before the opposition off loads the barge?"

"Not yet, sir. It has to be soon, we're in Senegal now, and we're running out of river."

"Concur. Careful out there and take care of them for me and Abdou."

"With pleasure, sir. Gargoyle out."

After hanging up, Morgan grabbed a quick nap at the front of the boat, sleeping so soundly that, when he finally awoke, he once again forgot where he was. Stretching, he looked around and marveled at the flora and fauna he saw along the river bank. As he admired the view, Petty Officer Sharpe, the newest and, at 19 by far the youngest member of Chief Shaw's crew, came up to him.

"Sir, what are those large floating things over by the river bank?"

"Those, Emilio, are hippopotami."

"Hippos? They don't look very cute or cuddly."

"Ha, far from it. Those animals are responsible for 500 deaths a year on the continent. Not something you'd want for Christmas, despite the song."

"Song?"

"'I Want a Hippopotamus for Christmas'."

"Never heard of it."

"Damn, I'm old..."

Now, after Chief Shaw's analysis, the boats had a destination, and the end to all this was neigh. Morgan moved from the control station to the boat's fantail where M. Hachette was eating from one of the boat's Meals Ready to Eat with a look of distain. He looked on with amusement as the French agent placed the MRE in a trash bag and grabbed one of the marulas included with the previous night's fresh food delivery.

"*Bonjour Monsieur Hachette! Petit déjeuner pas à votre goût?*

(Good morning Mister Hachette! Breakfast not to your liking?) Morgan asked with the somewhat passible French he took in high school.

"*Ah non. Ce n'est pas exactement le comble de la cuisine.*" (Ah, no. This is not exactly the height of cuisine.).

M. Hachette continued in English, "By the way, Gargoyle, your French needs work."

"You're not kidding. It feels like I'm gagging on something when I try to speak it. Switched to German in college. I have something I need you pass to your Reaper operators."

"Oui?"

"Chief Shaw looked over the charts and imagery this morning. He believes that the transfer will take place at or around Gouloubou, Senegal. There is a bridge there that's too low for the barge and tow boat to sail under, and there is a nearby clearing with road access for the trucks. We're still about 12 hours away from the area."

"Ah, merci. Chief Shaw and the rest of your U.S. Navy, eh, '*Les Gars de Bateau Sale*' are most impressive. Our *Commandos Marine* could use these boats. I'll pass on this information immediately."

"Thank you, sir. Our Dirty Boat Guys do indeed rock."

Morgan turned away as M. Hachette pulled out his satellite phone.

Aurora awoke in her cabin on the push boat to some good news. They will be at the rendezvous in about twelve hours. Another half day on board the rust bucket and she can get ashore to see to the offload of the five MLRS trucks and the on load of the next group of people bound for new lives in Europe. Then she'd board one of her father's helicopters for the trip to Dakar and a private flight back to Copenhagen. There was a knock on her door.

"Yes? Come in."

The push boat master entered the cabin.

"Good morning, Lady Aurora. We received a phone call from your father. Our operatives ambushed a group of Americans last night. They were in two boats in the vicinity of village of Tendaba, Gambia. They were re-fueling their boats when we attacked, but the boats had a pair of mini-guns that repulsed our people. We have to assume that they are still behind us."

"Do we have enough protection at our rendezvous site?"

"Yes, ma'am. Your father sent additional people when he received word on the American team."

"Thank you, Captain. Anything else?"

"No ma'am."

"Then that will be all."

The captain bowed slightly and left the cabin. *So, Morgan's nearby, nice. I have some unpleasant things in mind to do to him if I have the opportunity. He hurt father and me, hurt us dearly. And for that, he will pay, dearly.*

CHAPTER
THIRTY-NINE

Village of Gouloubou, Senegal
Sunset

The French Reaper operators contacted M. Hachette an hour prior to sunset, the barge had stopped at the clearing identified by Chief Shaw earlier in the day. With that report, Morgan and his team pulled the boats over to the north bank of the Gambia two kilometers upriver from the clearing and waited for the coming darkness. Morgan sent Galahad and his SEALs ashore to approach from the landward side, north, and west the clearing. They would also observe the offload of the five MLRS trucks and trailers and, when the trucks are clear, cue the attack. M. Hachette joined Galahad's team to attempt to affix the trackers picked up the day before.

"Gargoyle, Galahad," Morgan heard in his ear-piece as he stood on the river bank.

"Go."

"We're in position. The clearing is lit up like a Christmas tree, truck mounted lights at all four corners. We can see the barge's crane moving to land the first of the five trucks. There is also a cargo container sitting off to the side."

"Roger, can you see if there are air holes along the container's upper edge?"

"Stand by."

Morgan communicated to Dallas and Marvelous via hand signals to meet him on the bank. After a few minutes, Galahad's voice came back over the radio.

"Gargoyle, Galahad, several holes are visible on the infra-red. Looks like air holes. Break. I can also see our primary person of interest moving by the container."

Lady Aurora, excellent.

"Roger, copy all. Enemy strength?"

"Looking at about ten or so with side arms and SMGs split between the barge and the clearing. There is civilian helicopter in the clearing's Northeast corner and some off-road vehicles next to it."

Aurora's ride home no doubt.

"Roger, pass to M. Hachette he's go for his mission."

"Roger, sir. Out."

Morgan turned to Chiefs Shaw and Hurd.

"Dallas, Marvelous," he said. "When we get the word that M. Hachette completed his task, man the guns and get underway." Both men whispered a quick "Aye, sir," and returned to their boats. A few more moments passed then Galahad's voice retuned.

"Gargoyle, Galahad, M. Hachette is on the move."

Two kilometers from Morgan and the boats, M. Hachette crouched next to LT Coslick, the high grasses, and trees concealing them from the opposition. They observed the barge crew attaching the crane's hook to the second truck and trailer pair after the first pair landed ashore and moved away from the river bank. Galahad spoke into his whisper mike.

"Roger, sir, out."

He turned and whispered to the French agent.

"You're go, sir."

"*Merci, lieutenant. Bonne chance à nous tous.*" (Thank you, Lieutenant. Good luck to us all.)

M. Hachette moved quickly and quietly clock-wise around the clearing's edge. He stopped at the clearing's eastern edge, a few meters from the first MLRS truck/trailer combination. He crouched in the low grass and crawled silently towards the trailer. Once he reached the trailer, he placed one of Chop's tracking devices in the undercarriage in a place where it would both stay put and not be found without a deliberate search. With the trailer tracker in place, he moved to the truck and placed a second tracker, just in case. The job done, he crawled back into the cover provided by the trees. Looking back at the MLRS, he keyed his throat microphone twice, the 'mission accomplished' signal.

LT Coslick keyed his microphone twice in response acknowledging the French agent's transmission.

Morgan also heard the clicks and responded, "Roger, mission complete. Stand by, we'll wait until the last truck lands on the beach."

Morgan's team waited patiently and observed the landing of the final three MLRSs. After the fifth truck went feet dry, a group of drivers climbed into the cabs, started the engines, and lumbered towards the dirt road that turned north outside the clearing. This road led eventually to a paved road, which connected to the north-south N6 motorway.

Once the diesel engine noise of the last truck faded into the distance, Morgan keyed his mic and sent a one-word command to his team.

"Go."

CHAPTER
FORTY

Village of Gouloubou, Senegal
Sunset
A Few Minutes Earlier...

Lady Aurora walked around the clearing, watching the off load of the five MLRSs. Her father would be happy with the speed and efficiency of the barge crew and the local Jama'a Nusrat ul-Islam wa al-Muslimin militiamen as they moved the vehicles ashore. She also watched over the cargo container with the latest load of 'immigrants' heading to the brothels and sweatshops of Europe and, eventually, the Mideast and the United States. She was a bit disappointed, however that there were no candidates in this group for some 'distractions.' *Oh well, I'll be on my way out of here after the container is loaded on the barge for the trip back down the river. Guess Morgan couldn't make the party...*

The sound of several diesel engines starting caught Aurora's attention. All five of the MLRS trucks and trailers came to life and began their trek to join the JNIM forces in Mali, their ultimate destination. Aurora watched as they rolled away from the clearing and towards the dirt road, the sounds of their engines eventually replaced by the sounds of the surrounding savannah.

Good, now to get the container on the barge and myself on the helicopter.

She turned away from the edge of the water and walked towards her waiting aircraft. She saw the pilot leaning against the Agusta Westland AW189 passenger helicopter. Her father had spent what her late, English husband called a pretty penny in modifying the eleven square meter passenger area for maximum connectivity, with a large screen display and several tablet computers, and maximum comfort with leather seating and a built-in, well stocked, refrigerated bar, that made the aircraft's maximum range of 700 miles fly by smoothly. She waived at the pilot to get his attention when the sound of diesel engines returned to her ears. She began to wonder if the trucks were returning when all hell broke loose.

At Morgan's go, the two SOC-R boats started their engines and moved towards the clearing at full throttle. At the same time, Galahad and his SEALs began their assault, attacking Aurora's forces from both the western and northern sides of the clearing. Once the initial shock of the attack wore off, they began to return fire. Morgan had one the boats cover the clearing's southern side while the other attacked the barge and tow boat.

Morgan leaned toward Chief Shaw, "Bring the boat parallel with the beach to bring the 50 cals to bear."

"Aye, sir!"

Dallas turned the boat hard to port and kicked in astern thrust on the boat's waterjets that brought the boat to an immediate halt. On the deck, Petty Officers Hernandez and Haugen poured on fire from the GAU-17 and the M240 with Petty Officer Sharpe pounding away from the aft mounted M2. Chief Hurd and his crew flew by Morgan at speed as they attacked the tow boat.

Morgan keyed his microphone, "Keep your fire away from

the cargo container! There are people inside. Galahad, form a perimeter around the container, keep them protected!"

Galahad led one of his two squads of eight SEALs from the western edge of the clearing to the cargo container with one fire team of four SEALs forming a protective semicircle around it as the second fire team advanced on the barge and pusher boat. At the north-west corner, ENS Patel led his two fire teams directly towards the barge.

Aurora's forces fell back towards the barge and tow boat, but they were only trading space for time. She pulled a small radio from her belt as she stayed crouched down in the grass and out of the line of fire.

"Now!"

From the east side of the clearing, a heavy machine gun opened fire. The rain of 7.62-millimeter rounds immediately cut down ENS Patel and his fire team. The rest of the Patel's squad dove for cover along with Galahad and his squad.

"Rocket!" Galahad shouted.

One member of Galahad's fire team brought himself to his knees and brought a M136 AT4 Rocket Launcher to his shoulder. He sighted in the weapon on the machine gun's muzzle flashes and squeezed the trigger. The 84-millimeter rocket shot from the launching tube at a velocity of 950 feet per second and flew into the jungle. Its high explosive, dual purpose warhead impacted the ground just in front of the machine gun emplacement and exploded. The resulting explosion and fireball silenced the machine gun and shredded several of Aurora's men. Despite this, more men came out from the jungle, firing their AK-47s as they entered the clearing. Galahad keyed his mic.

"Gargoyle, we have several more troops coming out from the jungle to the east!"

Morgan received Galahad's update and directed his boat's fire towards the oncoming threat. The boat's mini-guns mowed down the rushing troops like so much high grass. With the threat eliminated, Galahad's fire team and the remainder of his second squad advanced on the tow boat.

Morgan began to turn his attention towards the cargo container when movement on the tow boat caught his eye. He saw one of the boat's crew lifting a long, cylindrical object onto his right shoulder.

"RPG!" Morgan shouted as he dove to the deck.

The rocket propelled grenade left its launcher and struck Chief Hurd's boat with devastating effect. The fully fueled, fully armed SOC-R exploded with a massive fireball, killing all on board. Morgan shook off the blast and jumped off his SOC-R and ran towards the tow boat.

"Covering fire!"

Morgan moved towards the RPG gunner as the boat's fire kept the pusher boat's crew's head pinned to the deck. Morgan intended to attack before the gunner had the chance to reload. He leapt onto the tow boat's deck, shooting a couple of its crew with his Mk 18 Close Quarter Battle Rifle along the way. He reached the gunner and raised his rifle to engage, but the gunner swung the empty launcher like a club knocking the rifle out of Morgan's hands. Morgan drew his Guardian II knife and plunged it into the gunner's abdomen. The gunner fell to the deck while holding his intestines in with his hands and bleeding profusely. Morgan grabbed him by the neck and belt, lifted him over the deck railing, and tossed him into the river. Instead of the expected splash, Morgan heard a dull thud followed by a roar, and finally a horrific scream.

Hippo! Holy shit!

Morgan saw the river run red with the gunner's blood as he was torn apart by the gigantic animal.

Ewww!

Morgan took a moment to look over the clearing and saw that despite the loss of Chief Hurd's boat and one Galahad's fire teams, it appeared that his team had won they day as many of the opposition lay dead or dying.

"Check fire!" Morgan called over his microphone. The fire from his men stopped as both the SEALs and remaining SWCCs assessed the situation. Over his earpiece, Morgan heard the voice of Petty Officer Haugen.

"I see Aurora! I'm going after her!" Judge shouted.

He jumped out of the boat and ran towards the woman.

"Judge! Wait! Stay on the boat!"

Morgan jumped ashore from the tow boat and ran towards Judge.

Judge approached the woman, who was pulling herself up slowly from the ground. She glanced behind her and saw that her helicopter, despite the firefight, was not damaged and ready to go. She raised a single finger in the air and spun it in a circle, the international signal for 'spin the rotors.' She turned towards Judge and smiled.

"Place your hands on your head and get back on the ground!" Judge shouted.

Aurora began to slowly raise her hands, but drew a FN 509 handgun from behind her back and fired a single round. The nine-millimeter bullet struck Judge directly in the forehead, killing him instantly. As Judge's body fell, Morgan shouted out as he ran towards the pair.

"Aurora! You bitch!"

Aurora looked directly at Morgan, blew him a kiss, gave him a quick wave, and ran towards the awaiting aircraft. She managed two steps before a shot rang out and she dropped to the ground. She dragged herself back up and limped towards the helicopter while holding her right leg. After a few more steps, the Agusta exploded and the subsequent shockwave knocked Aurora flat on her back. Morgan looked on in shock at both the wounded Aurora and the wreckage of the aircraft.

Holy fuck! What the hell was that!? I ordered a check fire!

Morgan was about to become rude on the radio when M. Hachette, holding his Heckler and Koch HK416 assault rifle, walked up beside him.

"*Il y en a toujours un qui essaie de courir. Oui*?" (There is always one who tries to run. Yes?)

"There is one indeed, *mon amie*. Do I have you to thank for the strike on the helicopter?"

"*Oui, Gargouille*. It took me a few minutes to connect to the Reaper pilots, but I passed on the helicopter as a high priority target."

"*Exceptionnel*. I'll take it from here."

Morgan walked over the prostrate form of Aurora, blinking his left eye three times as he did so. He drew his Smith & Wesson from its shoulder holster and stood over her, watching her over the pistol's sights as she breathed heavily. Morgan looked at her bloody right knee, shattered by M. Hachette's rifle shot.

"Well, that makes up for Lieutenant Kroll." Morgan grabbed Aurora by the hair and looked into her eyes.

"Who's bankrolling you, Aurora? You and Edward don't have the cash to afford the types of weapons you've been smuggling. Who are you working for?" Morgan asked.

"*Spis lort og dø*!" (Eat shit and die!) Aurora shouted. She then spat in his face.

Morgan then pointed his weapon at Aurora's left knee and squeezed the trigger. The 115 grain nine-millimeter, Hydra Shok hollow point round struck her left knee just under the patella bone. The round mushroomed to its full size as it tore through the knee's ligaments and cartilage. Aurora screamed in pain.

"You bastard!"

Morgan bared his teeth, showing her his oversized canines. She looked back at him in horror.

"That was for Judge. Now I'll ask again, who are you working for?"

"I can't answer that. That will sign my and my father's death warrants. We told you in Singapore, this is bigger than you realize."

"We can protect you."

"No, you can't. They will find us. They will find you. Both you and your little English whore are dead!"

Morgan realized that getting Aurora to talk was useless. Her loyalty to her father and fear of whatever organization they worked for was just too great. He pointed his weapon at her abdomen and squeezed the trigger again. This time, the round tore through her intestines before shattering her L3 vertebra. She howled in pain again, and blood began to flow from her mouth.

"That's for all the women and children you exploited. Last chance."

Aurora spat her blood on Morgan's glasses, one last act of defiance. Grabbing her by her hair, he finally pointed the Smith & Wesson at Aurora's left eye and whispered in her ear.

"This is for me ... milady."

He squeezed the trigger one last time. The bullet sent Aurora's brain matter into the Senegalese soil. Morgan tossed her now dead skull contemptuously to the ground, blinked rapidly three times, and keyed his microphone.

"This is Gargoyle, secure the people in the cargo container, and assess our casualties. Let's see where we stand."

Morgan moved to Judge's body. As he kneeled over him, Morgan choked back a tear and closed Judge's still open eyes.

"Damn it, Judge. You should have stayed on the boat."

Morgan stood up and began to see with a look of shock as what was left of his team begin to assemble. Of the sixteen SEALs and eight SWCCs, only ten SEALs and three SWCCs survived. They also had only one of their two SOC-R boats left. Morgan had the remains of his team gather the dead and see to the trafficked people in the container. Agency cleaners would arrive as soon as he passed the word to Langley, the mole no longer being a threat to the mission. As he supervised the clean-up, Morgan noticed M. Hachette walking away.

"Hey! *Où diable vas-tu?*" (Hey! Where the hell are you going?)

"Your mission is finished, *Monsieur Gargouille*, but mine is just beginning. *Bonne chance et bonne chance! J'espère que nous nous reverrons.*" (Good luck and Godspeed! Hopefully we'll meet again.).

M. Hachette headed towards the group of vehicles at the edge of the clearing. He found an apparently undamaged Toyota Hilux pick-up truck, started the engine, gave Morgan a salute, and drove away from the clearing following the MLRS trucks' path.

CHAPTER
FORTY-ONE

Peter G. Decker Half Moone Cruise and Celebration Center
Norfolk, Virginia
Four Days Later...

Morgan stood in the back of the Peter G. Decker Half Moone Cruise and Celebration Center's Grand Rotunda, his eyes, hidden by his Matsuda sunglasses, scanning the thickening crowd. The downtown Norfolk, Virginia venue was playing host to a fundraising luncheon for the People for the Ethical Treatment of Animals, or PETA. With its headquarters merely a mile and a half away, the use of the Half Moone facility made perfect sense.

The luncheon crowd began taking their seats, jockeying for ones with the best view of either the Elizabeth River vista visible through the two-story high windows, or the event's two speakers, Ms. Ingrid Newkirk, one of PETA's founders and the keynote speaker and the event's single largest contributor, Edward Rasmussen. Morgan and a team of F.B.I. agents, along with officers from the Norfolk Police department, laid in wait for Edward with an international arrest warrant and a set of hand cuffs. Looking around, Morgan thoughts drifted back to the events of the past few days…

A few hours after sunrise, Morgan's team had gathered their dead and wounded while stacking the bodies of the opposition along the river, including the late Lady Aurora. Once they finished, Morgan and Galahad gathered their men in the shelter of what was left of the tow boat, its hull now riddled with bullet holes, then headed over to the cargo container. Galahad placed himself in a 45-degree angle from the container's door, covering the entrance with his Mk 18 CQBR. Morgan opened the door and found about a dozen or so Africans huddled in the corner with four of them lying dead on the container's floor.

Morgan whispered as he took in the scene.

"Holy shit."

He called Galahad over.

"Paul, grab your medic and get back over here."

"Aye, sir," Galahad headed back to the tow boat.

Morgan called into the container, "Hello? Can anyone speak English? *Quelqu'un peut-il parler français?*" ("Can anyone speak French?")

A young man raised his hand, "*Je peux parler français.*" (I can speak French).

Morgan gestured with his hand, bidding the young man to exit the container. Morgan continued in French.

"Hello, my name is Robert. Can you tell me what happened here?"

"Hello, my name is Amder Ag Buzin. We all paid 5 million francs to be taken to Europe for employment. We were told that jobs awaited us. We were about to be loaded onto the barge when the bullets began to penetrate the container. These men covered the rest of us with their bodies to protect us.

"Shit. These men died heroes. Okay, we are here to help. We have medical personnel to help with any wounded. We can then get you

where you want to go whether that be home or somewhere else. Could you please pass this on?

"*Oui monsieur. Merci beaucoup.*" (Yes, sir. Thank you very much.) Amder said turning to the rest of the group.

Morgan left the container and met Galahad and his platoon's medic outside.

"There is one young man who can speak French. He's passing on the plan to the rest of the people. You speak any French?"

"No, but my medic does, at last well enough to get the job done."

"Good, let's get these people taken care of."

Galahad and his medic began to work as Morgan walked back to the tow boat. He met up with Chief Shaw and together they gathered any extra food and water they could scrounge for the people trapped in the container, along with any potential intelligence material and other important items. Once they finished, they carried what they had and passed it out amongst the people. Morgan was speaking with Amder when he heard the sound of helicopters. He passed the word to the team to take defensive positions, with Morgan himself covering the container. With everyone ready, Morgan took the time to look up and saw the source of the sound, two unmarked, Russian-built Mi-17 'Hip' cargo helicopters.

Ah, bless you Air Branch!

The two helicopters landed in the clearing and immediately lowered their cargo ramps. A four-man security team exited each aircraft and set up a perimeter. Once the helicopter's rotors came to a stop, a tall man with salt-and-pepper hair and dressed in a well-tailored, and quite incongruous, Tom Ford suit exited one of the Hips. Morgan looked on with an expression hovering somewhere between anger and disgust.

Jesus Christ, Stone. What the flying fuck is that son of a bitch doing here?

Morgan gave his team the all clear and walked up to the head of the Agency's Special Activities Center.

"Good morning, Malcom. Fancy meeting you here," Morgan said, sarcasm dripping like a leaky faucet.

"Morgan! What are you doing here?" Stone asked. "Ms. McCulloch sent me here to clean up a weapons smuggling operation, and she made no mention of you. I didn't authorize you participating in any missions."

"That's because I'm working for General Bailey and Ms. McCulloch directly on this operation. There's a leak back at Langley that, even using Navy assets instead of Maritime Branch personnel, almost ended this mission. So, we kept it quiet, and it's going to stay that way since there is one last target to get."

"You went over my head?"

"Well, more like climbed over your head and kicking you in the teeth on the way up…"

"Fuck you, you little prick! As far as I'm concerned, your Agency career is over. Nobody does an end around on me!"

"Well, we'll just see about that. Meanwhile, I have my team and a group of refugees to get out of here. You ready to help or not?"

"My instructions were to clean up the scene and extract the team to Dakar where we have a plane waiting, nothing about refugees."

"Well, they're coming with us, at least as far as Dakar. If you don't like that, we can always call General Bailey…"

Stone stared at Morgan with a look that would have killed lesser men. Morgan stared back with look that said, 'go ahead and call my bluff.' Finally, Stone blinked, both literally and figuratively.

"Fine. Get them on the aircraft as soon as the clean-up crew is done."

"Will do."

Morgan and his team assisted Stone's cleaners with sanitizing the area, collecting the bodies of the fallen and burying the opposition in-place. Morgan took the opportunity to spit on Aurora one last time as the dirt covered her corpse.

Burn in hell, you bitch!

Part of the clean-up included incinerating what was left of Chief Hurd's SOC-R as well as Chief Shaw's boat.

"Ah, it breaks the heart. She was a great boat," Dallas said. "The guys at Two-Two are not going be too happy with me, I signed for those boats."

Morgan replied with a friendly smirk, "Don't worry Dallas, they'll just dock your pay from now 'til doomsday."

"Wonderful, sir."

By late afternoon, the cleaners were finished, and all parties were ready to leave. Morgan turned to Amder.

"Okay Amder, time to get your people on the aircraft. Please let them know we are taking them to Dakar. From there, they are on their own."

"Thank you, Mr. Robert. I'll let them know."

Amder led the rest of the refugees onto the aircraft. Once they settled in, Morgan watched as his team boarded. He took one last look around, amazed at the work of the cleaners, and boarded the aircraft. The cargo ramp closed as the rotors came up to speed. The first Hip leaped into the air followed closely by the second.

Two hours later, the Hips landed near a hangar towards the back of Dakar's Blaise Diagne International Airport. They taxied towards a pair of fixed wing aircraft. One was a Boeing C-32 jet transport, a modified version of the company's 757 jetliner, and the second was a Gulfstream V business jet. Both operated by the Agency's Air Branch. The helicopters came to a stop and the cargo ramps opened. Morgan hit the tarmac and watched as his team and the refugees exited the Hips. Morgan walked over to Amder.

"Amder my friend, I have something for you."

Morgan pulled something from his cargo pants pocket.

Amder looked in wide eyed wonder at the stack of cash Morgan placed in his hands.

"I liberated this from the boat's safe. Please divide this amongst the rest of the refugees. Hopefully, this will allow you to get to where you want to be."

"Thank you, Robert! I'll never forget your generosity, and your humanity."

Morgan replied with a smirk, *"You are most welcome my friend, just keep the humanity thoughts to yourself please. I have a reputation to consider."*

He left Amder to see to his fellow refugees as he walked over to the Gulfstream. The front door of the jet opened, and Morgan saw a very familiar, and very attractive auburn-haired woman wearing battle dress come down the ladder.

"Sierra Hotel!" Morgan cried out.

Susan waved and as they met, then gave Morgan a big hug.

"Glad to see you in one piece, stories of the fight along the Gambia River are beginning to circulate."

"You and me both, Susan. You taking me back to the States in this lovely thing?" Morgan pointed to the Gulfstream.

"Yes and no. General Bailey sent this for you to get you back to the States as quickly as possible, but I have a job here to see to."

"Indeed. Anything you can tell me about?"

"Afraid not. Go ahead and board, the flight crew is waiting for you."

"Take care of yourself and good luck."

Susan said with a smile, "You too." She walked towards the hangar.

Morgan stood at the ladder and watched as Chief Shaw, Lieutenant Coslick and the rest of the team lined up to board the C-32. Morgan jogged over to the pair.

"Dallas, Galahad, you taking care of the remains?" Morgan asked.

"Yes, sir," Galahad replied. "We'll let you know about arrangements when they are made."

"Thanks Paul. I'd like to fly with you guys, but I'm needed back in the States as soon as possible. I have one more person to see to." Morgan said as he pointed to the Gulfstream.

"Good luck to you, sir," Dallas said. "I'm sure you'll hate every minute of your flight."

Morgan threw the pair a quick salute and ran back to the Gulfstream. When he arrived, he saw Stone arguing with the flight crew.

"Get out of my way! This is obviously my aircraft," Stone shouted.

"Sorry, sir," the aircraft captain said. "My instructions were to return only one passenger."

"Yes, me!"

The captain said, "No, sir, him," and pointed at Morgan.

Morgan flipped Stone a jaunty wave of his hand followed by a rude, single fingered gesture as he boarded the aircraft. The captain followed quickly behind him as the flight attendant pulled up the boarding ladder and closed the aircraft door. The last thing Morgan saw was Stone's expression of unbridled rage as the door sealed shut.

CHAPTER
FORTY-TWO

Peter G. Decker Half Moone Cruise and Celebration Center
Norfolk, Virginia

Morgan smirked to himself at the memory of Stone standing on the tarmac in Senegal.

That will never get old. Wonder if he ever got a flight back to the States?

He shook his head to clear his thoughts and focus on the job at hand. He looked around the rotunda again and listened as one of the PETA staffers conducted a quick sound check from lectern's microphone. Morgan conducted his own check, specifically his Beretta Nano tucked in his shoulder holster under the jacket of his light grey, sharkskin suit.

The flight back to the States was uneventful save for the debrief he held with General Bailey via the aircraft's secure video tele-conferencing system. It was friendly enough, but somewhat too long for Morgan's taste, especially in his exhausted state. General Bailey noticed Morgan's failing attention manifested in his drooping eyelids and bobbing head.

"Bob, you okay?'

Morgan shook himself awake.

"Oh, yes sir, just a bit tired."

"Get some sleep Bob, I have what we need to continue, especially the information on your warmer than expected reception. We've kept the action in Senegal out of the media, so Rasmussen doesn't know what happened. He's keeping his normal schedule as a result. Right now, he's in the U.S., touring the country raising money for homeless animals. We'll get him at his next stop."

"Where's that, General?"

"Norfolk. He's addressing a PETA fundraiser the day after tomorrow."

"Norfolk? Perfect! I know a guy. But that can wait a few hours. Anything else, sir?"

"No, get some rest. It's not over yet."

Morgan didn't hear the General's sign off as he immediately fell asleep on the cabin's couch. He also didn't notice when the flight attendant drew a blanket over his sleeping form.

Morgan awoke when the Gulfstream flew east of the Virginia Capes, and he had slept right through a re-fueling stop in the Azores. He grabbed an acceptable cup of coffee from the aircraft's galley and turned on his phone. He received a text from Chop:

Gargoyle,

I've made reservations for you at the Hilton Norfolk, right across the street from the cruise terminal. A package with your suit, roller bag, and other items is waiting for you there. I'll spare you the rude note the Copenhagen Chief of Station included with your things. You are definitely not on his Christmas card list. Also, your car has been moved from NAS Norfolk to a spot in the Town Point parking garage next to the hotel. Good luck!

Morgan smiled to himself after reading the message.

Well done, Chop! There's a great restaurant and beer garden on the hotel's roof.

Morgan sent a series of texts and placed a phone call or two from the aircraft's leather couch to arrange for a warm reception for Edward when he shows up at the fundraiser. As he was finishing up, Morgan heard the aircraft's captain over the speakers.

"Gargoyle, we're in final approach to Norfolk international airport. Please stow anything you may have pulled out and fasten your seat belt. The local time is 09:00."

The Gulfstream landed at Norfolk airport after flying an approach that took it over the Little Creek amphibious base and its air cushioned landing craft parking area. It taxied to the corporate aircraft terminal at the far end of the airport, opposite the main passenger terminal, and came to stop. The flight attendant opened the door and lowered the ladder. Morgan thanked the flight crew profusely as he exited the aircraft, especially for letting him sleep undisturbed. He entered the executive terminal, arranged a taxi ride, and when it arrived, headed downtown.

Morgan took the longest shower of his life after he checked into his room at the Hilton, scrubbing off nearly a week of sweat, dirt, and blood from his body. He examined the package Chop mentioned and was happy to find not only his suits but the rest of his clothing he left behind as well as his Beretta Nano and its shoulder holster. He dressed in his jeans and polo shirt and headed up to Grain, the hotel's beer garden. He grabbed a table along the roof's edge and enjoyed the restaurant's Cavalier burger and a Farmhouse Dry hard cider from Porter's Craft Ciders of Free Union, Virginia. He looked out over the Elizabeth River as he ate with the Norfolk Naval Shipyard on his left to the Battleship *Wisconsin* Museum to his right. In between the two sat the Peter G. Decker Half Moone Cruise and Celebration Center, the venue for the next day's event. Opened in 2007, the Half Moone Center served both as an event venue and as a point on embarkation for cruise ships that docked in downtown Norfolk.

After lunch, Morgan found his Corvette in the nearby Town

Center parking garage. He climbed aboard and started it up, smirking at the awesome engine sound reverberating through the parking structure. He set his satellite radio to the 'road trip' channel and drove to the entrance ramp for Interstate I-264. As a double play of Golden Earing's 'Radar Love' and 'Twilight Zone' blared out of the speakers, Morgan drove into the Downtown Tunnel, dropping a gear and giving the 'Vette some extra revs just to hear the sound bounce off the tunnel's curved walls. After exiting the tunnel, he took the exit from I-264 to I-464.

Morgan enjoyed the trip south on Interstate 464 with Cake's 'Short Skirt/Long Jacket,' Jan Hammer's 'Miami Vice Theme,' and Moby's cover of Lalo Schifrin's 'Mission: Impossible Theme' setting the appropriate mood for his ten-mile drive. Metallica's 'Enter Sandman' just ended as he pulled into the Norfolk-area F.B.I. field office in Chesapeake.

Though small compared to the likes of the New York or Chicago offices, the Norfolk field office was legendary in the Bureau for leading the investigation that brought down one of the most damaging spy rings in American history, the infamous John Walker Ring. Morgan pulled into a parking spot in front of the non-descript looking office complex. Only a high, wrought iron fence hinted at the building's true purpose. He walked into the lobby and approached the receptionist.

"Good afternoon," Morgan began. "Bob Morgan here to see Special Agent John Gomez." He handed her his U.S. Navy credentials as his position in the Navy acted as his cover while working domestically.

"Certainly, sir. Agent Gomez is expecting you. One moment please," the receptionist handed Morgan back his identification card and a visitor's badge.

"Thank you," Morgan said as he clipped on the badge.

A few moments later, a black-haired gentleman entered the lobby.

"Deeee Ceeeee Aaaaaaaaa!" the man shouted.

"Johnny Geeeeee!" Morgan responded.

The two men shook hands and exchanged a brief, manly hug. Standing a couple of inches shorter than Morgan, Special Agent John Gomez, F.B.I., had been, at one time, Lieutenant John Gomez, United States Navy, and had served with Morgan on the *Winston S. Churchill*. He left the service to pursue a career in federal law enforcement that led him eventually to the F.B.I.

"How the hell have you been, Bob?" Agent Gomez asked.

"Doing great, John. Between the Agency and Navy reserve duty, I've been busy lately."

"I can see that. What the hell happened to your eye? Last time I saw you, you had two."

"A long and interesting story for another time. Have a great story involving our favorite C.O. as well."

"Stone? Can't wait to hear that one."

"Quite, but like I said, for another time. Did your office receive the warrant for Rasmussen?"

"Sure did, just this morning. This guy is a real piece of work."

"You should have met his daughter, beauty and the beast in one luscious package."

"Damn!"

"Oh yeah. Can we go over the plan to get this guy?"

"Sure, come this way." John Gomez and Morgan entered the F.B.I. offices proper.

Agent Gomez's voice came over Morgan's ear piece.

"This is Gomez, our target and Ms. Newkirk have arrived."

Morgan moved further back against the Rotunda's back wall trying to make himself as inconspicuous as possible. He spoke into his radio.

"Remember, follow my lead hold your positions until I give the word. We don't want to spook him too soon."

A few moments later, Morgan saw the guests of honor enter the room amidst the applause of those present. After shaking a few hands, Ms. Newkirk and Rasmussen headed to the head table. Ms. Newkirk stood behind the lectern while Edward took a seat to her right. She adjusted the microphone and began to speak.

"Is this thing on?" she asked with a smile and the audience responded with a quick laugh. She continued.

"Good afternoon ladies and gentlemen and thank you for coming today. Your generous contributions to PETA today will ensure we continue to provide free dog and cat spay and neutering services for the foreseeable future." A quick burst of applause interrupted Ms. Newkirk. Once the room quieted, she continued.

"Thank you. I would now like to introduce today's guest. Mr. Edward Rasmussen is a native of Copenhagen, Denmark and the President and Chief Executive Officer of RDS Shipping. He has been a great friend to PETA, and the animal welfare community as whole, for many years. His contributions made our mobile veterinary clinics a reality, and his generous of donation of $1,183,990, that's an even 1 million Euros for our friends from across the pond, will keep those clinics on the road for the foreseeable future. Ladies and Gentlemen, Mr. Edward Rasmussen."

The audience began to clap in earnest as Edward stood up to take Ms. Newkirk's spot at the lectern.

"Thank you, Ingrid, and thank you ladies and gentlemen for the warm welcome!" "Edward began. "The proper care of our domestic companion animals has always been an important cause in my life as I feel how we treat these furry friends reflect on ourselves and how we treat our fellow human beings…"

Morgan tuned out the rest of Edward's speech, he'd heard it all before. He moved out of the shadows and towards the head table. In his peripheral vision, augmented by his prosthetic, he saw John Gomez and the uniformed Norfolk police officers enter the room. Once Agent Gomez was in position to the left of the main table, Morgan got Rasmussen's attention.

"Edward!" Morgan shouted. The crowd turned to see who

had interrupted the luncheon, and Edward looked at Morgan with a mixture of surprise and horror.

"Edward Rasmussen," Agent Gomez displayed his F.B.I. badge. "I'm Special Agent John Gomez, F.B.I." He pulled out a slip of paper from inside his suit jacket. "I have an international warrant for your arrest on the charges of weapons and human trafficking. The building is surrounded, so please come along quietly."

Rasmussen reached into his jacket, pulled out a Russian-made SR-1 Vektor pistol, and grabbed Ms. Newkirk by her hair. He pointed the weapon at her right temple as someone in the crowd screamed. He began to drag her towards the rotunda's massive windows and the emergency exit.

"Stay back! I don't how you escaped Aurora and her crew, but you won't get me, Morgan!"

"Edward!" Ingrid shouted. "What are you doing? Is this true?"

"Shut up you witch before I give you a nine-millimeter spaying!"

"Okay everyone, keep calm." Agent Gomez said into his radio. Morgan, Gomez and the officers formed a semi-circle around Edward and his hostage.

"Let her go, Edward," Morgan said. "There's nowhere to go."

Rasmussen reached the emergency exit built into the floor-to-ceiling windows. He leaned into the door's release bar, pushed Ms. Newkirk into Morgan and Gomez, and took off out the rotunda and across cruise terminal's outdoor Promenade Deck. A Norfolk police officer tried to stop him, but Edward shot him in the head. He ran across the walkway connecting the terminal to the nearby Town Point Park and the Nauticus museum with Morgan and Gomez in hot pursuit. Edward took the steps two at a time to stay ahead of his pursuers and turned left and ran across a wooden deck towards Nauticus. At the same time, Morgan and Gomez stayed after him with uniformed police coming around from the other side of the museum.

Edward cut through an open gate that led to the quay wall next to the Battleship *Wisconsin*. He turned right but seeing police officers coming from the opposite end of the quay, stopped short. He then ran up the gangway at the aft end of the battleship, climbed around a barrier that kept most people from climbing on board without paying, and hit the teak wood deck. One of the elderly museum docents tried to stop him, but Edward rewarded him with a quick push that knocked the poor man on his ass. He saw a door to his left that looked like it led to the interior of the ship. He opened it and saw a near vertical ladder leading down to the deck below. He immediately ran in, closed the door behind him, and lost himself inside the vast man-of-war.

Morgan saw Edward climb aboard the ship and assault the old man. He and Gomez climbed the brow as Edward entered the ship's interior. Once on deck, he stopped to check on the gentleman Edward had pushed past. The man wore a blue polo-style shirt with the Nauticus museum logo and a name tag that read 'Tom'. He also wore a U.S.S. *Wisconsin* ship's ball cap with a Chief Petty Officer's rank insignia pin and a gold lyre pin, the insignia of a U.S. Navy Musician.

"Are you okay, Chief?" Morgan asked using the man's former rank as he helped him up.

"Yes, sir, I'm fine. Only thing he hurt was my pride."

Morgan gave the man an amused smirk, "Roger that, Chief. Where does that door go?"

"It leads down to the second deck around the crew's mess."

"Can he access the rest of the ship from there?"

"Yes, sir."

"Shit, there are hundreds of spaces on this ship he could hide in. We could search for hours and never find him." Morgan thought for a moment. "Tom, is there any way we can get the visitors off the ship?"

"Yes, sir. There is a 1MC up forward in the old Quarterdeck shack. We can pass the word from there."

"Outstanding, lead the way."

Tom, Morgan, and Gomez moved along *Wisconsin*'s starboard side. Along the way, they passed a glass door mounted in what was a watertight door that allowed visitors into the interior of the ship via the Wardroom. The trio stopped at a watertight door located below Turret Two, the second of the ship's three 16-inch gun turrets. Tom opened the door and showed Morgan and Gomez the microphone for the ship's public address system, the 1MC.

"John, pass the word to get the guests off the ship. I'm going after Rasmussen."

"Pass the word, aye!"

"Just don't pass the word about divers working aloft." Morgan added with a smirk. He drew his Nano, ran back to the glass doors, and entered the ship. As he did so, he heard Agent Gomez's voice over the ship's speakers.

"On board *Wisconsin*! This is F.B.I. Special Agent Gomez. There is a fugitive on board the ship who is to be considered armed and extremely dangerous. All visitors are requested to depart the ship immediately via the forward gangway. I say again, on board *Wisconsin*! This is F.B.I. Special Agent Gomez. There is a fugitive on board the ship who is to be considered armed and extremely dangerous. All visitors are requested to depart the ship immediately via the forward gangway."

CHAPTER
FORTY-THREE

Battleship U.S.S. *Wisconsin* Museum
Norfolk, Virginia

Morgan stopped in the Wardroom and looked around.

This ship is too damned big. I need to bring that bastard to me.

Morgan looked to his right and saw a ladder leading up into the ship's superstructure. He experienced a momentary flash of brilliance and made his way up towards his goal, the Navigation Bridge.

Moving carefully, Morgan climbed up the ladder to the 01 level, the first deck above the main deck. He looked carefully over the watertight hatch combing before moving up to the next deck. He looked around and saw passageways that led to what were officers' staterooms and both the Captain's and Admiral's cabins. He moved up to the next deck, the 02 level, and found himself in a passageway outside a space with a World War Two-era armored watertight door. Holding his Nano out in front of him, Morgan entered the space and found himself bathed in blue light and surrounded by numerous equipment consoles, and the empty foundations for even more. This was *Wisconsin*'s Combat Engagement Center, the location of the weapon systems installed during *Wisconsin*'s modernization in the late 1980s. Morgan cleared the space and moved up to the next deck.

He stepped through another armored watertight door and entered a space with two, high-mounted leather chairs, a series of windows with brass crank handles, and a large, metal cylinder in the center. This was the ship's Flag Bridge, the space where an embarked Admiral and his staff would work. Morgan moved though the space and looked out through the windows. Out on the quay and on the exterior decks below, Morgan saw a small army of police officers, including a tactical team, setting up a perimeter under John Gomez's direction. Morgan continued from the starboard side to the port, checking the corners as he went. When he reached the far port side, he saw a ladder that led to the next deck up. He moved up to the 04 level and arrived at his destination, the Navigation Bridge.

Morgan entered the bridge's port side with widows to his left and a bulkhead mounted desk and phone to his right. Also mounted on the bulkhead above the desk was something he hoped he see, another 1MC station.

Perfect! I hope it still works.

Morgan picked up 1MC microphone handset and keyed it. He saw a small red light illuminate on the control panel and heard clicks come over the speakers.

Outstanding! It's showtime!

Morgan switched off the 1MC exterior speakers so that he would not be heard outside. He pulled out his phone, opened its video player application, and held the microphone to his mouth.

Down on second deck, Edward hid in an old crew berthing compartment. Accessible, but not refurbished enough to allow any of the guests to visit. He hid amongst the three-tier high bunks, what the sailors called 'racks,' and bided his time, waiting for the right moment to emerge and try to get off the ship. A small series of clicks caught his attention, then he heard someone speaking.

"Edward, this is Morgan."

Bastard! What does he want?

"Edward, I know you can hear me. This is being broadcast throughout the ship. Edward, I killed Aurora in Senegal. I extinguished the light of your life. Permanently. Would you like to hear her final moments?"

Rasmussen listened as he heard a shot, Aurora's screams and curses, another shot, Aurora's gurgling final breaths, and finally one last shot.

"That last shot went through her brain, Edward. Everything that she was, everything you loved, scattered all over Senegal. If you want me, come get me! I'm up in compartment 04-84-0-C, the navigation bridge. You know your way around ships, Edward. Come find me. I'll be waiting." The last sound from the speakers was a click as the microphone's key was released.

Edward wiped away a tear and screamed in rage. He moved out from his hiding spot and began to look for a ladder up to the next deck. He'll find that son of a bitch, the police and F.B.I. be damned. And when he does, he'll avenge the loss of his dearest Aurora in the most painful way possible.

Morgan returned the 1MC microphone to its holder. Time to prepare for Edward. The navigation bridge had two area of ingress, but he did not know which one Edward would use. Morgan moved from the bridge's port side and passed by an amazing sight, *Wisconsin*'s armored conning tower.

Part of the ship's armored citadel that protected all of the ship's vital command, control, and machinery spaces, the conning station looked more like a bank vault than a ship's watertight compartment. Constructed from 17-and-a-half-inch thick steel armor, the conning station held *Wisconsin*'s ship's wheel to control direction, an engine order telegraph to control speed, and was protected against direct hits from naval gun shells up to 16 inches in size. Two, electrically driven, watertight doors weighing 500 pounds each were the only ways in or out of the conning tower. Morgan decided that that's where he'll await

Edward as the steel armor would easily protect him from Edward's nine-millimeter rounds.

Rounding the conning tower along its starboard side, Morgan came to the work area of the Quartermaster of the Watch with a chart table on display to show museum visitors how ships navigated in the days before GPS satellites. Looking up over the chart table, Morgan saw what he was looking for, a cross beam up in the overhead. He removed his prosthetic eye from his eye socket and place it on the cross beam. Looking at the display in his Matsuda sunglasses, Morgan moved the prosthetic until he had a proper view of the starboard side approaches to the bridge. He moved to the conning tower watching the port side door. He then awaited Edward's arrival.

Edward growled to himself in frustration. He used the big yellow signs painted on the bulkhead in each space to mark his progress.

What did the sailors call them? Oh yes, bullseyes.

Each bullseye showed the deck, frame number, relation to centerline (port or starboard) and purpose of each space. Despite these signs, however he still became turned around on the 58,000 ton, 887-foot-long, and 108-foot-wide decommissioned battleship, and he was no closer to finding the bridge and Morgan.

He found himself on the ship's main deck, near to what was the ship's office. He then heard voices coming from a few feet away. He tucked his Vektor into his belt at the small of his back and walked towards the voices.

He entered a space that looked to him to be the officer's mess and saw five people. Three wore normal clothing while two were in the blue polo shirts and khaki pants like the old man he pushed to the deck. They stood around one of the mess tables while removing some sort of communications equipment. He walked up to the group, careful to keep his weapon out of sight.

"Excuse me," Edward began. "How do I get to the bridge?"

One of the staff members turned to Edward. He saw the name 'Larry' on the man's name tag.

"I'm sorry, sir. But the bridge is not open for general tours."

Edward pulled the Vektor from behind his back and kept all five people in front of him. One of the guests screamed at the sight of the weapon.

"I'll ask one more time. How do I get to the bridge?"

The other staff member, this one with 'Chipper' on his name plate, stammered out an answer.

"Just take the ladder behind us up four decks. It will take you right there."

"Thank you." Edward then opened fire.

Edward held his Vektor out in front of him as he stepped over the bodies and climbed up the ladder. Moving up through the decks, he finally ended up on the Flag Bridge. He looked at the bullseye and saw that he was one deck below the space where Morgan said he was waiting. He located a ladder on the starboard side and climbed up the next deck. Once at the top of the ladder, he moved forward carefully. Looking around he saw a small stateroom, the navigator's chart room with its large chart table, and in front of him a huge metal door, like a bank vault.

Morgan covered the bridge's port side access as his prosthetic covered the starboard side. Through the projection in his sunglasses, he saw Edward come up the starboard side ladder and onto the bridge.

Got you, you prick!

He silently shifted his position inside the conning tower and saw Edward moving with his weapon stretched out in front of him.

"Drop it Edward!" Morgan pointed the Nano out the armored doorway.

Edward turned towards the sound of Morgan's voice and fired three rounds. Two of the rounds hit the side of the tower and ricocheted harmlessly. The third hit the doorway and ricocheted into Morgan's Nano smashing the pistol and injuring Morgan's right hand. He tried to fire a fourth round, but the hammer came down on an empty chamber. He threw the empty weapon to the deck and came at Morgan howling in rage.

Morgan shook his hand after his Nano was hit and saw Edward rushing him. The pair fell backwards into the conning station. Morgan stood up and crouched into a fighting stance as Edward swung his right fist towards his head. He dodged the oncoming strike to his left, but a swift left jab by Edward struck Morgan in his still injured ribs. Morgan fell back as blow after blow stuck him in the head and chest. Edward shouted with every blow delivered.

"For Ivar!"

"For my people!"

"For my dearest Aurora!"

During the melee, the pair had moved completely around the conning station. Morgan's back now pressed up against the starboard-side armored doorway. Edward's right arm drew back for another head strike. Morgan dropped to the deck as Edward's fist flew towards his face, dodging the blow. The fist landed square against the conning tower's doorway. The full force of the blow intended for Morgan's face instead landed on the ship's armor, and the bones in Edward's hand shattered immediately. Cradling his now broken hand, Edward howled in pain. He stumbled out the conning station and ran inboard towards the chart house. Morgan jumped up off the deck and followed quickly, drawing his Guardian II knife from its belt sheath behind his right hip.

Morgan looked into the chart house and saw the navigator's chart table with a chart laid upon it. A beautiful sextant, a telescopic alidade, a stadimeter, a long empty wooden box, some books, and several old-time plotting tools sat arrayed on top of the chart. Edward, however, was nowhere to be seen. He moved carefully and noticed a small alcove to his left just before a large, black object came out from behind his blind spot and entered his field of view. The impact smashed Morgan's sunglasses, smacked the Guardian II from his hand, and knocked him onto the deck in a daze. Shaking his head, Morgan looked up and saw Edward toss a ship's spyglass onto the deck before grabbing Morgan by the neck. He was dragged to his feet and forced onto the top of the chart table.

"I don't need both hands to kill you, Morgan!" Rasmussen hissed. "You will pay for what you did to my darling daughter." With that, he began to squeeze Morgan's airway shut.

Fighting to maintain consciousness, Morgan began moving his right hand across the chart table. He felt something sharp, so he grabbed it and plunged it into Edward's neck. Edward shrieked in pain, and Morgan felt the hand around his throat ease its grip allowing Morgan to slip away and draw in air for his starving lungs. Once he caught his breath, Morgan saw what he stabbed Edward with, a pair of antique navigation dividers, part of the museum's navigation tools display. The divider's two nearly razor-sharp points were embedded in Edward's neck and had punctured his left-hand carotid artery. Baring his teeth in his malevolent smile, Morgan grabbed the dividers and pushed them further into Edward's neck.

"This isn't supposed to be fun, Edward, but seeing you like this does put a smile on my face."

Morgan pulled the dividers out from Edward's neck and dropped him to the deck. Morgan stood over him and watched as he bled out. He leaned down and listened to Rasmussen draw his final breaths.

"Do you have a valedictory for me, Edward?" Morgan asked, paraphrasing from one of his favorite films.

Edward whispered something that made Morgan's eyes go wide, but before he could ask anything else, Edward's death rattle reached Morgan's ears. A commotion in front of Morgan caught his attention as Special Agent Gomez and several Norfolk police tactical officers entered the bridge. Morgan called out to Agent Gomez.

"Johnny! In the chart room."

Agent Gomez entered the space and saw Rasmussen's bloody remains.

"Holy shit, Bob! What a mess! Are you okay?"

"A round grazed my hand, my ribs are screaming in pain, and I have one hell of a headache. Otherwise, I'm fine."

"So, what happened to Rasmussen?"

"His life just ran aground."

John Gomez shook his head with a combination of amazement and bemusement. Morgan continued.

"John, do you know anyone working counter-intelligence up in D.C.?"

"I have an academy classmate working C.I. up there. Why?"

"I may have a job for them…"

CHAPTER
FORTY-FOUR

CIA Headquarters
Langley, Virginia
Three Days Later…

Morgan drove up Route 123 towards headquarters feeling better than he had in in a long time. It's amazing what a night in your own bed can do for your disposition. He drove the Grand Sport past the main gates and found his favorite parking spot empty. He checked his phone and saw a text message, one simple word.

Ready.

As Morgan walked towards the lobby, the events of the past 72 hours ran though his head…

It took a good day to clear up the situation on the *Wisconsin*, but John Gomez and his team smoothed things out with the Commonwealth's Attorney while keeping Morgan away from the local media. While leaving the museum, Morgan saw why Rasmussen only had three rounds remaining in his weapon. The bodies of three museum guests and two museum staff members lay in puddles of blood on the port side main deck just forward of the wardroom. They had been a tour group and two guides down in the ship's engineering spaces. They had not heard Agent Gomez's announcement and had paid for it with their lives. More blood on Edward's hands.

When news of what happened at the Half Moone Center and the *Wisconsin* came out, things progressed quickly around the world. In Copenhagen, Danish police and security forces raided RDS Shipping headquarters and seized the company's assets. The Metropolitan Police Anti-Terrorist Branch, better known as SO-13 did the same thing in London while Sir Ian's children moved quickly to retrieve the inheritance stolen by their very wicked stepmother. In Singapore, the national police's Commercial Affairs Department and Special Operations Command raided RDS Shipping's Singapore headquarters and all the company's ships berthed in the port. In doing so, authorities intercepted another load of trafficked people on their way out of Asia. As for the people rescued from the *Aurora Express* and the container in Senegal, they all found their way either in the U.K. or back their countries of origin. When Morgan arrived at the lobby elevators one thought came to mind.

Just one more thing to do.

Morgan opened the doors to the Analysis Branch offices and walked into the thunderous applause of his co-workers, led by Clint Peters. Morgan smirked humbly, waived at everyone, and walked back to his corner cubicle. Clint followed close behind.

"Great job, Bob!" Peters said. "Glad you made it back, I had to settle for the swill that passes for coffee in the cafeteria while you were gone."

"Thanks, Clint. Brew you a cup?"

"Please," Peters said as he held out his mug.

Morgan put the mug in the Nespresso machine, put a pod in, and pressed the start button. As the coffee brewed, Morgan turned back to Peters.

"Things quiet here while I was gone?"

"Very quiet, downright boring at times. Now that you're back, what's next?"

"Well Clint, that's up to you. Right, General?"

Peters turned around and saw four people standing behind him. One was General Bailey; the second was Winston Flowers, a guy Peters knew from the Agency Counter-Intelligence Branch; and two people he did not recognize. One was a Hispanic woman in a sharp grey suit while the second was an African-American man in an obviously custom-tailored suit that barley contained his massive chest and arms. The woman reached into her suit jacket and pulled out a leather identification card holder.

"Mr. Clinton Peters? I'm Special Agent Christina Barco and this is Agent Tyrell Michael, F.B.I. Sir, you are under arrest on charge of espionage. You have the right to remain silent…"

"I'm aware of my rights Agent Barco," Peters said. He turned to Morgan who had stood up from his desk chair.

"How did you know?" Peters asked.

"Rasmussen mentioned that he and Ivar had a reception waiting for me in Berlin after I left Copenhagen. I only told one person that I was going to Berlin, you. Later, General Bailey found out from Chop that he spoke to you about a West African operation he was supporting when you two were talking in the cafeteria. That conversation took place just before my team was ambushed in Gambia and faced much stronger than expected opposition in Senegal."

Morgan hardened his expression.

"Why did you do it, Clint?"

Peters stood there silently with an expression that said, 'wouldn't you like to know.' Morgan turned around, grabbed the now full coffee cup, and smashed it against Peter's head. Between the impact and the scalding hot liquid, Peters dropped to the floor and screamed in pain. Morgan grabbed him by the collar and shook him mercilessly. Peters looked back at him in utter panic.

"Why Clint?! You were my handler, you piece of shit! My

friend! I trusted you with my life, and you almost ended it! Why?!"

Peters finally spoke. "My divorce! My divorce broke me both emotionally and financially. Someone approached me after the trial and offered to pay all my legal fees. I've been passing information to him ever since."

"Who does he work for, Clint?"

"I don't know." Morgan bared his teeth and shook him again, smacking the back of his skull on the floor. "I don't know! I swear!"

Morgan bared his teeth one more time and dropped Peters to the floor.

"Well, you'll have plenty of time to remember while you're sitting on your ass in the cell of some Supermax shithole. If there is any justice, you'll be ass-raped there at least once a week."

Morgan nodded to the two F.B.I. agents. He was through with Peters.

Agent Michael picked Peters up off the floor easily and cuffed his hands behind his back. The three counter-intelligence agents began to walk Peters out of the office, but Agent Barco turned to look back at Morgan.

"Any message for John Gomez?"

"Yeah, please tell John, I owe him a beer or three, and thanks."

Agent Barco flashed a bright smile that up until a few weeks ago would have worked on Morgan. She turned and began to walk with Agent Michael and Peters.

General Bailey placed his hand gently on Morgan's shoulder.

"You okay, son?"

"Aye, sir. Other than watching someone I thought was my friend get arrested for espionage after trying to have me killed, I'm just peachy."

General Bailey smiled at him gently.

"Peters was right, we do need to figure out what's next."

"I have a thought on that. Rasmussen whispered something to me before he died, a word I heard, or rather read before."

"Oh?"

"Yes sir, 'hantu'. It was the name of the file where I found the information on the shipment to Mali. I did some research on the word while I was still in Norfolk. It's a Malaysian word meaning 'ghoul' or 'ghost' or…"

"Specter?"

"Yes, sir," Morgan answered with a smirk.

"Sounds like something you need to look into. Can you have something for me in the next few days?"

"I'm sorry sir, but no. I'll be on leave for the next few days, burying a friend."

General Bailey nodded at Morgan and turned to walk away.

"General?"

Bailey turned back around.

"Helping the French with this cost us a lot in both materials and lives. Are we getting anything in return?"

"You see to your friends and figuring out who's behind the Rasmussens. I'll take care of the French."

"Aye, aye sir. Will do."

Monsieur Edouard Hachette hated the desert. He had enough of it serving in the Légion Étrangère, that's why he joined the DGSE. He loved Paris, the food, the wine, and of course the *belle femme*. Now he sat in the hot cab of one of the trucks that transported one of the Chinese MLRS in the middle of the Malian desert, the remaining four were now smoking craters in the border region between Mali and Senegal.

After taking his leave from *Monsieur Gargouille*, he tracked the two MLRS vehicles via the trackers provided by the CIA. Once the vehicles arrived at their destination, a Jama'a Nusrat ul-Islam wa al-Muslimin heavy weapons staging area out in the middle of nowhere, he directed French Special Forces, Air Force, and Reaper assets into the area. Between the three, every JNIM terrorist was eliminated and every heavy weapons system present, from heavy conventional artillery, to Surface-to-Air missiles, to armored vehicles, was destroyed. That is, all but two. During the battle, he had absconded with one of the MLRS vehicles brought over from Senegal while an associate, a certain Monsieur Lambert, who had been imbedded with the Special Forces team, drove away with one of the Russian-built, top-of-the-line S-400 SAM systems. Payment to the Americans for their recent help and the perfect candidates for some reverse engineering. They both now sat together in another patch of the God forsaken Malian desert waiting for their customer to arrive.

After running the truck's feeble air conditioner for what seemed like the one hundredth time in a vain attempt to keep cool, Edouard heard the sound of aircraft engines. He stepped out of the cab just as his associate did the same.

"*Mathias, avez-vous entendu ce que j'ai entendu?*" (Mathias, did you hear what I heard?)

"*Oui!*"

"*Dieu merci! Je pensais que la chaleur m'atteignait.*" (Thank God! I thought the heat was getting to me.)

The pair looked up and saw two, unmarked C-130 cargo planes flying low overhead. They watched as each landed on the flat desert floor and taxied up to the pair of vehicles. Edouard walked to the rear ramp of the lead aircraft as it was lowered to the ground. He saw a stunning woman dressed in black tactical paints, black tank top, a M-4 assault rifle across her ample chest, and pair of square lensed Ray-Ban aviator sunglasses with bayonet-style temple pieces. She took off a black ball cap and shook out a beautiful mane of auburn hair.

Eh bien, je suppose que ce voyage n'est pas si mal après tout. (Well, I guess this trip isn't so bad after all.)

She walked up to Edouard and flashed him a bright smile.

"Bonjour Monsieur Hachette, my name is Susan. I believe you have a delivery for me."

CHAPTER
FORTY-FIVE

Forest Lawn Cemetery
Norfolk, Virginia
The Next Day…

"Detail, attention!" shouted Lieutenant Coslick. At the command, three U.S. Navy SEALs from LT Coslick's platoon, resplendent in their full dress blue uniforms, snapped to attention.

"Ready!" The SEALs moved their M-4 carbines to the 'port arms' position.

"Aim!" The SEALs raised their weapons to their shoulders.

"Fire!" The SEALs fired their weapons simultaneously.

"Aim!" The SEALs prepared to fire again.

"Fire!" The SEALs fired their second volley.

"Aim!"

"Fire!" The SEALs fired the third and final volley.

"Present, arms!"

The SEALs snapped to the 'present arms' position. A few feet away, a bugler began to play taps. Standing at the grave site, Lieutenant Commander James Robert Morgan, also dressed in his full dress blue uniform with his officer's dress sword, snapped into a hand salute at LT Coslick's command.

Morgan began the day very early, waking at 04:30 to beat the traffic on I-95 South. He laid his dress blue jacket and dress sword carefully in the back of his 'Vette, climbed in, and headed for the highway. After a surprisingly smooth drive down both Interstates 95 and 64, Morgan arrived at his first destination, the Hampton National Cemetery in Hampton, Virginia.

Carrying a printout from the cemetery's website and a small bouquet of flowers, Morgan parked the Grand Sport, put on his dress blue uniform jacket and his cover, and walked up a small rise. At the top of the hill, he found what he was looking for, the final resting place of Lieutenant Douglas M. Kroll, United States Navy. Morgan missed Doug's service as it took place while he was underway on *Arlington*, so he took the opportunity to pay his respects on the way to his next destination. He placed the bouquet on the ground in front of the headstone, whispered a few words of thanks, and snapped a hand salute. Morgan dropped the salute, returned to his car, carefully placed his uniform jacket in the back, and left the cemetery.

Morgan crossed the Hampton Roads Bridge Tunnel, exited Interstate 64 at the Granby Street exit, and arrived at his final destination of the day, Miles Memorial United Methodist Church in Norfolk's Ocean View neighborhood. After parking, Morgan put his service dress blue jacket back on, threaded his sword belt through a zippered slit on the jacket's left side, clipped the sword scabbard to the belt's sword hook, buttoned his jacket, placed his cover square on his head, and headed inside. Immediately after walking through the front door, one of the church's ushers pulled him aside.

"Sir," the usher began. "You need to remove your hat while inside the church."

Morgan looked at the man with an expression that said,

'Trust me, I know what I'm doing,' and tilted his head towards his sword.

"Sir, I am under arms. The cover stays on."

The usher saw the sword, nodded his head.

"Sorry, Commander, didn't see your dress sword. My apologies."

"No need, sir. You're just doing your job."

Morgan took a seat towards the front of the church to the right of the center aisle, which gave room for Morgan's sword to hang outside the pew. Once seated, Morgan looked around the church with a sense of utter astonishment. He saw hundreds of people begin to fill the pews and the balcony above. He finally remembered why. Judge volunteered his off-duty time helping veterans apply for housing assistance, education, and health care. He worked particularly with homeless vets to get them whatever they needed to get themselves off the streets. Now, Morgan saw the fruits of Judge's work. Hundreds of people paying their respects to a man who improved their lives immensely. Additionally, dozens of sailors in their dress blues entered the church, most of whom wore the either the Crossed Silver Flintlock and Cutlass emblem of the SWCC community, or the SEAL gold trident on their chests.

Morgan shifted his vision back to the front of the church and saw a woman and two children sitting in the front row, Judge's family. If Morgan remembered correctly, they were his wife, Melinda, who went by Mindy, and their two children, 12 year old Maria and 10 year old Martin Jr. Morgan stood up, unclipped his sword, and walked to the front of the church.

"Mrs. Haugen? Good morning, I'm Lieutenant Commander Bob Morgan. I served with your husband."

Mrs. Haugen stood up and offered her hand, "Hello, I'm Mindy. Judge had mentioned you several times, Commander. He was right, you do look like a pirate."

Morgan shook Mindy's offered hand with an amused smirk.

"Please call me Bob, and I get that a lot. Mindy, allow me to pass on my sincerest condolences on your and your children's loss. Judge was a great shipmate and even greater man."

"Thank you, Bob. Maria and Marty already miss him. Were you there when he died? I can't get a straight answer from anyone on what happened."

"I was there, but I cannot give you any details. But what I can say is that his sacrifice was not in vain as he saved the lives of hundreds of people from all over the world, including trafficked women and children, and that the people responsible were dealt with, permanently. You and your children should be very proud of him and his service. If you need anything, please let me know." Morgan passed Mindy his U.S. Navy business card with his personal point of contact information.

"Thank you. But Judge's friends have been amazing, so we're good at the moment."

"Outstanding," Morgan said quietly.

He took his leave of Mindy and returned to his seat a few moments before the minister asked everyone to be seated. The church's organ began to play as Judge's flag-draped casket, pushed by Chief Shaw and Petty Officers Hernandez and Sharpe, moved down the aisle. Once the casket was in position, the three took their seats in the front row.

The service began in earnest with the minister offering a few words, and a succession of those Judge had helped over the years stepping up and speaking of how he had helped them and to his amazing character. The last to speak was Chief Shaw. He told tales of how Judge, always the family man, did not partake in some of his crew's more interesting activities while on deployment, as well as all that Judge did in support of his team and the SWCC community as a whole. Chief Shaw ended his eulogy with a reading of 'The Watch'.

For sixteen years
Martin Haugen stood the watch
While some of us were in our bunks at night

Martin Haugen stood the watch
While some of us were in school learning our trade
Martin Haugen stood the watch
Yes, even before some of us were born into this world
Martin Haugen stood the watch
In those years when the storm clouds of war were seen brewing on the
horizon of history
Martin Haugen stood the watch
Many times he would cast an eye ashore and see his family standing
there
Needing his guidance and help
Needing that hand to hold during those hard times
But he still stood the watch
He stood the watch for sixteen years
He stood the watch so that we, our families and
Our fellow countrymen could sleep soundly in safety, Each and every
night
Knowing that Martin Haugen stood the watch
Today we are here to say
'Judge... the watch stands relieved
Relieved by those you have trained, guided, and led
Rest easy, Judge, you stand relieved... we have the watch..."

"On Time, On Target, Never Quit!" Chief Shaw shouted.

As one, Morgan, all the Dirty Boat Guys, and all the SEALs shouted back.

"HUZZA!"

The sound of taps faded in the distance and Morgan dropped his hand salute. The minister once again said, "Please be seated," and Mindy and her children sat in seats directly behind Morgan. Petty Officers Hernandez and Sharpe picked up the flag from the top of the casket and began to fold it carefully. Once it was in the proper triangular shape, and after three polished, expended rifle cartridges were inserted into the folds, Petty Officer Hernandez slowly handed the flag to Chief Shaw as Petty Officer Sharpe slowly saluted. Chief Shaw returned the salute slowly and accepted the flag. He executed an about face maneuver and faced Morgan. He slowly saluted and passed the flag to Morgan. Morgan returned the salute slowly and took the flag from Chief Shaw. Morgan executed his own about face, to face Mindy and her children. Morgan knelt on his left knee in front of her and offered the folded flag.

"On behalf of a grateful nation…"

Morgan now drove home, getting off Interstate 95 North at the Occoquan exit to take Route 123 and avoid the dreaded Beltway. The last things Morgan wanted to deal with was, specifically, traffic and, in general, people. He was in a particularly foul mood and felt like crap. So foul that he kept his radio off during the entire trip north. None of his music, neither on satellite radio nor on his phone held any interest for him at that moment. Visiting the grave of one friend and burying another all in the same day took an emotional toll on the normally unemotional Morgan, and all he wanted to do was go home and go to bed. He could have used Cat at his side during todays' service, but she was "on assignment."

Guess that's the downside of falling in love with someone in the community. You never know when, or if, they'll be in contact.

He pulled the 'Vette into his parking spot, pulled his Smith & Wesson from the car's center console and placed it in his inside-the-waistband holster. He pulled his uniform jacket from the back of the car, put it on, picked up his sword and cover, and headed for his door. As he reached for the doorknob, he saw that the door was open a crack. He carefully and quietly placed his sword and cover on the porch, opened his jacket, and drew his weapon. He opened the door slowly and with his weapon raised moved into the vestibule. He moved from the vestibule and entered his living room where came to a sudden halt at what he saw.

All the living room lights were off except for his reading lamp at the corner of his couch and dozens of candles flickered all around the room. He lowered his weapon and looked around with amazement and not a little confusion. He heard a velvety smooth voice come out from his kitchen.

"Hello, James."

Morgan turned towards the voice and saw Cat come out from the shadows. She wore a form fitting green cocktail dress, beige silk stockings which allowed her paw print tattoo to be visible on her right ankle, and black leather high heel shoes. A single gold bracelet graced her left ankle. Her fingernails, as the song said, 'shined like justice' being painted a color that matched her dress. She held a hardcover book of some sort in her left hand.

"Oh my God! Cat!"

Morgan ran to her while holstering his weapon. He swept her up into her arms and kissed her with more raw emotion and passion than he had ever done before. Eventually they broke their kiss, and Cat held her hands gently against his cheeks.

"You shaved off your Van Dyke."

"Dress uniform."

"Better."

"How did you find where I lived…? Oh wait, never mind. I forgot. You're a spy."

"Quite," Cat replied with a smile. "Come on then, get out of that jacket and get on the couch."

"Yes, ma'am."

Morgan took off his dress blue jacket and hung it in the vestibule closet. He stepped outside a moment and brought his cover and sword back into the condo and placed them in the closet as well. He loosened his tie and began to take off his shoes. He looked up and saw Cat sitting on the corner of the couch right under the reading lamp. She had taken her shoes off and was now patting her lap.

"Ready?" she asked.

"Wasn't I supposed to buy you dinner first?"

"That's okay, you can buy me breakfast," Cat replied with a conspiratorial look.

Morgan laid on the couch and placed his head in Cat's lap. She leaned in, kissed him, and moved a lock of hair away from his good eye.

"Ready, sailor?"

"Absolutely."

Cat opened the book that laid on the arm of the couch, "*Casino Royale*, by Ian Fleming, Chapter 1, 'The Secret Agent.' *The scent and smoke and sweat of a casino are nauseating at three in the morning. Then the soul-erosion produced by high gambling— a compost of greed and fear and nervous tension — becomes unbearable, and the senses awake and revolt from it. James Bond suddenly knew that he was tired. He always knew when his body or his mind had had enough, and he always acted on the knowledge…*"

EPILOGUE

64th Floor
Guoco Tower
Tanjong Pagar Neighborhood
Singapore

Elyas bin Agus, known to his organization as Raja Hantu, the Ghost King, stood at his penthouse's window, the entirety of Singapore's City Centre lay at his feet. Not bad for a kid who grew up in the slums of Kuala Lumpur, scrapping by just to survive. The former Islamic radical later turned his focus to matters of business, both legitimate and illegitimate.

Now he lived in a fabulous penthouse, formerly owned by some glorified vacuum cleaner salesman, in the heart of Singapore. Though his efforts, hard work, and not a few acts of violence, he built Hantu into one of the largest, covert enterprises in Asia, if not the world. He had his hands in many legal and not-so-legal activities, all of which made him huge, mostly untraceable, profits. He stoked the fires of conflict around the world, all in support of his bottom line.

The loss of Rasmussen, his lovely daughter, and the capabilities RDS Shipping provided, put that bottom line at risk. Lady

243

Aurora's skills with people in particular will be missed. Her charms made making deals much easier. He'd find out whoever it was that destroyed his pipeline into western Africa, and he'd make them pay. But first, he had to tie up a few loose ends. He pulled his phone from his custom-tailored suit jacket and dialed a number.

"*Ini adalah Raja Hantu. Adakah kita masih menemui Mr. Peters?*" (This is the Ghost King. Have we found Mr. Peters yet?)

"*Baik Raja. Dia ditahan di Penitenti Amerika Syarikat, Lee, Virginia sementara menunggu perbicaraan.*" (Yes, Raja. He's being held at the United States Penitentiary, Lee, Virginia awaiting trial.)

"*Baiklah. Melihatnya, dia tidak pernah melihat bahagian dalam ruang sidang.*" (Very well. See to it he never sees the inside of a courtroom.)

"*Baik Raja. Saya sudah mempunyai seorang lelaki dalam kedudukan.*" (Yes, Raja. I already have a man in position.)

Elyas bin Agus disconnected the call. Hantu's covert action department will make short work of Mr. Peters. They have the best operatives in the world, recruited from Special Forces units, law enforcement organizations, and intelligence agencies from all over the globe. It's amazing how many agents from the CIA, FBI, MI-5, MI-6, Russian SVR and FSB, Israeli Mossad, and China's Ministry of State Security are willing to leave those organizations to come work for him. Those organizations needed to pay their people better. Be that as it may, those operatives all worked for Hantu now. Anything Mr. Peters may, or may not, know about the organization will die with him, and those well-paid operatives will ensure that it'll look like an accident.

Bin Agus returned to his desk. Peters had been dealt with, but he still had much work to do. He was on the verge of the largest, and most ambitious operation Hantu has ever conducted. An operation that will earn him billions, and with those billions, unprecedented power. Once bin Agus had that power, he would shake the world.

ACKNOWLEDGEMENTS, NOTES, AND GENERAL MUSINGS

Thank you for reading Nautical Strike, and for making it this far! Writing a book is hard, and writing a book of fiction is even harder. I would not have made it this far if it were not for three great people. The first is my thriller writing sensei, Mr. Brian Drake, author of the Scott Stiletto, Steve Dane, and Sam Raven series of thrillers. He took the time to help this budding author get things right and not, hopefully boring the readers. The second is my editor, Ms. Tracey Govender (http://www.-booksculpt.com). She's the one who took my pile of words and punctuation marks and molded them into a coherent story. Anything to the contrary is on me, not her. Third, I thank Mr. Miika Hannila and the fine people at Next Chapter for taking a chance on this fledgling thriller writer. The fourth and final is Emily at Fantasy Name Generator .Com (https://www.fantasy-namegenerators.com). If I was stuck trying to come up with a name for a character, I'd visit her site and use her awesome name generator to find just the right name based on the context I planned on using at the time.

I would be remiss if I didn't thank our man in Singapore, Lim Lo Suy. Lim answered many questions about all things Singapore, and he coined the title for the head of Hantu, the Raj Hantu. Big thanks go to Paul Ray Heinrich, beta reader and shipmate. Also, I must thank Cynthia Kidd, formerly of the U.S. Army's Test and Evaluation Command, now with the U.S. Navy's Operational Test and Evaluation Force. She was kind enough to use her Army experience and knowledge to review my use of the Army's Maritime External Air Transportation System. If I got it wrong, it's all on me. Of course, the biggest thanks to my amazing wife, Kate who has to put up with her loving husband having his nose in a thriller at all times of the day.

Thanks also goes out to Doug Demuro, whose You Tube video review of the McLaren Artura assisted me in listing its many 'quirks and features' in the course of the story (https://www.youtube.com/watch?v=t_lrA3Uz1Tw); and Ryan George of Screen Rant's 'Pitch Meeting' You Tube series for the expression 'super easy, barley an inconvenience' (https://www.youtube.com/user/ScreenRant).

It's an author's prerogative to put the people he likes/loves into his books. If it isn't, well it is now. Several of the main characters are named for the people most important to me. The first is, of course, Catherine Sarah Roberts named for my awesome wife, Kathryn Sarah (Roberts) Adamcik. Unlike her fictional counterpart, she goes by Kate as opposed to Cat. My dearest found it rather surreal seeing her name in my story, despite the slightly different spelling. And yes, she has the front paw prints of one of our kitties tattooed just above her right ankle, just like I have one of the two emblems Morgan has tattooed on his upper arms on one of my upper arms (I'll let you guess which one).

Next is General Bailey's secretary, Ms. Coleen Biggins. She is named after my first crush, junior prom date, and all around best female friend from my high school days. Just like her fictional doppelganger, she's a raven-haired beauty who's now the mother of two back in my home town of Cleveland, Ohio.

Speaking of General Bailey, he's named for a real retired U.S. Marine Corps Lieutenant General. The then Colonel Bailey and I deployed together on the USS *Bataan* (LHD 5) when he was Commanding Officer of Second Marine Regiment (Task Force Tarawa) and I was *Bataan*'s Navigator. At one point in the deployment, he presented me with one of his regiment's t-shirts as a thank you for taking his Marines to combat and back. That shirt is now framed and hanging on my office wall along with several other souvenirs from my time in the service.

The CIA cyber security expert Morgan works with is named for the Information Resources representative I deal with at Operational Test and Evaluation Force, Lloyd Decker. Before moving to the command's IR department, Lloyd was the Lead Test Engineer I worked with during the first Operational Assessment of the Navy's latest navigation system.

The alias Morgan used, Robert L. Curry, is named for the son of one of my best friends from my days at Ohio State, Captain Roger L. Curry, United States Navy, retired. Roger and I were in The Ohio State University Navy ROTC unit together and we both were in the unit's Rifle/Pistol team. He, as the only Ohio State University student I knew with a Federal Firearms Dealer's license, was the source of the first firearm I ever owned, a Smith & Wesson 6904 nine-millimeter (I still own that weapon over 30 years later). He and his wife Heather are parents of three great kids the youngest of whom is Robert. Talking with his dad, Robert appears to be a history-guy like me, so hopefully he'll appreciate being in this book.

The NATO Amphibious Task Force Commander, Rear Admiral Martin 'Mallard' Allard is named for my skipper on the *Bataan*, former A-6 Intruder, and F/A-18 Hornet pilot, U.S. Navy Captain Martin Allard. Captain Allard was the first, and only Commanding Officer I ever had who insisted on being addressed as 'Skipper' instead of Captain while in command. Skipper Allard worked hard, played hard, and we as a crew followed him to war and back, gladly.

The two SEAL lieutenants, LT Doug 'Doug' Kroll and LT Paul 'Galahad' Coslick are both named for two now-former US Navy lieutenants. Doug and Paul worked for me during my last tour in uniform as the Operational Test Director for the *Ohio*-Class SSGN conversion program at Operational Test and Evaluation Force. As a Surface Warfare Officer testing submarines, both LT Kroll and Coslick, both submariner officers were there to advise me on how things work on a submarine, and to ensure I didn't do something stupid while underway ("Hey! What does this valve do?").

Two characters named for two important people in my Navy career were Chief Special Boat operators Michael 'Dallas' Shaw and Marvin 'Marvelous Marvin' Hurd. Chief Shaw is named for Chief Gunner's Mate Michael 'Dallas' Shaw, my division's Leading Chief Petty Officer when I was Gunnery Officer on the destroyer USS *John Hancock* (DD 981). To me, Dallas Shaw is the epitome of the U.S. Navy Chief Petty Officer and one of the reasons I stayed in the service after my first sea tour. Chief Hurd is named for Aviation Maintenance Administrativeman (AZ) Second Class Marvin Hurd. Petty Officer Hurd was a US Army Vietnam veteran, a native Clevelander like me, and was one of my recruit company commanders way back in 1984 who taught this then-17-year-old kid how to be a Sailor. He was also a boxing fan, hence his character's call sign.

The final two character are listed in the dedication. I served in the early 1990s with the then Lieutenant Joe Acevedo on the *John Hancock* where he was the Supply Officer while I was Guns. Using him as the basis of Morgan's gadget guy at the CIA was the only choice. He was a great SuppO and shipmate, and it saddened me to hear that ten years later he had passed away from a heart attack while serving at the Naval Support Activity, Bahrain. The final character, SB1 Martin 'The Judge' Haugen is named for Senior Chief Engineman (Surface Warfare) Judge Haugen, USN (ret.), and yes, his real first name was Judge. He served with the Navy's boat units at the tail end of the Vietnam War and became a teacher Portsmouth, Virginia school system after retiring from the Navy. He passed away in March of 2017 after a motorcycle accident, and like his namesake in the book, his service was packed with over a thousand people, many of whom he helped as a part-time veterans' councilor.

I also added a few cameos including Neil, the owner of Streats; Rear Admiral Dennis Fitzpatrick, USN (ret.), my

Commanding Officer on the aircraft carrier U.S.S. *John F. Kennedy* (CV 67); Commander Jon Dachos, USN (ret.), a Surface Warfare School Department Head course classmate, and *Bataan* shipmate whom I promoted to Captain and Commanding Officer of *Arlington*; Tom, a fellow volunteer at the Battleship *Wisconsin* museum; Chipper and Larry, two other members of the Battleship *Wisconsin* Museum staff (sorry guys!); John Gomez, a shipmate from my time in uniform at Operational Test and Evaluation Force and a real life Naval Criminal Investigative Service agent; and finally my best friend from high school, Jerry Biggs (again, sorry Jer!). We'll see more of Jerry and John in my next book.

Oh yeah, one last thing. Everything regarding the U.S. Navy, the CIA, etc. came from either open source material, my personal recollections, or my rather vivid imagination.

Thanks to all of you!!!!!

WHO'S RESPONSIBLE FOR THIS?!?!?!?

 Mr. Robert A. Adamcik was born and raised in Cleveland, Ohio and graduated with a degree in History from The Ohio State University in 1989. Upon graduation, he was commissioned an Ensign in the United States Navy and served for 20 years as a Surface Warfare Officer, serving on six ships during the course of Operations Desert Storm, Southern Watch, Stabilise, Enduring Freedom, and Iraqi Freedom. He retired from the Navy as a Lieutenant Commander in 2009, but still serves on board a ship as a volunteer tour guide at the Battleship *Wisconsin* Museum. He resides in Norfolk, Virginia with his wife Kate and their several dogs and cats.

To learn more about Robert A. Adamcikand discover more Next Chapter authors, visit our website at www.nextchapter.pub.

Printed in Great Britain
by Amazon